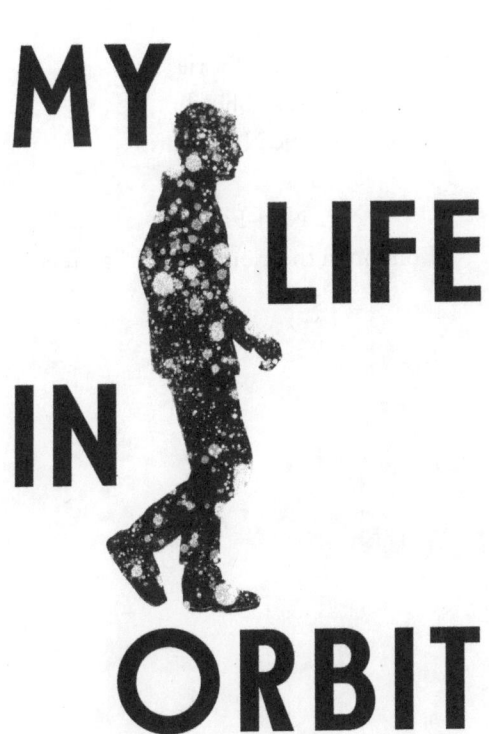

Also by Richard Blandford

Novels
Flying Saucer Rock & Roll
Hound Dog
Whatever You Are Is Beautiful

Short Stories
The Shuffle
Erotic Nightmares

Non-Fiction
London in the Company of Painters

MY LIFE IN ORBIT

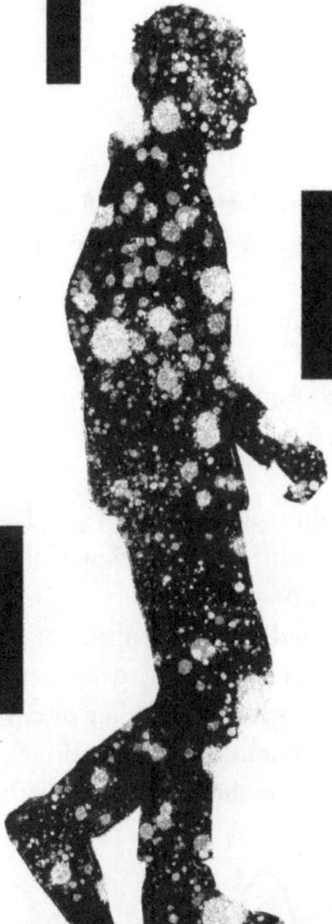

RICHARD BLANDFORD

*Published in the UK in 2024 by Everything with Words Limited,
Fifth Floor, 30–31 Furnival Street, London EC4A 1JQ*

www.everythingwithwords.com

Text copyright © Richard Blandford 2024
Cover © Holly Ovenden 2024

Richard has asserted his right under the Copyright, Design and
Patents Act 1988 to be identified as the author of this work.

This book is sold subject to the condition that it shall not, by way of trade
or otherwise, be lent, resold, hired out, or otherwise circulated without
the publisher's prior consent in any form of binding or cover other than
that in which it is published and without a similar condition, including this
condition, being imposed on the subsequent purchaser.

*Printed and bound in Great Britain by
CPI Group (UK) Ltd, Croydon CR0 4YY*

A CIP catalogue record for this book is available
from the British Library.

ISBN 978-1-911427-37-7

Song of Myself, 51

The past and present wilt—I have fill'd them, emptied them.
And proceed to fill my next fold of the future.

Listener up there! what have you to confide to me?
Look in my face while I snuff the sidle of evening,
(Talk honestly, no one else hears you, and I stay only a minute longer.)

Do I contradict myself?
Very well then I contradict myself,
(I am large, I contain multitudes.)

I concentrate toward them that are nigh, I wait on the door-slab.

Who has done his day's work? who will soonest be through with his supper?
Who wishes to walk with me?

Will you speak before I am gone? will you prove already too late?

Walt Whitman

Atom Comics. I can tell you a thing or two about them.

Since 1959, there have been 31,284 Atom Comics published. Some of these sparkle with imagination, wit and a surprising level of philosophical insight. Many of them do not, and are derivative, repetitive and uninspired. The art has been, at various points, visionary and boundary-breaking, but is often simply hackwork. Nevertheless, I have read every single one.

I could tell you their history, how they began in New York in 1940 under their original name of Quality Tales Comics, a subdivision of a larger magazine publishing house, and soon flourished under the editorship of Joe David (born Joseph Davidov). That they initially specialised in war comics but diversified into romance, horror, sci-fi, crime and mystery titles as tastes changed in the post-war years. How an upsurge in interest in the superhero genre in the late 1950s led David to rename the company Atom Comics (a reference to the atomic tests happening at the time) and, working primarily with the artists Ben Hammer (whose name perfectly encapsulates his dynamic and action-packed drawing style) and Mo Lightman (who drew in a more sinuous, lyrical manner), launched a new set of titles – *Ghost Frog, Radio Girl, The Silent Scissor, The Super-Absorber* and *The Trout*. About the ingenious way the stories interwove, with the heroes occupying a shared world, characters drifting from one title and into another with a freedom never before attempted in the medium.

I could go on to explain how the company survived the resignations of Hammer and Lightman, and the eventual retirement of David, and continued throughout the ensuing decades, introducing more characters and titles to greater or lesser success, before developments in computerised special effects led to the unexpected arrival of Atom Comics movies in the last few years, achieving a commercial dominance that the comic books (always a cult concern) never managed.

But none of this really matters. What does matter is what happens on the letters page of *The Super-Absorber* #7, published in 1960. A reader complains that on the second panel of p. 16 of the previous month's issue, the titular hero's costume features white zigzags across the shoulders, rather than the customary yellow. This is surely a mistake, the reader says, expecting an apology, if not a refund of the 10 cents he spent on the comic book. It actually is not a mistake, replies writer/editor Joe David, and that in fact, that particular panel occurs in 'a differing reality' in which the Super-Absorber has white zigzags across his shoulders, and not yellow.

The 'differing reality' (DR in fan terminology) rationale was, from that point on, used to explain any momentary deviation from the norm readers found in Atom Comics. Even an audience of mainly prepubescent boys could see this as an obvious ploy on the part of David to cover up the inevitable mistakes that would occur in a medium relying on fast turnaround of production. But this is not the end of it.

Some older Atom Comics fans, unable to leave behind childish things, became aware from conversations with Mo Lightman at early fan conventions that he was a follower of the nineteenth century mystic, medium and probable con-artist Micajah Culp.

Culp's esoteric ideas are seen by some as a precursor to the many-worlds interpretation of quantum mechanics, perhaps coincidentally proposed just two years before the launch of Atom Comics. In any case, throughout the sixties, there was a growing tendency among fans to take the 'differing reality' statements seriously, with a consensus emerging that any Atom Comics story may be jumping back and forth between them, the break from one to another not always even noticeable. Reading Atom Comics while 'high' and looking out for the invisible leaps between realities became a countercultural pursuit. When a few of these stoned fans eventually emerged as the next generation of Atom Comics artists and writers in the early seventies, it was obvious they were deliberately inserting discrepancies in the text and pictures in order to suggest shifts from one reality to another (David, nearing retirement at this time, remained tight-lipped about the seriousness of his 'differing reality' declarations. Goodman, whose sinuous art style had become increasingly eccentric under the influence of Culp, had already quit Atom Comics some years before and was now avoiding all public statements, while Hammer, at the time of his own resignation, said only of the issue that he wanted to work for a publisher where 'no one writes you a thirteen-page letter when you make a mistake'). By the mid-eighties, the idea of 'differing realities' was explicit in the stories themselves, starting with the multi-part 'Infinite Atom' crossover event and carrying on to the present day, the intricacy now their main selling point.

And so, 31,284 comic books. Nearly all of them containing discrepancies that suggest to the eagle-eyed reader that the story has shifted from one reality to another, slightly different one. Atom Comics readers of the world have come to rely on me to identify all these shifts, logging in my online database exactly when they occur while employing a numbering system to denote each reality, a system that requires constant revision with each new publication or revelatory rereading of a back issue.

But not for much longer. For contained in the letters pages of the most recent batch of Atom Comics was an announcement. While the Atom Comics films would continue, the comics company itself was shutting down, the whole enterprise ending in just one month. There was no explanation given. Fans across the world were stunned, the centre of their lives ripped out from them.

I knew why they were stopping (although I would never tell).

Inadvertently, I had helped kill them off.

I remember when I first called it Daddy. I was very young (any older and I would have been too self-conscious to adopt such an affectation), and it had told me the rule was to run around the outside of an emptied-out paddling pool. Sitting on the side, bathing their feet in the absent water were two women in sandals and sundresses. Friends, I should imagine, having a lazy day out. They were older than Lori, which to me then meant they were very old, but were probably younger than I am now as I tip into middle-age. I was running as close to the edge of the pool as possible, without actually being in it.

To get past these two, sitting serenely and enjoying the day, I would have to run around them. But going around them was not the rule. The task that had been set was to run along the edge. If they were on the edge, the only acceptable compromise would be to run over them. And while I knew it was not acceptable to run over people, I also knew that the commands that came from the voice that was not a voice (more an urge) had ultimate authority.

And so, that is what I did, or attempted to. When I came to the first of these women to block my path, I did not slow down. I did not deviate. I carried on running, or attempted to, over her lap.

Immediately, my foot caught in her sundress and I tripped, my head landing fortuitously in the bosom of her companion. Both women shrieked, but due to my then-pocket size and my characteristic lack of momentum, the impact was not that severe, and both swiftly recovered from the interruption.

'I'm sure Mummy and Daddy don't think you should be doing that!' said one of them as I carried on running.

My mother, Lori (a name she chose for herself and by which I always knew her) was on a bench with a book some way away and had not seen. I had not consulted her about the plan. Even then, I knew such things were private.

But the woman had mentioned my daddy. As far as I was aware, I had no daddy. One had not been mentioned by Lori up until that point. So was that voice (that was not a voice) then my daddy? In which case not only did he approve, but it was his idea. From that point on, I have always half-thought of that voice as Daddy. An annoying mental tic that has never gone away, even though the original conceit faded almost as soon as it appeared (as did any childish pleasure I might gain from running. Perhaps not coincidentally I became a stationary creature soon after).

Although I have never been a daddy, I am, it improbably turns out, a father, at least in the tiniest sense of the word. I will meet her for the first time today, at two o'clock, in my least favourite coffee shop on the high street. This is not the sort of thing that is meant to happen to someone such as myself. I come from little and lead to nothing. And yet, here I am, putting on the special clothes I bought for the special meeting with this young woman (whose hobbies include horse riding, exercise classes and something called street dance), and who is, it is very strongly argued, my daughter.

It has gone nine. I am running late. After breakfast, I got stuck in the shower for nearly an hour. This was a long one, even for me. It's not that I believe a shower should last for that amount of time, although I have them religiously (I must not contaminate). It's just that once I have persuaded myself to enter and adjust to the watery world, it can take me that long to face the challenge of transitioning to dryness. And so I exist in a state of limbo, not really wanting to stay, but unable to leave. It is only when I catch a glimpse behind the shower curtain and find the bathroom white with steam that I can bring myself to turn the dial down to nothing and get out (it's the transition from one state to another that is the problem. Where, exactly, is the border? When does one thing definitively stop being itself and become something else? The edge of the paddling pool before the pool itself. Or, how far, for instance, must lips stretch before they change from impassivity and make a smile? These are more things that bother me. And I have trouble smiling).

The showers have gotten longer since the library burned down. But then, without a schedule to stick to, everything has expanded. I have been trying to get dressed now for more than fifteen minutes. So far I have managed to put on my pants and one sock, achieved several minutes ago after a slow start. I have been standing in front of the chest of drawers since then, going over a list in my head. Not a list of useful information that might help me during the course of what will inevitably become one of the most important days of my life. It's a list of comic books, precisely those published by the Atom Comics company in March 1976.

...*Beware The Pummelor!* #2 (DR0001, DR1005)
Ghost Frog #193 (DR0001, DR0009, DR0632)
It's Radio Girl! #19 (DR0084, DR0228, DR0794, DR0917)...

As this happens, I flap my hand rapidly, while my body shakes and my mouth makes all sorts of shapes I would never make in public (the thought of doing so seems pornographic). According to the informative leaflet they gave me, this is a way people like me have of relieving anxiety, and it is true. I have barely thought about meeting my daughter for all the time I have been doing it.

The spell is broken when I hear my landlord (about whom I have suspicions) moving about downstairs, coughing and shouting at his enormous and farcical dog as it repeatedly blocks his way in the cramped living space they share. Before the dread can get me, I reach for the second sock, and stand with it in my hand for several more minutes, it flapping and shaking with me as I once more think of Atom Comics, this time those from September 1981, when a crossover event occurred in that year's annuals for the first time – beginning in *The Trout Annual* #17 (DR0001, DR0033, DR0285), continuing into *Combustible Man Annual* #2 (DR0001, DR0777, DR0931, DR1108) and concluding in *Ghost Frog Annual* #19 (DR0001, DR0435), DR0777, DR1033). This forms a particularly thrilling sequence, and I shake and flap that much more before I am again released, this time by the all-too-familiar sound of the landlord's flatulence seeping through the cardboard-thin floor. The other sock finally on, I pull open the wardrobe where my special new clothes hang.

The shirt has a very pleasing pattern. Dark blue squares

contain three sides of a light blue square containing two sides of a dark blue square containing a light blue square containing a dark blue square and inside that (implicitly if not in reality) a light blue square and inside that a dark blue square and so on. The infinite within limits. The most beautiful completion.

Of course I am nervous about the day. My hands shake as I take the shirt from its hanger, and not with pleasure. But it is not just the meeting with my daughter that makes me like this. There is also the ritual of the haircut I must have this morning. That it is with the same barber that I have gone to at the same time every week for near the past two decades does not make it any easier.

Haircuts distress me. It's always been this way. Lori was the first person to cut my hair. She let it grow long and girlish for several years, until it became a matted mop blocking my vision. I don't remember it at all, but she once told me in one of her rare moments of nostalgia that I screamed and screamed, as if the scissors were actually going into my skull. This does not surprise me. Even now, every snip feels like a violation. I can only imagine what it would have been like for a young child with no idea of what was happening. Would I have known the hair would eventually grow back? Or that the cutting would stop with the hair and not move on to other parts that stuck out (bodily incompleteness being a particular childhood fear of mine)?

Despite my cries, and against her better nature, Lori persisted. And eventually, after no doubt causing me to question my belief in the very existence of love, the cut was finished. How long it took me to recover (if I ever truly did), I do not know.

Several months later, the awful ritual was repeated.

Although this time round I would have understood the limits of this assault from my only source of nourishment and care, the sense of violation would have surely been the same. According to Lori, I shrieked again throughout that second cut, and every subsequent one that followed at six-monthly intervals.

When it came time to start school, the shaggy bowl Lori was so adept at was not considered acceptable. Knowing that she had reached the limit of her haircutting ability, and hoping I perhaps might respond better to a stranger, I was somehow sweet-talked into visiting the local barber.

I know that the pole outside, revolving and sending the red and white stripes into infinity, would have stolen my heart. How could something represented by such perfect order be bad, I must have thought. This alone could easily have persuaded me to pull myself onto the booster seat, and sit back with the plastic cape wrapped around me.

As Lori told it, I did not respond better to a stranger. Without the protective layer of maternal comfort, the horror of the exercise hit me all the harder at the first sight of the scissors. I bawled, I thrashed, I climbed under the bench, bringing down a shower of magazines on top of me as I went.

How long was I under there, in my new kingdom comprising only myself, a wooden bench frame and a scattering of men's magazines? Probably less than half an hour, but my dim recollection is of a much longer time. I remember it as days. Days of refusal. Refusal to move myself from the corner I had curled up in. Refusal to engage with the pleas from Lori as the barber gradually slipped from a jovial acceptance of the situation to insistence that it all get wrapped up as he did have other customers, you see. For in that eternity under the bench,

I had discovered something. If the world around me would not behave, and insisted on jabbing me with scissors and slicing off parts of my actual body and letting them drop to the floor, I could shrink the world until it was just myself. Until external reality came to its senses and treated me properly, I could simply deny it, so long as it kept its distance.

It did not keep its distance. The situation was eventually resolved when the now quite angry barber picked up the bench and flung it to one side, destroying my new kingdom forever. Thankfully, he was no longer interested in finishing the job he had started, and the haircut had to be completed at home, with Lori's fears of operating beyond her level of competence fully realised (she would turn her hand to many activities over the years as a matter of necessity, but not achieve elegance in all of them). I would start school with a haircut that defied all sense of shape and order. It would still be some years before I saw that Lori's arguments in favour of barbers had merit, and grudgingly agreed to go once more (although to a different barber and a different pole).

Today's cut could easily wait a week. I could skip it without consequence. But you've got to maintain the system.

My new mobile phone mimics a penny whistle for my attention. I have only had it a few days. The first one I have ever owned. Up until this point, the merits of being bothered when you left the house had escaped me (not that the landline rings now). In truth, it scares me. A tentative step into a century that still makes me nervous well into its second decade. But once a message from my daughter (who communicates in more ways in one day than I have mastered in a lifetime, but does not think she has ever used an old-fashioned telephone), went unread by me for a full five hours, and I caved to the inevitable.

So far, I have done little with it. The only number saved in it is hers (the purity of that appeals). I have downloaded no 'apps'. But I have let it tell me about my emails. Sure enough, the whistle is informing me of yet another critique of the latest updates to the database. I already have dozens I need to reply to, all from users unhappy about my latest adjustments. I don't get much thanks for the work I do. Not that I do it for the recognition.

It has been suggested to me that I should get a cat. It would break the monotony, the cat-suggester said. They would provide company, and fun. What this well-meaning individual failed to understand is that the monotony is entirely by design, and while I sometimes feel bowed down under its suffocating pressure, it brings its own comfort. Besides, the idea of a living creature being dependent on me to keep it alive is inherently stressful. It is hard enough to keep myself fed and watered. I have never really looked after anybody or anything in my life.

Other reasons for not getting a cat are that, firstly, the cartoonish dog downstairs would no doubt be driven insane by its sensed presence and, secondly, that I cannot think of any criteria for choosing a name. I am not sentimental, so do not wish to honour anybody I have known or admire by naming a cat after them. And I have never found any aspect of a cat's appearance or behaviour so humorous I would wish to immortalise it. Perhaps the titling of a hypothetical cat is something I could talk to my daughter about as we drink the expensive coffee and eat the nice cake.

Without being consciously aware of doing it, I have placed one of my legs in my new trousers (a lighter colour than I have ever worn on my lower body, they are smarter than jeans, but not smart enough for work. I have no use for them after today).

But now I am stuck again. Tugging fruitlessly at trousers that can never be said to be properly on until I can bring myself to lift my other leg. But it does not lift. Something is holding me back. Too many things are out of alignment.

Firstly, today is hotter than it is meant to be. It is late spring, but summer wants to arrive early, I can tell. My new clothes are heavy on me, and I haven't even got them on properly yet.

Also, I have nearly no money. I'm only on half-pay while I wait for the library to re-open in its new portable location, and after the phone and the clothes, all the money I have in the world is in my wallet. Once I have treated my daughter (who no doubt hangs out in coffee shops with her friends for hours, ordering the stranger drinks I cannot even pronounce) to the most expensive cup of coffee in town, there will be little else to keep me going until the next depleted amount appears.

But there is something bigger than these irritations. An unshakeable sensation of freefall. That the guide rope I had been clinging to all my life somehow got burned up in the library fire. Of what little destiny I had being fulfilled, in that act of mildest heroism. I am in unwritten time, and I am scared.

The trousers are on. In one final burst of concentration, so are new shoes, laces tied (did I really need new shoes? Will she be looking at my feet?). Time elapsed, too many minutes.

I will make the bus on time. I will arrive at the barbers on schedule at nine forty-five (my schedule, not the barber's. He does not care what time I arrive).

I am not always like this (I am always like this).

Although I never really change, I am sometimes also my own opposite ('Do I contradict myself…'). And while I hesitate to ever classify myself as anything in particular other than an exception to any rule (I have lived a life in brackets), I have to admit I have been given labels in the past by others (although not often with enthusiasm, and rarely do they stick). But now in this after-time, I have new labels, and a new name. I do not enjoy my new title, but it has to be said that, in the moment of my christening, it gifted me with a clarity I have never before possessed. It was only then I could truly see the long crawl that led to the slight rise. When all the shaking and flapping of years gone by added up to a something that was more than nothing. When, in the heat of fire I was temporarily elevated and earned the name of Fantasticus Autisticus.

Stepping out from the barbers into the mid-morning sun, my legs are weak from it all. The infringement of the shaver. The forced familiarity. The inevitable question of what I was doing this weekend and my habitual inability to come up with an answer that would strike someone such as a barber as legitimate.

As I do every week, I need to sit down and recalibrate. Read a little (I have a *Radio Girl: Secret Signals* omnibus with me in my satchel). Perhaps also work my way through my inbox of complaint. It is time to start orbiting.

After the entry point of the barbers, my orbit continues up the left-hand side of the high street, passing the launderette which I do not use (the landlord lets me do one wash a week in his machine, his gargantuan dog licking the exposed small of my back as I bend down) and the peculiar 'reading room' of uncertain spiritual persuasion next door, before reaching its first port of call – the town's comic shop. I will always stop here. There is a small cafe area at the back where cups of powdered coffee and ageing biscuits can be bought very cheap. This makes it my favourite coffee shop in town.

Slightly further on is my second-favourite coffee shop. This is an optional stop, only taken if a roleplaying game in the comic shop back room gets too overheated. The coffee is nicer, but the price is not. There is little to interest me for a while until the old Methodist church, a building much too big for the number of Methodists now found in the town. This is also only an occasional stop (the religious element is not an attraction) as its doors are only occasionally open. But when they are, they sell second-hand books to raise money for their decaying building, and every so often a gem can be found amongst the dross.

Once past the church, the high street descends into a row of boutiques, selling nothing I could ever afford to buy (or interest me if I did), but it is here that is the location for my least favourite coffee shop in town, where I will nevertheless in just a few hours be meeting my daughter (who grew up in a home where no one worried about money – at least, the price of a cup of coffee) for the first time.

Beyond this, the high street reaches its farthest point, the road becoming another and pointing to the left, up to the train station and beyond that, the library that is still nominally my place of work.

I do not usually make it this far. In the normal course of things I cross over the road at the expensive coffee shop, where it narrows and favours the pedestrian with cobbles instead of tarmac, to where on the other side is the town's main bookshop, where everything is new and not dog-eared and tea-stained. I never buy anything in there. I don't know anyone who does. But we all like to look.

I then move in the opposite direction, heading the way I have just been, but now on the opposite side of the road. There is a department store here which is very much an optional stop. I only go in here if an item of clothing has worn away to rags and is in need of urgent replacement. I bought my new special clothes here. I even used the changing rooms. I'm hoping no more special clothes are required between now and death. I can say no more about it.

There are more shops like this before the high street begins to cater more to my level of income. A budget supermarket followed by what is known only as 'the cheap shop', an otherwise nameless bazaar where all sorts of oddities wash up, on sale for prices so low it has to be wondered whether criminality is involved somewhere.

Most of my needs are catered for by these two shops. But it is not to them that I go next. My orbit has a complication. I first go past them, crossing the road again, and to a charity bookshop, before crossing back again to another similar shop (beyond is the bad part of town to which I never venture), only then going back on myself to visit the cheap shop and the supermarket, and then catching the bus back home. I knew from past experience it would be practically impossible to navigate the charity shops with bags full of shopping. Daddy was not happy with this imperfection in the orbit, taking it away from the concept of a perfect lap (again with the laps), but it feels like he's accepted it now. He doesn't shout too loudly when I cross the road, anyway.

It does not make sense to be orbiting today. I could easily get on the bus back home and come back later. But an orbit always begins with a haircut, and a haircut has been had, so an orbit must follow (I don't make the rules).

And it's not just me who orbits (although I admit I probably take it the most seriously). There must be at least twenty others like me that I recognise by sight, and possibly many more that I don't, routinely travelling with little sense of purpose round the centre of this small town. People who don't quite belong where people are meant to, in the usual families or clubs or circles or workplaces.

We aren't all friends, exactly, in the usual sense of the word. We don't often arrange to hang out. But as we each make our own individual circuit of the town centre, we sometimes fall in step with at least one other, and a brief companionship of sorts arises. Rarely will you get a group of more than three, but sometimes, maybe once or twice a year, six or even more of us will achieve perfect alignment, and from a distance you might think of us as our own fragile community, ready to be blown into the wind by the slightest breeze.

I see one of them out of the corner of my eye, orbiting in the opposite direction to me. A studious-looking young man of no fixed institution, his long hair a bit too unkempt for acceptance. We nod awkwardly and carry on. He is not someone I talk to. I only know him as someone who knows Olly, which isn't enough for a conversation (sometimes I think Olly is the fulcrum of the orbiter world. Without him, none of us would even acknowledge each other).

As I approach the comic shop now, the thicker-than-I'm-used-to fabric of the shirt weighing heavily on me all of a sudden, I know that Olly will be there, holding court in that back room, cadging cups of coffee off his acolytes. I am not in the mood for Olly. I very rarely am. But I am perhaps more comfortable in his presence than that of others. He is probably my best friend, in that I talk to him about things I don't talk to anyone else about, even if he mostly doesn't listen.

I arrive. Marcus, the manager, looks drawn from sleepless

nights, his skin as grey as his favourite and ancient Radio Girl T-shirt.

'I still can't believe it,' he says.

Needless to say, he is talking about the imminent closedown of Atom Comics. It has affected him badly, and not just because of the inevitable loss of trade.

'It is a shock,' I say, but no more.

He presents me with a batch of comics and clears a space on his desk.

'I expect you'll miss them too,' he says.

I make some sort of noise but say nothing. It's too difficult a question to answer.

Marcus recognises my importance in the online Atom Comics culture, allowing me special browsing rights. I can read all the new issues as they come in, as long as I purchase one on occasion (this was not one of those). It does not take me long. I have been doing it for so many years, and have read so many, that I can now absorb each comic book in a matter of minutes, making note of DR shifts in my head as I go, ready to add to the database when I get home (I never make notes. That's when the errors creep in). This week, there are seven new Atom Comics. I have read all of them in twenty-two minutes.

As I flick my way through the small pile, I can hear Olly's voice booming out from the back room. 'You seriously rate that film in its theatrical release version? You total prick. There's a fan edit that's better. It gets rid of everything that doesn't work and puts all the bonus stuff that you need from the Blu-ray where it needs to go. You can torrent it. I'll send you the link...'

The young people who come here all listen to Olly, even

though he's only a few years younger than me and habitually insults them. He knows all about the new things – the films, the TV shows, the games – although he's never paid for any of them, priding himself on not having set foot inside a cinema for eighteen years (even I have benefited from his expertise regarding covert downloads). He doesn't do books, however, being very much a visual learner.

I put off going back to see him for a few minutes longer, even though I can see him well through the open doorway that leads to the back room. The comics are soothing, meditative. Olly is not. But I know, in his way, he is necessary.

'Heeee's…

Fantasticus!

Fantasticus!

Fantasticus Autisticus!'

He's seen me. And now there he is, singing the song he came up with after the fire, doing a little dance at the table. The surrounding teenagers turn to stare at me like I'm a newly discovered species of animal.

I don't think the song is Olly's, not properly. It's his version of another song. He's explained it to me but I don't understand. I don't know much about music. After peripatetic trumpet lessons in school led to a most traumatic experience, I almost fear it. Olly knows about all the music.

As the song and dance finally reach their conclusion, the youths scatter, sensing that grown-up business, of a sort, is now occurring. I pull out a chair and sit down opposite with my small plastic cup of powdered coffee.

'Alright, Fantasticus, you magnificent wanker. How's life treating you?' The insults I don't even hear anymore. But it's that particular name he's given me that jars, despite its peculiar resonance. You never know where you are with nicknames. They can turn from signs of affection to cruelty without a letter being changed. That's one thing you learn in school. But still I let it go. I know from experience, you can't stop Olly from doing anything he's already doing. You just have to wait for the idea to burn itself out. It may take days, it may take a lifetime, but it is the only way.

I shrug (I have three physical gestures of communication – nod my head, shake my head and shrug. Anything beyond that is ostentation) and make a noncommittal noise in reply. I will say something but not yet. You need to let Olly blow off a little steam first, or there's no hope of getting through. Neither of us look each other in the eye. This is one of the good things about Olly. Unlike nearly everyone else, he doesn't expect it because he can't do it himself. I can't do it because on the rare occasions I've tried, the person's gaze has ripped right through me, uncovering my darkest secrets, exposing all to the light and leaving me with nothing. Olly, on the other hand, can't do it because his eyes have a tendency to veer in different directions. He once told me (not that I'd asked) that his field of vision was one of constant overlap and an occasional blind spot in the middle. Growing up, he never realised things were meant to be different because it was all he ever knew. I knew what he meant.

''Ere, Fantasticus, what do you make of the new *Combustible Man* film, what with you being an expert on that Atom Comics stuff. I pirated it last night and I thought it was the weakest one, although it's definitely better than *Atom Agents*, which was wank. Stevo over there liked it though, didn't you, you tosser…'

The films based on Atom Comics do not interest me. While

they share characters and some basic plotlines with their source material, they make no use of the differing reality concept at all and, therefore, I do not consider them canon. Olly does not understand this. There is no point trying to answer his question with this. Not only because he is still talking and cannot be stopped, but because I do not have the capacity to interrupt people, even those who cannot interrupt themselves. Consequently, I have spent a lot of time waiting for people to finish their sentences.

'...anyway, this major dickhead online says he's seen a leaked version which is thirty minutes longer, and I'm like, fair enough, I'll look into it and I do that and there is no leak, there is no extra half hour, just this guy talking shit...'

Olly is wearing his nice suit today. Perhaps he has a job interview. Or perhaps he just feels like wearing his nice suit. He has several, all from charity shops, and this is the only one that sits sensibly on his body. He goes for job interviews a lot. Sometimes he even gets the job, but never for long. At least, never long enough to get out of his parents' attic conversion.

'...so yeah, what do you reckon? *Atom Agents* or *Combustible Man: World on Fire*? What would you go for?'

'I would have to say... *Combustible Man: World on Fire*.' I have seen neither.

'Yeah, that's what I thought. I'll tell this prick you said that, because you're the expert.' I feel like protesting against my reputation being used to settle a daft internet argument, but it doesn't matter. He is moving on. 'Did you hear about what happened to Ahmet?' he is saying now.

Ahmet is another orbiter. A quiet and happy man, overly apologetic about his own presence as he feeds his enthusiasm for old horror paperbacks. Ahmet can always be found protected by his puffa jacket, hood up, whatever the weather. He lives with his brother, who helps him to not spend all his money at once (perhaps a little too well) and gives him odd tasks to do around town while he circles. His path crosses mine at various points and we do the usual orbiter nod. People like Ahmet. I don't mind him.

'Some prick conned him out of money in one of the charity shops. Asked him if he could borrow twenty quid for two hours. Never gave it back.'

'That's bad,' I say, because that is the sort of thing you say when someone tells you this type of news, I have learned. It is bad, though. Twenty quid would be a lot of money to Ahmet. It's a fair amount to me. This twinge of sympathy reassures me that the worst things people have said about me over the years aren't totally true.

'Yeah, happened yesterday. Said I'd keep an eye out for the bloke. I'm pretty sure I know who it is he's talking about. Right shifty fucker. Listen, do you want to wander round town, see if we can spot him?'

A wander is not an orbit. And my orbit has begun.

I shake my head.

'I'm seeing my daughter later,' I say.

Olly's face is a blank. Slowly, a penny drops inside it.

'Oh, yeah, I remember now,' he says, relieving me of the worry that the hard work I put into sharing such sensitive personal information not that long ago was for nought. 'But you're not going right away, are you?'

'Well, no, we're not meeting until two, but…'

'It's only half-ten now. You could walk around a little bit with me, couldn't you?'

'I don't know. It's a big event. I need to be in the right frame of mind. And I've got emails…'

'Yeah, you could do an hour though. Come on, let's go. Oh, actually, let's get another cup first. I'd pay, but I'm broke until Monday.'

Olly exists in a perpetual state of being broke until Monday. Even on Mondays. I, on the other hand, with even a half-income, makes me wealthy in the orbiter community. I sigh. The urge to orbit is strong, but the iron will of Olly will always be stronger. I reach for my wallet.

'You're a star, Fantasticus,' he says. 'But don't forget the biscuits.'

'This would be easier with a car,' says Olly, as we head down the high street, towards the shabby end where the second-hand shops are. We've been walking for over quarter of an hour at a snail's pace, and I haven't been able to think of a good enough reason to get away. That I am not following my orbit, even a truncated one that avoids food shopping (even I know you are not meant to turn up to a meeting with your long-lost daughter with groceries) is making Daddy mutter. Not to mention that it's not even midday and the heat is already prickly, while my new shoes are rubbing on the back of my ankles. Yes, it would be easier in a car, but orbiters don't drive. We wouldn't be orbiters if we did.

We've passed several others of our firmly pedestrian kind, none of whom have seen the man in question. Some of them know who he is though, which at least means that he is not a dream. Meanwhile, Olly's head is shifting from side to side, scanning the streets for this particular miscreant I wouldn't know from Adam. 'Oi, Fantasticus, imagine driving down here in a Ferrari with the top down. You'd have to learn how to drive, though. I can't because of my eyes. Why don't you drive, Fantasticus?'

'I never got round to it,' I say. This is not the whole truth. The reason I have never learnt to drive is because the idea of sitting behind the wheel of a vehicle designed to accelerate at great speed seems insane, and I don't understand why everyone who's ever tried isn't dead. I can't say this to Olly, though. It's not the sort of thing he'd understand.

'Hang on,' says Olly, 'isn't that Teigan? The one you thought you stood a chance with? But then you talked to her and it went wrong?'

He's right. There she is, on the other side of the street, in a light yellow summer dress even I recognise as stylish (that she thought to look out the window first before choosing her clothes strikes me as some kind of marvel). My stomach somehow leaps and shrivels at the same time at the sight of her as she stands alert, as she always is, scanning her environment for any potential threat.

Yes, I did show a brief interest in Teigan. But it was very casual, and certainly not a concerted effort on my part to end the dry spell I have been in for... some time. And there was that one time I bumped into her when I just happened to be where she would likely to be on a particular day, and I walked with her and we talked a little bit and then we slipped into a long silence which I thought demonstrated a level of comfort in each other's presence but apparently, I was later informed by a third party via the fourth party of Olly, she found deeply awkward (although I maintain that if she found it really so unpleasant, she could have easily lifted the silence by saying something herself).

What it is about her I find appealing, I am not sure. It

would be nice to think it's because I want to protect her from whatever the perceived threat that constantly worries her might be, but that doesn't sound like me at all. Maybe it's because I can't imagine her making any big demands, although I already seem to have failed to provide the basics she did expect. And I like the fact she has a distinct look that has nothing to do with fashion. Short faunlike hair (no fear of the scissors for her), and the very best charity shop clothes that she can make look as if she's just bought them in one of the boutiques at the top of the high street. An attention to detail. My type of thing. Anyway, it seems like I'm not her type of thing, so it's all in the past now, a whole month and a half ago. Before the fire. Before the email. I have moved on, and have other things on my mind (although I do still think about her quite regularly).

'Oi!' shouts Olly, and whistles loudly with his fingers in his mouth. She looks up, startled. 'Teigan, over here!'

She glances both ways as if looking for an escape route. Finding none, she gives us a reluctant wave of recognition. Before I can stop him, Olly is striding over the road towards her, not looking at the traffic. It parts for him in both directions, like the Red Sea. The world works like that for Olly. In small ways, anyway. I wait for a safe moment to cross and follow, once again surviving that particular dance with death.

I don't know why Teigan is an orbiter. Her clothes hang from her body in the way they should, and she can do all the superhuman things women are meant to do, like painting her nails and wearing make-up in a way that doesn't make her look like a clown. I could easily imagine her in an office, behind a till or even in an estate or travel agents, persuading someone to spend far more money than they should. But something stops her joining in all that, getting in the way of her giving the appropriate smile. Something keeps her permanently worried about some unseen enemy that could get her at any second. Whatever it is keeps her down here, on the tatty end of the high street, with us.

'Alright, Teigan,' says Olly, while he's still some feet away. Chivalrously, his habitual insults never extend to the opposite sex. 'How's it going? Me and Fantasticus here are just cruising, looking for some bloke we have to duff up, what are you up to?'

'We're not going to beat anyone up,' I say, across the respectful distance I am keeping.

'Yeah, you know Ahmet, right?' continues Olly. 'Some prick conned him out of twenty quid and we're going to get it back.'

'That's terrible,' she says, her voice delicate as a dried-out leaf.

'Yeah, so we're going to find him and we're going to say, give Ahmet his twenty quid back, plus interest, or we're going to smash your brains out with this lead pipe.'

Olly mimes swinging said lead pipe in the air, making Teigan duck and hide her head in her hands.

'We won't be doing that,' I say, pointlessly.

'So you're more than welcome to join me and Fantasticus here, keep an eye out for a shifty fucker, wears a baseball cap, carries a rucksack. What do you reckon?'

She looks still more alarmed, her head darting in all directions. Remarkably, this habit of hers makes eye contact so unlikely I can look directly at her with far greater ease than with anyone else I know. I notice her chin has a slight cleft, and the bridge of her nose is remarkably flat. I don't often notice these things about people.

'I can't, I think,' she says. Just that.

'Well, if you change your mind, you know where to find us. Battering some joker in an alleyway until he gives us the fucking money!'

Olly's voice is a roar now that bounces off the buildings. In that moment, his unemployed status strikes me as natural and right.

'We're... we're not going to be doing any of that,' I say to Teigan, as she edges away sideways.

I'm expecting nothing more. She gives so little at the best of times, and this is not one of those. But then, she turns her head, almost so that she's looking at me, and says, 'Why are you... why does he call you Fantasticus?'

The personal nature of the question thrills and invades in equal measure. I thought there was no coming back after the walk of silence, but there are, it seems, moments of grace and here she is, taking an interest in something about me. But the words do not come. Sometimes, they just don't.

'It's... it's a long story,' is all I can think to say. And what follows is a silence so deep even Olly cannot think how to fill it.

'Oh, OK' she says, her gaze dropping far down to the ground, as if I've just smashed something over her head. 'Anyway, I've got to go.'

And she does go, skittering down the road away from me as fast as her legs will take her without breaking into a run.

'Oh, mate, you screwed that up massively.' Olly has started up almost immediately. 'She was so giving you an opening and you totally bottled it. Don't know how you're coming back from this. I was bigging you up to her the other day actually after the mess you made, but you might well have properly fucked it now. Sorry, mate. Just calling it like I see it.'

I don't say anything. I clench my fists and try to contain my fury. My anger at myself for getting it so wrong. At Teigan for not being able to read my mind and see my inner pure self. At Olly for being there to witness it all. Next thing I know I find I'm trying to squeeze the anger out of my legs.

'You alright, mate? Your face is all weird.'

I'm in public, and I'm doing one of the things I have always done and that I taught myself not to do in front of people many years ago (the squeezing is the shaking and the flapping's irate cousin). Something that must never be seen is happening on the street. Doesn't matter if I have a doctor's note explaining it. You can't go around doing things like this in front of bus drivers and the like. It has no place in their world.

I release my grip and try to breathe normally. I'm conscious my face is probably now some horrible grape-like purple.

'What was that about? Is that one of the things you do because you're Fantasticus Autisticus?'

I say nothing. Obviously, he's right, but the idea of having my behaviour held up for inspection like this revolts me. There is nowhere to go but in. For a moment, I am once again in my own personal kingdom underneath the barber's bench. Nothing can touch me here, not even Olly's incessant river of speech. His voice becomes just a noise like a road drill or a seagull. Annoying but not something to think about.

I am rescued from further enquiries when Olly spots Ahmet rifling in the cheap bins out front of the charity bookshop opposite. He calls out to him and once more crosses the road back to where we were, the Moses effect occurring for him as usual. Again, I follow him cautiously, and get the blare of a car horn for my troubles.

'Ahmet. Hey, Ahmet, you loveable fucker. Me and Fantasticus are on the case. We're going to get your money back, don't you worry about it.'

Ahmet lifts himself out of the book bin, barely emerging from his puffa jacket shell.

'Oh, don't put yourself out,' he says. 'My mistake. Should have been more careful. This sort of thing keeps on happening to me. I'm too trusting, that's my problem.'

'Don't talk shit, Ahmet. This guy fucked you over. No one fucks over one of my mates. Anyone does that, I give them one chance. And after that, they'll be lucky if they aren't pissing through a straw. Fantasticus is the same, aren't you, Fantasticus?'

'Um, not really, but...'

'Well, it's very kind of you,' says Ahmet. 'But please don't put yourself out.'

'Not putting ourselves out, not at all,' said Olly. 'Anything for you, Ahmet, you're a mate. Seen anything you like?'

'Well, there is a good book here that I would like, but I don't know if I can get it.'

'How much is it?' says Olly.

'You can buy three books for one pound. I have five pounds. But my brother gave that to me for the special soup he likes.'

'Don't look at me, mate, I'm broke until Monday. But Fantasticus will get it for you, won't you?'

'Um... yes,' I say, searching for and finding my last spare pound in the coin purse of my wallet, trying to hide the notes I need for later when I see my daughter (I keep my wallet in the front pocket of my trousers, not the back. People think this is strange, but they're the ones sitting on their wallets).

I give Ahmet the pound. He buys three books, but he only wants one – a long novel about killer crabs – and so gives Olly and me a book each before he hurries on his way to the next stop, his protective shell of a jacket shining in the sun. I can only wonder how hot it must be inside.

I look at the book Ahmet has given me. It's a children's book of fairy tales – a cheap modern reprint of a much finer, older edition, chocolate stains marking the outer pages from beginning to end. I know this book. Seeing it again almost makes me feel nostalgic for a very different time. Almost.

'You can have mine, too,' says Olly, handing me the book Ahmet has just seconds before given him. 'I don't want it. Print is dead. Everyone knows that.'

The book is the hefty hardback autobiography of a television gardener. I do not want it either.

'Right,' says Olly, 'back on the case, pardner.'

'I've got to get on,' I say, as I struggle to fit the two new books in my satchel. The fairy tales book is too tall, the gardener's book too fat. I give up and tuck them under my arm.

'But we haven't found the geezer yet, Fantasticus. He's taken twenty quid of Ahmet's money! Does that not strike you as a serious injustice in need of rectification with extreme prejudice and also extreme violence?'

'Yes, well, no to the violence. But I'm meeting my daughter—'

'Yeah, but that's not until later. You said. Listen, it's against all my principles but I'm willing to compromise, yeah? Just this once because it's you. We'll split up. You take this end of the high street, I'll go back the other way. We'll meet up in an hour back at the comic shop.'

'Uh. Yeah, sure.'

'I've given you my number, yeah?'

'Yes,' I say. It is a lie (the number is written on a scrap of paper in my desk drawer) and slips out easily, as it requires no emotion to back it up. I can tell false facts with ease, but cannot fake the feelings behind them, I have discovered. It would be no bother to take the number now. But then the purity of that phone address book, with its one number, would be gone.

'I'll see you, then. One hour. Laters, gators.'

Olly swiftly turns and heads back in the opposite direction, the flaps of his suit jacket lifting slightly in the wind behind him. I wait until he's far enough away in the distance, and head for the nearest bench. It's not the best part of town to sit. It gets rough at this end, before you run out of high street entirely and you end up in the bad part of town I don't like to walk through. But Olly's stalking the good part of town, so that's that.

I put the books and magazine down next to me, get out my phone and read the first email. Some pushy American is complaining about my decision to place three pages of *The Silent Scissor: Death by a Thousand Cuts* mini-series #3 in DR 7641, when due to the curious spelling of 'jasmine' as 'jamsine' on a billboard, these pages should occur in DR4410, the setting of *Junior Atom Agents* #32, pp. 16–22, where the same spelling occurs not once but twice. I reply to him, politely but firmly, that the same variant spelling can potentially occur in multiple DRs, and that is not in itself enough to assume that they are one and the same. If further evidence comes to light, then I shall reconsider, but until then, my decision remains unchanged.

I open the second email. I do not read it. My mind has already journeyed elsewhere.

I am thinking about my daughter (who has many friends and smiles with natural ease in the photos she has sent me. For my part, I do not like having my photo taken. It feels worse than a haircut. There is only one photo of me taken in the past decade. It is for my work identification badge. I sent her that in response). I am thinking about how I have not told her what I am. I will have to tell her. I haven't been able to hide it up until now, even when neither myself or anyone else knew what 'it' was. It would be best to just say it up front.

But the word in and of itself explains nothing (there are so many different varieties of us). It does not explain the library, or the database or what I am doing in that shoebox of a flat. It does not explain the orbiting or the overpriced comic book in my satchel or how I accidentally helped make her in the first place.

Daddy awakens (although he's never really asleep, just dozing). He has an idea (that is a command that is a system as always forever and ever until we both go down together). Tell it to her. Everything. Think of it all now, while you wait, and then write it all down at a later date, such as tomorrow (don't worry, you won't forget a single word. You never do). It could be a book. A book for one reader. Perhaps just a lengthy pamphlet. But it must all be in your head before you see her. That is the rule (Why is it the rule? Because it is the rule).

I don't know if I like the idea. I can see the benefits, but it seems so big a task. And would she really want all of it, my entire life? Wouldn't she be happier with bullet points? Oh come on, it's not about what she wants.

The words are already filling my head by the second, like

a tape playing too fast. The moment to raise an objection has gone (but was never really there). The new task fills me up. I belong to it now and never mind everything else. It was not there and now it is and it is all there is. It has been like this since the beginning.

And in the beginning…

In the beginning...

In the beginning... there were blocks. Wooden, with a dark, smoky taste, good for gnawing on with my baby teeth, breaking through the gum. Six blue. Six green. Six yellow. Six red (red were the best). They came in their own trolley, fitting neatly into a tray fixed above red wheels, with a blue handle I suppose the infant me must have pushed as I learned to walk, although I don't remember the pushing. The blocks were the thing, and all the potential orders contained within them. One line of red on top of one line of blue on top of one line of yellow on top of one line of green. Or a tower of blue next to a tower of green next to a tower of red next to a tower of yellow. Or one block yellow, one block blue, one block red, one block green and then back to yellow again, repeating potentially on into infinity.

The satisfaction of a system properly realised would fill my mind and body. I would shake with delight. The blocks would fill the world until there was no world beyond. No front room, no sky, only them. Perhaps Lori still existed in such moments, but only as a living object I could share my joy of the blocks with. It would have been only us there, in that flat I remember being immense but must have been so small, as it filled with blocks in my mind like a tidal wave, covering every surface, converting it all into something both endless and complete.

It wasn't an intellectual thrill, but sensual. I was in love with any order that consumed me. And the order would be my world until another took me over and its predecessor would seem ugly and alien if I ever looked back on it, although I rarely did.

I wonder when the first time was I ever held onto a system for too long, after I had stopped believing in it, but still finding it all but impossible to push it away. When did the demand first outlast the joy, and the innocence of the blocks came to an end?

And before the beginning...

Who my father was is a secret Lori took to her grave. She never felt the need to tell me, and I never thought to ask. He announced his irrelevance by his absence, was how I must have seen it. Did he even know I existed, and would it have changed anything if he did? I doubt it. Even if he had met me, I was not the sort of child a distanced parent would likely demand to have in their life.

And so all that can be said about my father is that Lori knew him, in at least one sense, while studying at a polytechnic in a town that was not her own in the 1970s. A fellow student perhaps. Or a tutor (it was after all the 1970s).

It could be hypothesised that my father was tall. I am taller than Lori was, and I do not recollect any of her relatives being giants. My skin is defiantly pale, while Lori tanned dark and easily. So, a tall pale man, possibly (if it is indeed hereditary) behaving awkwardly in social situations (although evidently not that awkward). Still out there, maybe. But it doesn't matter. He will never look for me. I will never look for him.

Who my mother was (and with whom I share no perceivable

characteristics) is a lot easier to answer, at least superficially. One thing I can tell you about Lori was that she was always young. I don't think many people think of their parents as young when they're growing up, but she always was. All the other kids' mums were older, even when they weren't really. There was just something about her that always stopped her fully crossing into the adult world. A freshness, a brilliance almost, however many hours she worked, however many years actually passed. It was only towards the very end that a tiredness crept in that showed her youth was ending, and when it was gone so would she.

But that is for later. For now, what needs to be said is that she came from a family of box stackers, fish canners and drivers of milk floats (who would never call her Lori), and was the first of them to ever make it to higher education. That her attempt at a degree in the Humanities was derailed by my arrival. How her status as an unmarried mother was greeted by her family, back when such things were so often shameful, is another thing I do not know. Lori did not dwell out loud. Her attitude was to always move forward, to the next thing and the next thing and the next. I do now wonder if she could have been secretly looking back as she gazed into space, clutching cups of tea that went cold in her hands, as I have caught myself doing much the same of late on a few occasions (I cling to this look of hers as one of the few specifics I still have. Not many years gone, and I already struggle to remember precise things she said, or the manner in which she said them. A few fragments, none big enough to share and be understood. I can give you the gist – a sketch of her, but I cannot quite bring her back to life. I can, on the other hand, tell you in detail the contents of every issue of Ghost Frog: Underworld #1–49).

But a lot of the time she was not gazing. She was in productive motion. Decorating. DIY. Making. Sewing, sawing, baking. Life to her was a thing that could be mended, altered and improved. Her naturally black hair (the later streaks of white did not age her) was nearly always pulled up and covered by a scarf to stop it dropping down and becoming entangled in whatever she was working on at that moment. And when she wasn't working little domestic miracles and I was old enough to be left, she would be at work, job after job, always learning, always adapting, although never that well-paid. Launderettes, cafes, toilets. She did them all, grafting as well as any. Always keep moving, seemed to be the message of her life. She was a survivor, until suddenly she wasn't.

Finally, when all work was done, it would often be just the two of us, sat on the sofa watching a black and white TV drinking milky tea, or days out at the library (which I found exciting more for the little numbered stickers on the side of the books than the books themselves), or on the bus to bird sanctuaries and nearby woods, both on sunny days and in pakamac weather. We spent a lot of time learning the names of plants and trees. I don't remember any of them now. What the difference is between a beech or an ash leaf has been pushed out of my brain by too many years of other categorisations, and I wonder now if Lori was even that interested in trees, or whether it was just that trees didn't charge to be looked at. Nevertheless, she embraced it all with enthusiasm, as she did everything she set her mind to. An enthusiasm that I now see was often the only thing that stopped us from sinking. Maybe it would have been good if she was less enthusiastic about some things, like the boyfriends (her type liked to present themselves as creative or spiritual or enigmatic – woodworkers, karate teachers, artists of some type – but became tiresomely oafish once their feet were under the table). But again, I'm getting ahead of myself.

Her family I only vaguely remember. They were there a fair amount in the beginning, I think, before they started disappearing. Lori moved back in with her parents with me for a while after I was born. She'd get a little council flat of her own by the time I was a toddler (where the blocks were). I can still see the living room of that flat's wallpaper – squares within squares of orange and brown that were nearly as exciting as the bricks. Black and white squares of linoleum on the kitchen floor. Artex swirls on the bathroom ceiling Lori made herself.

And I recall relatives visiting us among these patterns, or us going to them in homes that had patterns of their own. I can just about conjure a grandfather who smelt of pipe tobacco. A grandmother who smelt of mothballs. Cousins who were children, like me (but not like me). Other cousins who were older. The aunts and great-aunts, an occasional uncle. I would end up being jiggled on a knee, or given a raspberry on my belly that covered me in spit. The talking, the cousins playing games I didn't understand, the chink of spoons swirling sugars into endless cups of tea – it was all just noise.

Only one time did the noise come from me. It was a Christmas Day. We were at my grandparents'. Big family gathering. Seemed like a hundred people in that room, although it was probably only slightly more than ten, when some uncle-by-marriage reached down apropos nothing at all, interrupting whatever fantasia of patterns I may have been engaged in, and ripped the nose right from my face.

'Got yer nose!' he said, smiling, as if this was anything to smile about.

And there, sure enough between his index and middle finger, was my nose, red and bulbous.

I instinctively covered the gaping hole in the centre of my face where my nose had only recently been and screamed for Lori. Not being able to immediately locate her – she may have gone to the toilet or been helping in the kitchen – I ran frantically in search. Along the way, I must have somehow run into the bucket in which was planted the diminutive but very real Christmas tree, because it fell down behind me, the glass of several lights smashing as it landed. A small electrical fire broke out which, following panicked shouts, was sensibly extinguished by a level-headed aunt (no doubt using the knowledge gained in the type of workplace where electrical devices caught fire with some frequency), ripping Nan's thick blanket from her legs before it could spread and take the entire tree. However, the flames had already heated a cousin's present of a smiling orange space hopper. The explosion that followed resulted in more screaming and one suspected heart-attack scare. All the while, I ran and cried, oblivious to the chaos in my wake, my focus solely on the pressing issue of my missing nose.

Finally, Lori emerged and tried to calm me by reassuring me that my nose was in fact still on my face. I knew better. I had seen it, throbbing with blood between the fingers of my mutilating uncle. Eventually, said uncle, muttering how he didn't know the kid couldn't take a joke did he, was persuaded to place the nose back on my face, his fingers magically sealing it so that it did not leave a scar, confirmed to me when a mirror was held up. Gradually my howls subsided as I was distracted by some lesser present for the bastard child (definitely no space hopper for me), as the charred tree was raised again, the burnt carpet doused in water and hidden under a flattened box and *calm was restored to the room (save for the fit of anger from the cousin who had lost the gift they had only just inflated, punching the sofa as a stand-in for myself).*

And after that, the disappearing began. Visits became fewer. We went to theirs less. They came to ours not at all. This may be an order I have placed upon a much more chaotic pattern of withdrawal. But one thing I do know is that the Christmas after was not spent at my grandparents' house. We spent it alone, in our little flat, with the patterns in the wallpaper and the floor and the ceiling. I remember, because we had no tree, but a Christmas pot plant Lori had decorated with tinsel. And there were definitely much fewer presents. A child doesn't forget that.

Perhaps it was, after all, the stigma of unmarried mothers, hanging so heavy as it did back then. Or perhaps it was the realisation between all parties that bookish Lori with her strange child, who would not play with his cousins and instead stared at the carpet and did not know how to take a joke, could have no place in that family, which was all about talking and playing and noise and jokes that were cruel and not funny.

Then, one day, we were not going to live in that flat anymore. We were going to move to another town, not too far away, but not too near. There was more work there for Lori once I started school. An uncle (not the nose uncle, another one), drove us and everything we owned in the world down the motorway, the first time I had ever been on one, to our new town and our new flat, which was very much like our old flat but with fewer patterns (I did not understand I would not see the new patterns ever again. Their loss was my first bereavement. I feared long journeys from that point on, which at least meant Lori saved on holidays). Once the uncle had helped unpack, he was gone with a wave I expect was insincere, and I never saw him again, or the rest of them. Grandma would die and Granddad would die, as would the odd great-aunt or uncle, and Lori would sometimes go back for the funeral, but she would never take me. And there was never a present at Christmas or a card on a birthday, for Lori or for me.

I don't have too much to show from before I started school. Nose, fire, space hopper. Barbers, scissors, bench. Blocks, wallpaper, carpets, little else. I know I was sent to some sort of nursery for a few hours most mornings. I can catch the odd scrap of that – the texture of a toy, the colour of a bean bag. I think there were patterns there. I think I was happy. The mild, floating happiness I feel in the shower in the minutes before the skin wrinkles and I find it hard to leave. I cannot think of any child other than myself being there, even though there must have been.

It is with school that

My phone whistles and I rip it from my pocket to read the latest message from my daughter (who has been on a foreign holiday nearly every year of her life, while I have never been on a plane). She says that she's having a little trouble getting away and she won't be here until 2.30, at the earliest, but looks forward to seeing me then. I feel sickened and relieved. More time to wait. A bit more time to sort this all out, this everything.

My thread is gone, and what I have summoned already no

longer seems good enough for the task. A few facts, a lot of feelings, but the intended subject of myself seems to have fallen through a hole in the middle somehow. I am missing something vital, but I don't know what (Daddy agrees).

In an effort to trigger some kind of thought, I flick through the opening pages of the autobiography of the television gardener. After a brief preamble about his disbelief at winning at some awards ceremony, his approach to making sense of his life is similar to mine. Starting as close as he can to the beginning, he recalls the first time he was fascinated by a plant, age three, describing its leaves, the stem, the petals, the stamen. I see the flaw. Although he does not know it, the plant is not the point. He let that plant take him over. He surrendered to it. It's been pulling his strings ever since. Why did he not resist? But then, why did I let myself be hollowed out time and again and be used by the blocks, and the carpet, and the Artex ceiling, and the comics, and the database, and the shower, and the haircut and everything else...

I am not like the TV gardener. I know when I have been seduced. And the why of it is not such an interesting question, at least in my case (the TV gardener should still consider it). After all, is there any other answer other than the brutal and boring truth that my brain is unusual and I have a propensity towards this behaviour? But to put it like that, I feel diminished. There is surely more to me (is that too bold a claim?). There must be another way in.

I put the gardener's book to one side and the cover of the book of fairy tales that was underneath looks up at me. Illustrations by Raymond McGiveney. Like Mo Lightman, a Vibratist. His pen and ink drawing of a writhing dragon predates his introduction to the movement and is full of the violent angst that would soon disappear completely under its influence. I wonder for a second if I am strong enough to flick through the pages of this book I studied once (not as a child, but as an adult), but the chocolate stains restrain me, holding a large chunk of the pages together and making the job impossible.

But it does set me thinking about fairy tales, and what I learnt about them all those years ago, following the rabbit hole that began with this very book. A way of telling a communal truth through lies. For children now, but for adults originally, reinforcing mysterious wisdom through patterns of narrative. Princes and princesses are laid low and raised high. A sleep like death is ended with a kiss. Events, commands, things, people, all coming in threes. (The first usually wrong in one way, the second in another, with satisfaction only achieved with the third.) What does it all mean? Everybody knows, but no one can explain.

What personal fairy tales could I have told my daughter when she was young? What lies, and what truths within? Would I have been able to use them then, to say something of the very few truths I know? Was there any story I could have told, that would have enlightened her young mind at all? Anyway, it's too late now. She's all grown up and I missed it.

The sound of running footsteps on the pavement is followed by the smell of sweat, heavy breathing and a shadow falling. Bent over me is Olly, drenched, wheezing and unable to speak. If he has a job interview today, the chances of him getting it have weakened considerably. I wait for him to catch his breath.

'Fantasticus,' he gasps eventually, in a voice that sounds like it is being squeezed through bellows. 'I've found him. He's in the launderette.'

'Oh,' I say. 'Good, I suppose. What do you need me for?'

'Back-up.'

'I... how am I meant to back you up exactly?'

Olly is hefty. I am not. There is no useful physical force I can apply in most situations, let alone a confrontation of any kind.

'Block his path in case he tries to get away when I duff him up. What do you think?'

I hadn't given serious consideration to what I'd do if we ever found this person, as the event seemed so unlikely. Standing about while Olly commits an act of violence does not seem like an option, but neither does stopping him. It's a tough one, and I have to be careful. I have the capacity to be superhumanly stubborn, but in some circumstances, I can be bamboozled into doing practically anything (this goes some way into explaining the existence of my daughter.) I give it some thought.

'I... I'll go with you,' I say. 'If you ask him for the money nicely, with no violence.'

'Oh, fuck off,' says Olly.

'Fine, I will.'

'OK, OK. No violence, but I'm not going to be polite. I'm going to swear. Even if he gives the money back straightaway, I'm still going to swear at him.'

I sigh. Nothing will stop this seeming anything other than a bad idea.

'Don't worry,' says Olly. 'Nothing from the top drawer. Come on, let's go.'

Despite still not having his breath back, Olly starts to run. I did not think there would be running. There cannot be running.

'I'm not running,' I say.

'What? We've wasted enough time already. He was only doing a short wash. We don't even know if he's drying. He could be gone any minute. Let's go!'

'I can't meet my daughter drenched in sweat. I can't run. I'm sorry.'

Olly shakes his head. 'And there was me thinking you knew what was important in life. I'll run on. You follow. But get there quick and back me up, yeah?'

I shrug in agreement and watch him resume his staggering run for a number of metres, before he grabs his side, shouts out 'Aggh! Got a stitch!' to the passing world, and carries on at a brisk hobble, before disappearing into the thin crowd of midday shoppers.

I have half a mind not to follow him at all. But I did say I would. I also said I would keep an eye out for the man and didn't, and it was only luck that Olly was too caught up in the chase to wonder why I was sat on a bench staring at the front cover of a book of fairy tales. And Ahmet should get his money back, I suppose. I start walking, but not too fast. Still, it is too hot, my shoes are rubbing, and I can feel the first thin prickle of sweat on my skin.

The launderette is halfway between the charity bookshop and the comic shop. From a distance, I can see Olly standing outside, nursing his stitch like a war wound in-between coughing fits.

'Too late,' he splutters. 'He was here when I got here, but he left.'

'Did you ask him for the money?'

'No.'

'Why not?'

'Didn't have back-up, did I? I didn't have your phone number, and you didn't check in…'

Despite the ridiculousness of the situation, I feel bad. And it is nearly lunchtime. I hadn't really thought about it, lunch out not being part of my established orbit, but I should eat something before meeting my daughter, now that she is going to be late. Acts of altruism don't come naturally to me (among other things, they open up a whole dialogue of potential reciprocation that is fraught with danger), but Olly looks like he's going to die unless someone hydrates and nourishes him.

'I'm going to get some lunch,' I say. 'Would you like to—'

'Join you? Yes, I would. That would be very kind of you. You're paying, yeah?' Life fills Olly's cheeks at the prospect of a free meal. I do some sums in my head at just how big a chunk this will take out of the money as Olly enthusiastically leads the way to my second-favourite coffee shop in town.

'The point is, all films are made up of ideas, yeah? And ideas belong to everyone. Like, Einstein never owned the Theory of Relativity. No one had to pay him every time they used it. He thought of it, but it belonged to the world. So, if someone thinks up a great idea for a blockbuster movie, same thing. Why do I have to pay to see it? It belongs to me already.'

Olly, his energies revitalised by the burger and chips I have bought him (I am having an omelette), is explaining why he hasn't paid for any of the thousands of films he's watched over the past decade. He has been speaking for some time, as he has many reasons. I am not really listening. I am making up stories. Not fairy tales, exactly. But stories you might tell a child, like the ones Lori used to read to me before I could read for myself (and then only books of facts about trains and planets and dinosaurs). Stories that could explain my own childhood, without the dreariness of the bleak facts, such as they are. A sideways way in, that may get closer to the elusive thing I am reaching for (Daddy also likes the idea, a bit too much. I sense a trap). It's pointless, evidently. The child for whom I am mentally writing has grown and no longer exists. But I have never let futility hold me back in these matters.

'Think about it this way, right. The money I pay for a cinema ticket wouldn't pay for one meatball of a big Hollywood film director's lunch. And the free publicity I do for them by talking about their films online increases their audience. So they should be taking me for lunch. To a really nice place as well, not a shithole like this, no offence...'

THE MACHINE IN THE PLAYGROUND

There once was a boy (who was me, but also not me from the moment I set him apart and put him in a story, with all the inevitable simplifications and necessary manipulations of storytelling inherent in that) who lived at home with his mother in a small house in a big pile of houses, one on top of each other. The weight of all the other houses on top of their house squashed it down nearly flat, so there was hardly room for them at all in it, but they didn't mind. They were very happy in the house, which was full of the most wonderful patterns that made the boy dance with excitement.

One day, the boy's mother said, 'Son, it is time for you to start going to school.' The boy did not want to leave the house and the wonderful patterns, but his mother said, 'You must go to school, because we are very poor and I cannot look after you all day anymore. I have to work, washing other people's houses and clothes, to make money for us to buy food to eat.'

And so, the next day, the boy's mother took him to school. 'You will be happy here, if you do two things. The first thing is, do what you are told by your teacher so they are not angry with you. Second, you should play with the other children, and become their friend.'

The boy did not have any trouble doing what he was told by his teacher. They were very happy with the way he stood up, sat down and put his hands on the desk in front of him, the way they told him to.

The second task his mother had given him was much harder. You see, the boy could see no other children. The classrooms, the corridor, the stairwells, the dinner hall were completely empty, except for himself and the teacher. Even the playground was empty, besides the dinner lady, who rang a bell just to tell the boy when to stop playing by himself, dancing the way the bricks in the wall and the railings told him to and go back inside for his lessons.

There was one thing in the playground, however. A giant machine, so big it nearly filled it. It was covered in dials and levers, and made lots of whirring and clunking sounds. The boy did not know what the machine did, only that it was very loud.

The machine puzzled him so much, he asked his teacher one day, 'Please, Miss. Could you tell me what that big machine is in the playground that makes all that noise?'

And his teacher said to him, 'Why, that is no machine. What you see in the playground is the other children. Pull the levers in the right way, and you will see that I am right.'

The boy tried to pull the levers, but they would not move. Not only that, he could not tell if they were meant to be pulled up, down, to the left or to the right.

He said this to his teacher, who replied, 'You must pull them in just the right way, and in the right order, and then you will see the children. I'm sure you will work it out very soon. It is not hard!'

There were many levers, perhaps hundreds, on the machine. No matter how hard he tried, he could not pull them in the right way, in the right order.

'That is strange,' said his teacher, when he told her again once more that the levers would not move. 'All the other children could see how to pull the levers, and the right order, on the first day of school. You must not be trying. It is your fault and there is nothing to be done about it until you stop dancing with the bricks and railings, and try harder to work it out yourself.'

The boy was very sad, not because he wanted to play with the other children that much, he was happy enough dancing to the patterns of the bricks and the railings, but because his mother had told him that he should and he wanted to make the teacher happy. But however much he tried, he could not do it.

Still every day the boy went to school and stood in the playground, pulling levers this way and that, still hoping that he would finally find the right way to make the other children appear.

Years went by, and the boy had nearly given up all hope and thought he would never see another child, when he pulled one of the many levers and, just for a moment, the machine looked less like a machine and more like children. Not very much, the children he saw were like ghosts, and he could still see the levers and dials, but children they were, running around, playing their games and screaming in a way that sounded like pain but he knew could not be.

Spurred on by this breakthrough, he carried on pulling the levers this way and that and, over time, the machine became children a few more times, until finally, they were children all the time but still a machine whose levers he had to pull but mostly did nothing when he did. And it did not get that much better than that for years and years THE END

THE INVISIBLE BOY AND THE TRUMPET

There once was a boy who was invisible. He lived with his mother in the middle of a tall tower, and like other boys, he had to go to school. Although the other children knew he was there, because his name was on the register, they could not see him, and carried on as if he was not there at all. Sometimes they would bump into him, or sit on him by accident, and they would remember then, but then they would quickly forget, and would continue playing their games without him.

His voice was invisible too. Even though he would speak, it would be as if no sound had come out of his mouth, and after a while he just stopped trying, as being silent was the same as making noise, and was less effort.

The boy was sad that he was invisible, and with an invisible voice, but he got used to it over the years, and accepted it would be the way things would always be for him. But then, one day, something unexpected happened.

A man came to the school and asked all the children if any of them wanted to learn how to play the trumpet. The boy was excited by this idea. 'People can't hear or see me, but they will know I am here if I play the trumpet,' he thought.

The boy stuck his hand up, but the man could not see it. So he shouted as loud as he could that he wanted to play the trumpet, but the man could not hear. 'There's only one way I can get his attention,' the boy thought, and sat on the man's chair. When the man sat down, he found he was sitting on the boy.

'Who is in my chair?' the man said. 'It feels like there is someone there but I can see nobody.'

'Oh, that boy's invisible,' said one of the other children. 'We only know he's there if we sit on him.'

'Perhaps he wants something,' thought the man.

'Would you like to play the trumpet?' he asked the boy.

The boy nodded, but the man could not see his nod so he tugged on his sleeve instead.

And so the next day, the man took the boy to a room in the school full of musical instruments of all different kinds. 'Here,' the man said, and handed the boy a big, shiny, brass trumpet. 'All you have to do to make a sound is you take a deep breath, hold it in, put your lips to the mouthpiece, and blow like you're making a raspberry. If you do it just right, the raspberry will go into the trumpet and come out the other end as a big noise.'

The boy did as he was told. At first, the noise that came out was only a raspberry, but by listening carefully to what the man said, he blew and he blew until finally, a big loud trumpet blast came out the other end.

'Well done,' said the man. 'That is the first step. Now I will show you how to make different notes and play a tune.'

But the boy was not interested in that. All he wanted to do was make the noise. He blew and he blew and he blew, making the loudest noise he had ever made. The man had let him take the trumpet home with him to practise and so he made the noise there until the neighbours complained to his mother and, although she liked the idea of him learning an instrument, she had to tell him to stop. In a way, the boy was pleased they had complained. It meant they knew he was there.

One day, there was a poster up on his classroom door, with a pen attached to it by a piece of string. The poster read

ACTS NEEDED FOR
SCHOOL TALENT SHOW

The boy thought for a minute. If the whole school heard him playing the trumpet, then the whole school would know he was there. Perhaps he would stop being invisible.

The boy put his name down on the poster to perform in the talent show, although all anybody saw was the pen moving in mid-air.

'I cannot wait for the talent show!' the boy thought, as he counted the days. At last, the other children would see him, and he would be like everybody else.

Finally, the day arrived. All the children from all the school sat cross-legged on the floor in rows from the front of the school hall to the back. As the talent show began, and act after act of singers, dancers, comedians and magicians went before the school, and each was rewarded with a large round of applause, the boy waited impatiently in the wings. 'In just a few minutes,' he thought to himself, 'that applause will be for me. Just for existing.'

It was time for his act at last. The teacher in charge announced him, and he stepped out onto the stage with his trumpet, which was the only thing the other children could see, floating along in front of the curtain.

The boy blew. And he blew. But because he had not taken the time to learn any notes or tunes, as they did not seem to him to be important, the sound that came out of his trumpet did not seem pleasant to the other children. Loud as the noise was, soon he heard another noise above it. They were laughing. All the children were laughing.

The boy left the stage, confused by what was happening. There was no round of applause for him. The laughter followed him into the wings, where the other acts were laughing too. He tried to do a trick he had taught himself when he was little, and make the world around him so small only he was in it, so he could not hear the laughter. It did not work.

For a while, he was not invisible. Other children would see him, in the classroom, in the playground, but only to snigger and nudge a friend as they remembered the day of the talent show.

And then, as time passed, the invisibility came back. He could no longer be seen by the other children and he was glad THE END

THE MAGIC NEWSAGENT'S

Once there was a boy who had a mother but not a father. Then one day, his mother introduced him to a man. 'This is your new father!' she said, and the man moved into their home but he didn't stay long and they were on their own again.

A little while later, the mother introduced the boy to another man. 'This is your new father!' she said, and the man moved into the home. He stayed a little while longer than the first, but he was always shouting and one day he nearly hit the boy after he got in the way and so his mother told the man to leave and they were on their own again.

Eventually, the mother introduced the boy to a third man. 'This is your new father!' she said, and the man moved into their home. This man was a kind man, and he bought the boy many toys and treats. His mother was happy that this man liked to spend time with the boy.

On a particular day, the man took the boy to the shops with him. They came to one shop that sold sweets, crisps, fizzy drinks and newspapers.

'This is a newsagent's,' said the man. 'I am going to buy myself a newspaper. If you like, I will buy you a comic.'

The boy did not know much about comics. He had seen some before, but had never properly looked at them.

'How about this one?' said the man, pointing to one with lots of drawings of people with silly faces doing silly things on the cover.

The boy shook his head. 'No,' he said. 'It is too silly.'

'Well, how about this one?' said the man, this time holding up a comic full of pictures of war and explosions.

The boy shook his head. 'No,' he said. 'There is too much war in it.'

The man smiled. 'How about this one?' he said, holding up a comic with a shiny cover and a picture on it of people in strange costumes, blasts of mysterious energy coming from their hands. 'I used to read this when I was a boy. It's awfully good.'

'Yes,' said the boy. There was something about that comic. It felt like it was calling to him. 'I will have this one.'

And so the boy walked home reading Ghost Frog #292 *(Part 6 of the 'Infinite Atom' crossover event), nearly bumping into lampposts and falling into the curb. He did not understand the story, why these people in funny-coloured outfits were hitting each other and zapping each other with beams of fire that came out of their hands and heads, but that was what he found exciting. That it was part of a bigger story, an intricate system of narrative that spread out in untold directions (as by chance this was the Atom Comic in which the 'differing reality' concept was finally made explicit), through potentially infinite dimensions. This is what he had been waiting for all this time, he realised. What began with the ordering of coloured blocks and the patterns in the carpet and carried on through memorising lists of dinosaurs and planets and their moons had led him to this. A world contained in stories to explore, full of its own secret patterns, its own mysterious order to be uncovered. This was something that seemed to be made just for him. The boy tried to stop himself shaking and flapping with excitement in the street but he could not.*

Anyway, one day the man disappeared from their home and his mother said he wasn't his father anymore THE END

'...should be begging on their hands and knees for me to watch that video of their film someone did on their phone. Listen, Fantasticus, we should get a move on. That bloke's not going to find himself, is he?'

I do not think I am cut out for children's stories (Daddy is on the fence). It is perhaps best that my daughter (who in her photos radiates with the joy of life) did not have me telling her these things when she was little. I doubt much wisdom would have been imparted, except that it is best to learn to actually play a musical instrument before giving a public performance.

Back to my ridiculous reality. Olly has finished his plate, and I grasp I am still expected to be taking part in this pursuit of his.

'I can't help anymore, Olly...'

'You can, though. You said she was going to be half an hour late. So you can give me another half an hour, at the least, can't you?'

'I have emails,' I say.

'They can wait, can't they? This prick could have spent that twenty pounds by tomorrow.'

'He's probably spent it already. In the launderette.'

'Nah, an arsehole like that would hold onto it for pleasure. Dole money for the launderette, nicked money for booze and weed.'

'But what can we do?' I say. 'We don't know where he's gone now.'

'Yeah, well, we would do if I had you as backup. But I couldn't tail him because I was looking for you.'

'If you had me as backup you wouldn't have needed to tail him.'

'Exactly. It's your fault both ways. Listen, this is the plan, right. We'll go to the launderette, we'll talk to the people there. See if any of them know anything about where he's headed. Get heavy with them so they'll spill the beans, know what I mean?'

'You can't get heavy with innocent people in a launderette. You'll get arrested.'

'Right, that's why I need you there, Fantasticus. Rein me in, stop me from busting a few heads. You know what I'm like when I get angry. And anyone who protects a dirty fucker like that is as bad as he is, in my book anyways.'

'Fine,' I say. 'I'll go with you. But you need to be quick.'

'Oh, I'll be quick alright,' said Olly, pushing his chair out. 'I'm chomping at the bit to get hold of this creep and...' He clutches his chest and winces alarmingly. It would be the sort of moment the average man would ask his friend if he was OK. But I am not the average man. So I simply stand and watch, waiting for the situation to reveal itself. 'It's alright,' he says eventually, through a faceful of pain. 'Not a heart attack. Indigestion. I think. Maybe a heart attack. No, indigestion. Let's go.'

Once again, I let him lead the way, at a pace that somehow manages to be frantic and glacial as he negotiates his urge for justice with digestive discomfort. Eventually I can't help but overtake and hold the door open for him.

'Thanks,' he says, and for a second, he sounds genuinely grateful, before the hunt once again consumes him and he barrels up the street, still grabbing his chest as he goes. It's hotter. My rubbing shoes are more than hurting. Why couldn't I have stayed on my orbit? More to the point, why couldn't I have stayed at home?

At least this sun is as high as it's going to go, I think to myself, as I follow Olly down the high street towards the danker end of town yet again. No one in the launderette knew anything. The manager was about to throw Olly out for annoying her customers when he'd shouted 'I know where the fucker is!' and bundled me out onto the street.

'Where are we going?' I say.

'Think about it,' he says, 'He wants to spend Ahmet's money, right? But he's got a bag of washing. He's not going to his dealer or down the boozer with a great big bag of laundry, is he? So he's going to go home first. Now, where does he live? Easy. He's a scummy wanker. Where do all the scummy people in this town live? One place, Gaskill Towers.'

His logic is not sound on quite a number of levels, and I can't help thinking that were it not for parental support, Gaskill Towers is exactly the sort of place he'd be living himself, but as usual, I do not tell him any of that. I let him rant and ramble as we pass the charity bookshop and the bench where I sat down, and into the end of town I really don't like. I barely notice any of it. Daddy is haranguing me, saying I'm wasting my time and attention on my friends instead of focussing on what's important – the book for my daughter (who has never mentioned reading as one of her hobbies). I want to flush away everything about it but still it squats unwelcomely in my head like some repellent oversized toad. Daddy wants to know what the problem is.

Autobiography failed. Imagination failed. I've got nothing left, Daddy. Why can't you just let it drop?

'You alright, mate? You're doing that arm-squeezing thing again and your face is all scrunched up. You were doing that earlier when we were in the cafe, by the way. You having flashbacks or something?'

Christ, it's happening without me even knowing now. Why is it spilling out like this? Who has seen it? The shame makes me want to do it again.

'It's nothing,' I say. 'Let's just do this thing we're doing.'

We carry on down to where the buildings get shabbier, past the last of the shops (strange places with whitewashed windows that sell something but no one's sure what) before it switches to residential buildings, if bed and breakfasts can be counted as that. If he's anywhere around here he'd be in one of these. Another thing I don't tell Olly, or he'd be ringing every doorbell.

Eventually, these too give way to more modern developments. Blocks of low-level flats from previous decades, their utopian optimism washed out by the rain years ago. Kids on bikes cycle up and down outside. I know they can smell my fear. All children can, but particularly these ones.

There is a dangerous crossing by a flying saucer of a roundabout, and on the other side stands Gaskill Towers, a collection of monumental slabs propping the sky up.

Compared to these beasts, the block I grew up in with Lori is a quaint little stump. I don't think I've ever seen them in the sunshine before. But then, I never come here.

There is grass surrounding the towers and their accompanying concrete pathways, filling in dead space and not looking at all at home in its current situation. Olly plonks himself down on it. I stand.

'Make yourself comfortable, Fantasticus, we're going to be here quite a while.'

'I can't be here quite a while, I'm...'

'Meeting your daughter. Yeah, I know, I know. It's not like you never mention it. But you'll be here long enough for this shifty fucker to come out of one of those towers, and for me to get him in a wrestling hold and have him begging for mercy. There are no rules round here, Fantasticus, except survival of the fittest.'

I wonder how Olly can possibly see himself as the fittest as he breaks into a coughing fit so violent it threatens to bring up his lungs. I still do not sit.

While he fixes his gaze on the towers ahead, psyching himself up for battle, I find myself inching towards the shade of a tree, where I put down on the ground the books I have been cradling under my arm for what seems like hours now. The idea of simply ditching them seems obscene and against the natural order, which is that books are passed on and used again and again, even though the fairy tale collection, with its chocolate stain holding some of the pages together, is by anyone's definition, a dead book. For this reason they are still here with me, weighing me down until Olly lets me stop long enough to find them a new home.

But in my satchel is my *Radio Girl: Secret Signals* omnibus.

It is something I definitely want to hold onto. This one story provides a particularly thorny knot in the task of identifying all the various differing realities contained within Atom Comics. A twelve-part maxi-series from the turn of the century by the fourth generation writer/artist creative team of Chuck Rayner/ Tanvi Mukherjee, it explores differing realities both explicitly and implicitly at a complex level. The story is this. Radio Girl (specifically that of DR0001), a radioactive mutant hero created in the initial atomic event that marks the beginning of Atom Comics continuity and who has the power to receive and transmit radio waves from her own skull (which she can convert into an energy field of incredible destructive and protective power) picks up mysterious coded transmissions from an unknown source. Eventually the code is broken with the help of the renegade antihero, the Codemaster, who in exchange for help in his ongoing conflict with the mob enforcer Billhook, informs Radio Girl that the signal is a message from herself, calling for help. The source of the signal is found to be a black hole, and therefore from a differing reality (black holes are gateways to other dimensions in Atom Comics cosmology).

Having obtained the Universal Door from the immortal being and Moon resident Multiplus, Radio Girl uses it to guide her to the reality from which the signal emanated. She finds herself in DR0794, home of the Radio Girl who featured prominently in Radio Girl comics of the mid-seventies. (And can be identified by the spelling of her birth name as 'Rebecka' rather than 'Rebekah'.) This Radio Girl has herself received a distress signal from the Radio Girl of DR1172, star of nineties Radio Girl comics (notable for her much larger bust size). Tracking down this Radio Girl who reveals that she herself received a distress signal from that of DR7758 (short-sighted), it is established that each is warning the next of an interdimensional being, crossing realities and slaying the Radio Girl who inhabits it.

At this point, the story becomes more intricate, as it becomes clear that we are no longer following the adventures of the Radio Girl from DR0001, but that from DR2045, who has a notable birthmark on her neck and PTSD from her encounter with the Creeping Brain in the *Radio Girl: Blood on the Dial* graphic novel (1996). This means that all the other Radio Girls she is encountering cannot be those that have just been met by the Radio Girl of DR0001, but a second set following similar paths in their own respective differing reality. Identifying all these Radio Girls is a particular challenge, becoming only more so as the story switches to other versions of Radio Girl a further six times (at a conservative estimate) before the story's conclusion, in which an army of Radio Girls (at least 587 appearing in one splash panel alone) confront the antagonist, revealed to be Multiplus himself (his motivation is obscure). Only by combining the force of each Radio Girl, every one unique in slight or significant ways, and forming a single Radio Girl, known as Radio Girl Prime, with their contradictions resulting in a devastating blast of positive/negative radio energy, can the immortal Multiplus be (temporarily) defeated.

Untangling all that is a lot of work. Of the 1,612 Radio Girls definitely featured or implied, I have identified a mere 224 with their correct DR numbers. It is so tempting to concentrate on this. I even open to the page I have got to and actually start, standing there uncomfortably with sore ankles under the unsatisfactory shade of a thin tree.

But as I misbehave and concentrate on the wrong thing and

Daddy starts to shout even though the whole database was his idea too, I see that the problems arising from one task present a possible solution to another, and I am in fact being good after all. I understand the problem with the book now. Coherent linear narrative flattens me out, and I end up making too much sense. But despite all the systems and the order, I am a truly nonsensical person. My current situation more than bears this out.

Fragmentation. Contradiction. What if I embraced these things? Present a version of myself and the life I have lived that is made up of broken shards, without even attempting to piece them together and form a complete mirror. No Fantasticus Prime, just a collection of variants.

> *Do I contradict myself?*
> *Then I contradict myself,*
> *(I am large, I contain multitudes.)*

These are not words you would find in any Atom Comic, but I learnt them once, and they seem useful to me now.

But let us not be too hasty. There need to be parameters or there is just chaos (and we are nothing without a system, says Daddy). There is still much to say about my life as a nonsensical child, before we discover the nonsensical man I have become.

I can take the pain of standing no longer and crouch, hovering above the ground so as to avoid grass stain on my new trousers, and think about how, years ago, when I was still unformed (as if I am formed now), I was

SLOW

I was a slow child, physically. Every task – moving from one side of the classroom to another, eating, getting changed for PE – seemed to take me that much longer than anyone else. It was as if time for me was passing at a different speed. In games, I was the easiest child to hit with a medicine ball, and in any race across the gym, I was always trailing behind. If ever forced to take part in any group dance performance, my movements would lag, possessing a perfect rhythm of their own unconnected to the one established by the music (that I passed through the care of quite so many educational professionals, without arousing enough curiosity in a single one of them to ask why I was quite so below the expected standard seems quite remarkable in retrospect).

Although I was slow, I never quite ground to a halt. However far behind, the finishing line would always be reached. I can't easily say why. It's not as if I saw any inherent merit in the task set. A race could just as easily not be run as run, and everyone involved would likely be all the better for it. But still, the idea of simply abandoning a challenge, faking some leg injury or asthma attack as some other children did, was not for me. Once I was locked into the system, even if it was a stupid system established by some track-suited sadist of a

PE teacher, as always, it had hold of me. Every race, regardless of whether it incorporated some impossible element involving a skipping rope or beanbag, and despite the certain humiliation I would be subjected to simply for trying, had to be completed.

For years, this quality of unquenchable persistence went unrecognised. Then, at some late point in my school life, cross-country running was introduced as an activity, and to the surprise of the tracksuit of that year, along with the entirety of my classmates, I was good at it.

It took me a while, on that first race three times round the local park, to notice that I wasn't doing quite as badly as some of the other, less athletically gifted boys. But it was on the second lap, when I found myself overtaking a group who were competent that I realised something odd was happening. By the third lap, even though there were pains in my legs and stomach the like of which I had never before experienced, I could see that it was only the genuinely sporting boys, the ones who endlessly excelled, ahead of me. It was an unbelievable situation for everybody, so much so that the PE teacher refused to accept it and sent me round for an extra lap, joining the stragglers from whose ranks I had only just escaped and nearly exploding my lungs in the process.

Although I never came close to winning any of the cross-country races that followed, I would occasionally scrape into the top ten, on one occasion nearly into the top five. And while I never enjoyed the experience of pushing my body to the point of being ripped apart, I do admit treasuring the memory of one tracksuit turning to another and saying, 'He'd crawl over the finish line if he had to, that lad'. He couldn't have remotely understood the implications of what he was saying, but he was right.

FAST

There was one time I was fast.

The school was by a reasonably quiet road, albeit one that was a regular bus route. To help us navigate our way across at the end of the school day, a lollipop lady was on hand to hold up what traffic there was with the customary sign on a stick. We were always expected to wait for the lady to lead us across, even though the road was often clear and the lady was in no hurry at all, each time delighting in talking to the children about their day for what seemed forever before finally making the crossing. The other children did not seem to mind this, and willingly gave up information in response to this barber-like curiosity.

I, on the other hand, was always impatient to get home from school quickly, back to the familiarity of home, the warmth of a black and white TV, and a big pile of Atom Comics to be read again. And on this particular day, the lollipop lady was even slower than usual, the pointless dribble of conversation drawn out for what seemed like forever to my undeveloped mind (I'm not certain the time would pass any quicker for me now).

Something inside me broke. I just had to get to the other side of that road, to where the comics, the squash and the biscuits were. I just ran. Straight into the path of an approaching bus.

The horn blasted. The lollipop lady shouted. At this point, I should, according to the logic of survival, have quickly turned and returned to the side of the curb to be admonished and stay alive. But I was not following that logic. I was following Daddy's. And Daddy was telling me to get to the other side of the road.

My legs moved at a speed they never had before and never would again. I made it just as the bus roared by. I could hear the lollipop lady still shouting at me as I kept on running, perhaps genuinely upset that she nearly witnessed a death, perhaps merely vexed that I nearly cost her her job.

For a while after that, children would point at me and mutter about how I was 'the kid who nearly got run over'. At least it stopped them going on about the trumpet.

FRIENDLY

This might seem odd, considering my earlier, barely disguised and somewhat mawkish metaphor of the machine in the playground, but I did, eventually, make some friends, of sorts. It started with one. A new kid. His name was Wayne. He was cool, and could play sports, his skin actually tanned, and he was maybe slightly American. He didn't know of my baggage as being the boy who had only recently danced by the bricks and the railings and didn't care that much about the opinion of others if and when they ever told him about it. But somehow, we got talking, and there must have been something he liked about how I phrased things, or my general demeanour (I cannot be sure, but I think our initial interaction may have been something to do with the broadcasting of the first attempt at adaptation of an Atom Comics character, a short-lived and unsatisfactory TV version of The Trout, which ignored the noir feel of the original comics and played it for laughs. I remember Wayne being impressed that I had knowledge of the character's origins. Despite Atom Comics being ostensibly aimed at children, there seemed to be no other child in the entire school who read them). Anyway, there was something he liked, and somehow we were friends. Real, actual friends. We would spend time together, and I would enjoy it. I would say things, and he would like to hear them. It felt like the sun had come out after years of overcast and miserable days.

That was the golden age, I think, when Wayne and I would just chat, about what, who knows now. And like all golden ages, it couldn't last, although of course I thought it would forever, not knowing the nature of golden ages at that time. Wayne, however, could not resist the call that all tanned, cool boys hear, that of the soggy sponge football. One day I came out in the playground, and Wayne was not waiting for me. He was effortlessly tackling, heading, kicking and all the other things footballing lads do with a group of similarly able athletes. He asked if I could join in, and not wanting to lose their new acquisition, they miserably said yes. But my coordination being what it was, I could not make a meaningful contribution, and was placed in defence, which is more insulting than being put in goal. After a while, I sloped out of the game, and watched.

I would watch Wayne playing football a lot. Although I could still command his attention in transitional moments, it was clear he had moved on. I spoke to him less and less, and eventually barely at all. I would eventually form other fragile friendships, but none as briefly intense as that first one.

Some years ago he requested me as a friend on social media via the account I had reluctantly set up as a point of access for the database. I accepted the request. He did not message me, and I did not message him. He sees my posts that give nothing away about my life at all, save that I have updated my site yet again. I see his. I don't know who this strange man is who talks about his family and his kite-surfing and his exciting new employment opportunity with some company that makes electric fans. I never found out why he looked me up – whether he was curious what had happened to me, or if he was simply collecting old friends like stamps. What would happen, I wonder, if I messaged him now? Would his response be friendly and expansive, or the curt reply of someone impatiently working through their to-do pile? Would I get any reply at all, or would the icon on my screen tell me that the message had been read but left to hang in the breeze? But there's nothing to say, really. There's enough evidence on display for us to both know the truth, that while he has grown into the adult he was always destined to be, as indicated in his choice of the soggy football over me, I have remained the same. The boy in the playground who could not play football and knew too much about comics. That boy has not moved from where he left him.

A THIEF

I was always a good child, careful to do whatever teachers or responsible adults demanded of me. Only when the limitations of my body and the peculiarities of the mind got in the way did I displease them, and even then never intentionally. I was always trying. Having said this, I was also a shoplifter.

I stole Atom Comics, obviously. There were over thirty published a month, and the little amount of pocket money Lori could afford to give me barely stretched to one a week. The local newsagent's only ever stocked a few, but there was a big shop in town that would have many more. Every weekend I would beg Lori to take me in, and she would leave me in the shop (that sort of thing happened back then) and I would speed-read as many as I could before she would gently drag me away (Lori did not actually like me reading Atom Comics. She felt they were too violent, and featured derogatory representations of women. She was right, of course, but I was barely focused on the action or the characters at all. If Radio Girl's costume was ripped until it became just a wisp of material, or if The Pummelor should bash open a man's skull, then this was as significant as the cups they might drink their coffee from, mere filling between the dimensional shifts that were of far more interest to me).

The limitation of time meant that I would still only be reading, at most, a third of the Atom Comics published in a month. As I always strive towards a state of completion, however impossible, this caused much pain.

It wasn't that I didn't know stealing was wrong. That was a lesson I had absorbed at a very early age when the attempted taking of a biscuit I hadn't been offered resulted in the hard slap of the hand from a stern and vengeful aunt. It's just that I thought, and Daddy thought too, it more wrong that I should be kept from reading every Atom Comic published simply because of financial limitations.

At that time, I had a zip-up jacket, acquired from a charity shop and belonging to the fashion of a previous decade. It was already too small for me, but Lori couldn't afford a new one, and so I was still wearing it a good year after it should have been passed on to hang on another poor child as a badge of shame. Its very tightness became a virtue in my eyes. I discovered that I could place up to three comics within it, next to my jumper, without them falling down (it could actually hold a few more, but the bulge then became overly noticeable and stiff-looking, as if for some reason I had shoved a tea tray under my shirt).

The next Saturday came, too slow, too fast. I knew I had to do it. Even though every stop on the bus ride into town felt like a step closer to the gallows, there was no backing down. I must become a criminal and that was that. Atom Comics, and Daddy, demanded it.

And there I was, in the shop. Lori left me alone in front of the wide rack, stuffed with Atom Comics. I had a strong urge to turn and run after her, begging her to take me away from this madness that engulfed me. But I did not. Instead, I carried out my usual ritual of speed-reading two or three of them. Then, seeing that time was slipping away and Lori would be back soon, I lifted another three from the rack with a shaking and sweating hand and, too nervous to even look side-to-side to see if I was being observed, I placed them inside my open jacket and pulled up the zip.

Although the zip sounded as loud as a road drill, it miraculously made it all the way up in one swift motion, without the material getting jammed or the teeth failing somewhere to interlock. As it reached the top, and a tiny flap of skin on my neck got caught for a moment, nearly making me cry out, I realised I had done it. The comics were in the coat. And no one was grabbing my shoulder.

At that point, I had a thought. Lori, who I had never previously deceived, would wonder why I had not spent my pocket money on my usual comic a week. To pull off the job, I would have to go right up to the counter with the comics stuffed inside, act as if nothing was untoward, and hope they didn't fall out when I reached out my hand with the shiny pound coin. It was the biggest risk I could take, but the whole operation depended on me going through with it.

There was no queue. It was just a straight walk from the rack to the counter. I began to move. I had to resist the urge to hold the comics up, and rely on the sheer outgrown-ness of the jacket to hold them in place. It did its job magnificently, and all too soon I was there at the counter, trying to hold in any shakes, tics or twitches that would have given away my guilty nature.

Behind it was a sad-eyed man, old enough to have been something else before he washed up working the till in a newsagent's. He took both, gave the comic back with my change and, as I took it while struggling to maintain a trustworthy level of eye contact despite the pain, he winked at me. I followed the gaze of his open eye, and it was clear he could see the tea-tray bulge from under my jacket, a lot more noticeable in the fluorescent glare of the shop lights.

He said nothing. He smiled slightly. I walked away and waited for Lori back at the rack, my skin burning with the anticipation of his calling shop security and them whisking me away to some back room. But they never came (I now suspect they did not exist). Reliable as ever, Lori appeared and, not thinking at all that I had for the first time betrayed her trust (something I felt so little guilt about, it made me wonder if I had ever been truly good), led me out of the store, giving me some bags to carry to the bus stop. The jacket stayed wrapped around me like clingfilm, and the comics made it all the way home without discovery. I slipped them out as I undid my coat and hid them under the Yellow Pages, until it was safe to collect them and add to my already substantial collection.

I was more brazen the next week, and less afraid. I managed four. A different person at the till, this time a bored student who didn't even look at me. The week after, a smiley teenager let me get away with five.

It would perhaps be more narratively satisfying if I were to get my comeuppance, the comics falling to the floor as I paid, or a store detective making me unzip in front of Lori and exposing my shame.

But it did not end any of those ways. The conclusion to my criminal career was far more mundane. I was waiting for Lori, nonchalant now almost, reading a comic at the rack with a full six under the coat , when I felt what I knew from the familiar pressure to be her hand on my shoulder. She beamed with triumph as she pulled something fake fur-lined out of a bag. A coat, from the charity shop. Practically new, she said. She was sure it would fit me. Now we could throw out the silly tight thing I was wearing.

I tried to crack a smile. It did not come. Although there was certainly some relief that fate had tipped my hand away from such a risky venture, I was sad that something I had taken such pride in had been so abruptly terminated.

Sometimes I wonder if my life would have been better had I stayed on such a course, as being good produced so few positive results. But then I think, no, my inability to lie convincingly would have tripped me up at the next level, and a fall would have come soon enough. Better the path taken. It was the best of all possible worlds. Although I sometimes yearn for the impossible ones all the same.

POSH

Throughout my childhood, Lori and I were continuously poor. Although she changed jobs with some frequency, the increase in wages she pursued was always so minuscule it never registered in terms of any sort of real life benefit. Why Lori's obvious intelligence never lifted her from the most low-salary jobs I am not sure, but I suspect that consciously or unconsciously, she knew she would not be able to commit herself. I was not a child who could be left with their friends because I rarely had any, and the neighbours' kids would never like me, rolling their eyes whenever I was dumped on them. And I could not be a latchkey kid, learning how to make my own tea, because my coordination was then so bad it was likely that, if left unsupervised, I would set the flat on fire.

Our flat stayed small, the block it was in remained unpleasant, the clothes we wore kept on emerging from charity shops, or worse, from Lori's own sewing basket (sometimes we would experience little islands of affluence if one of Lori's boyfriends moved in. But as they never seemed to last, I learnt quickly never to get used to the colour television they would invariably take with them when they left).

The school I went to was not in a good area. Many of the other children who went there were poor. But somehow we managed to be even poorer than them. The other poor kids' clothes would make their way to Oxfam and I would end up wearing them. For this I was mocked.

Despite being the poorest of the poor, in the eyes of other children, I was also posh. This was partly down to the way I carried myself, with a tentative nervousness that made me appear not of 'the street'. But it was mainly down to the way I spoke. I did not have the regional accent proper to someone of my class. Instead I talked in a very precise upper middle-class manner. This wasn't intentional. It was just the way it came out.

Added to my natural state of distance, it created the impression I thought I was somehow 'better' than the other children. I did not think this (although one always has suspicions). In any case, it meant that I spent much of my school years existing in a peculiar double state. Both the lowest and the highest, looked down upon while apparently thinking myself too good.

Now I know this is common for people like me. But back then there was no explanation. Just a sense of fitting nowhere. Classless, not in the bohemian sense, but because no class would have me.

It brings you down, that sort of thing.

FUNNY

At some point towards the end of my school life, I found out I could be funny. This I discovered by accident. A boy asked if I knew what they were serving in the dinner hall that day (I was an obvious recipient of free school meals). The answer was macaroni cheese, but in that moment I had a mental blank and could not think of the word 'macaroni'. Try as I might, I just could not summon it. To bring an end to the peculiar silence that my mental block was creating, I tried to work round the problem by describing macaroni. 'It's that pasta that looks like worms, and also like tubes,' I said. 'And cheese.'

The boy burst out laughing, so much so he slapped my back at the humour of it all. This had never happened to me before. 'Good one,' he said, as he walked away, still chuckling to himself.

I had not intended to be funny. I'm not sure I had ever intended to be funny in my life before. But I saw great opportunity in this unexpected development. The boy's reaction, after all, had been nothing but positive. Even my best social interactions at that time were laced with some wariness towards me. If I could just understand what I had done, I reasoned, then perhaps I could do it again, and again after that. And life would be good, or in that direction.

Breaking it down, I came to this conclusion. I had been funny because instead of saying the thing I had been expected to say, I had said something else. But this thing had in some way related to what I had been expected to say, while also inadvertently passing some comment on it. By saying the macaroni was like worms, I had inadvertently implied that it was unpleasant, thus reflecting the commonly held opinion, perhaps held by the boy himself, that our school dinners were horrible (and by adding the coda of 'and cheese', I had returned to a state of normality, while the jarring interjection of worms still lingered, creating the queasy imagery of worms covered in cheese). The key to being funny then, was to combine the expected with the unexpected, using the latter to in some way comment on the nature of the former.

But how to incorporate my new discovery into everyday discourse? I ruled out confronting people and simply launching into it. It would have been too shocking if I, someone who had not begun a conversation with anyone in ten years, were to start doing so now. It would be impossible to subvert what was expected if nothing was expected at all. Instead, I opted for imitating my initial victory, and to answer all questions in a funny way.

It did not work straight away. There were a few initial attempts where my humorous answers were met by dead stares and mouthed insults, which was discouraging. But it was not long before I scored another hit. I was asked if we were to have our usual science teacher that day, or if the supply teacher we had had the week before would be carrying on.

'Oh, they're not coming back,' I said. 'They've fallen in a beaker and they can't get out.' Now, this was funny for two reasons. Firstly, the supply teacher in question was quite short.

Secondly, they were incompetent. By claiming they had fallen into a beaker, I was drawing attention both to their size and their proclivity for accidents. This joke was received well, and I was rewarded with a brief conversation where I was treated roughly as an equal, laced with no remarks about my poverty, poshness, general strangeness or the incident with the trumpet five years ago (I do not pretend that this or any other joke has stood the test of time. I present them here purely as historical evidence).

'What did you get in the spelling test?'

'Sevren out of tern.'

Not all my jokes were appreciated (scandalously, the above was not), but over time, I gradually earned a reputation as something of a wit. This paid off socially. I would be asked to join dinner tables. I would be waved over to groups in the playground. My company would be sought out. Incredibly, my plan had worked.

And for a while – a few weeks at least – this was my life. A court jester, always to be relied upon to provide a quip in any situation, following my magical formula. I wouldn't say I was popular, as such (that would be too much of a stretch). But I had a role.

Until, one day, it stopped working. I would say a thing, but the laughs did not come. The smiles became fainter. No matter how hard I tried, my funny answers to serious questions no longer elicited the response they once did. Kids seemed to be almost annoyed, as if they genuinely wanted an answer to the question and not some humorous response. I even tried saying funny things spontaneously without any set-up, but that went down even worse. After a while, I would no longer be called over, and eyes would glaze over when they would see me.

I did not understand it at all at the time, but I understand it now. You can only give people so many jokes before they want something more from you. To stop skimming the surface, show them something of yourself, an interest in them. A reciprocal back-and-forth that forms bonds. But I wasn't going to do that. After all, I don't give pieces of myself away to just anybody. In the end, all I had to offer was schtick. A one-joke act who fell off the bottom of the bill.

And that's showbusiness.

ANGRY

At some point, I stopped trying to be funny, or even to be liked, and got angry.

'Alright, how's it going?'
'How do you think? Fuck off.'
'Have you got a pen I could borrow?'
'No. Fuck off.'
'What's your problem?'
'None of your fucking business. Fuck off.'

This alarming development and serious reduction in my vocabulary was, I see now, a symptom of fast-fading hope. I had made myself as appealing as possible, but I was still not passing muster. If I am still abject in my best light, I must have reasoned, then I may as well be that at my worst. And to that end, I made myself the disgusting object I assumed others saw me as.

I'm ashamed to say this anger spilled out into my relationship with Lori. For years, I had barely said a cross word to her. Even though I found the disturbances to our home life brought by the various here-today, gone-tomorrow boyfriends jarring, and the consequences of our poverty were all too present in my school life, it never occurred to me to bring them up. And she in turn never saw my obsessions and peculiarities as problems. We existed in a state of dual acceptance.

That all changed somewhere around the end of school and before the shift into sixth-form. Nothing she did was good enough. The food was bad, the clothes she made were dreadful. The flat was mouldy and everything smelt.

Most of the time she took it on the chin, but one evening I wouldn't stop about all the watches, bikes and birthday presents other kids had and I never did (and never really wanted) and made her cry. As she sat there and sobbed, I knew I should apologise and comfort her, but I didn't. I didn't know how to. The idea that I could have any emotional effect on anyone at all seemed absurd. Yet the crying was undeniable evidence. Childhood interactions should have prepared me for this, but due to their paucity I had nothing I could reference. So I just let her weep until she stopped, and I was nice to her for several days after.

In some ways, all of this was a typically teenage thing to be happening, but there was more to it than that. Looking back on it now, I see my anger towards Lori was because I sensed that something was going very wrong. I was poised on the brink of adulthood, a world that was, as the other kids foresaw, a place of jobs, sex and relationships, and yet on fundamental levels relating to these things I was barely functional. Too uncoordinated for manual labour, too socially inept for an office. Unable to make a friend, but still expected to form a romantic bond, exploring someone else's body when I could hardly tell where my own limbs were going. From all sides, it seemed I was expected to carry on marching into maturity, however badly equipped I was for the expedition.

None of this could be articulated at the time. There was

no conversation, no vocabulary through which it could be conveyed. Everything I felt about myself, in fact, existed outside available language. And so the pain that had grown out of sight over time could only be conveyed in blasts of misdirected rage, hitting the one person on Earth who could be said to care about me at all.

The anger only came to an end when, after a gap of several years, Lori got a new boyfriend, Derek. As fake dads went, he was probably the best of the lot, except perhaps the mysterious one who bought me my first Atom Comic. More laid back than most, with a job so dull I can't remotely remember it, he did not attempt to present himself as someone in any way unusual. This change from the usual pattern was inarguably better for Lori, who seemed at last to be learning from past mistakes. For me, his very presence was an irritant when I just wanted space to rage in.

It was early days in their relationship, nothing too serious. Still, he had begun to hang around the flat a fair bit, and it was not long before he witnessed one of my explosions. By this point, they had become so habitual, I would think nothing of launching into one in front of an audience. He waited until Lori was out of earshot, and simply said to me, 'Can't you just stop?' With that one question, I saw myself as I must appear to others, and immediately disappeared under an avalanche of shame.

Once I had dug my way out, the anger had subsided, replaced by a sad, numb silence. I took my first load of exams and did well. Not because I was preparing for my future, but simply because exams were there to be done. As usual, a system was in place and all I could do was follow it. By doing well I had earned my place in the local sixth-form, and the chance to do more exams. Lori was keen for me to go, perhaps because sixth-form could lead to university and my fulfilling the dreams that were crushed for her by my existence. Or perhaps she sensed that exiling me into the world of work at my tender age would crush me. Meanwhile, the long summer that was probably meant to be the best of my life but wasn't dragged along as I carried on reading my Atom Comics, avoiding the summer job Derek, now semi-permanently installed at the kitchen table in the mornings, hinted I could get if I looked for it. When autumn finally came, my passions were raised again, but not in anger. This time, I was

IN LOVE

Although I had always gone to a mixed school, you would not have known it from my attempted social interactions. I only ever attempted friendships or even basic interactions with boys, not for any latent homoerotic reasons (I was a most unerotic child), but because girls seemed so many stations of difference away, that as an activity it did not seem worth bothering with (that girls did not generally play football or jokingly engage in casual violence may have in fact made it easier, but this did not occur to me at the time).

The move from secondary to sixth-form changed things in ways I was not anticipating. Classes were smaller, and there was no uniform. I was no longer facing a blazered-wearing mass. Instead, individuals began to appear in front of me, with their own style, their own unique expression, even their own ideas. That girls could, in their own way, be as distinct as myself (even though my own particular form of individuality was well on its way to the state of blankness I carry to this day) was a shock to the system.

I had somehow been railroaded into taking something called Communications (I would have been happy to have taken all science and maths subjects as I was strong in those and generally weak in the humanities, but the aim was to make each student well-rounded. I fear I have still yet to attain the spherical form the college had hoped for me, although I admit I have since attained some interesting bumps). In this class, we learned how people communicate via reciprocal gestures, enthusiastic body language and a steady maintenance of eye contact. I did not like this class. I left each day with a feeling I could not begin to describe. I had to drag myself to it for every lesson, and anyone with any sense would have quit. But I did not have sense, because in that class was Juliette Cass.

Juliette was from the other side of town, where the houses were nice enough to have gaps between. Possibly the only girl attending to wear tweed and never trainers (boots in the winter, sandals in summer), she interested me strangely in a way no one, male or female, ever had before. She was not beautiful in the conventional sense, not that I'd yet given a moment's thought to what constituted beauty, but her green eyes flashed with an intelligence I had only ever before seen on television programmes about science. Juliette read difficult books for pleasure, like Lori, and while I saw no reason to do that myself (still perfectly content with Atom Comics as they courted a more mature audience), the fact that she did intrigued me. When the tutor asked us for our opinions, Juliette was one of the three students who would answer, as the rest slumped dumbly in their seats.

There was one detail about Juliette, and not a particularly distinctive one, over which I fixated. On her neck, most days, she wore a somewhat chunky silver cross. Whether it was for religious or aesthetic reasons, I had no idea (although from the sheer heft of the thing, I now assume the latter). Like beauty, religion was something I had at that point not given much consideration to. Lori had brought me up with no faith, although eastern philosophy permeated her reading, her attitude to interior decor and her suspicion of any medicine that had passed a clinical trial. What religion I had been exposed to had bounced right off (perhaps I needed no system for living imported from outside when I had Daddy making me such intricate creations). Still, Juliette had a cross, and it hypnotised me every time I saw it. Why? I simply cannot tell you, other than it was the one thing I knew that belonged to her that served no practical purpose (unlike her tweed jacket or her pencil case) and therefore a symbol of her very essence. Gazing at it bathed even the psychological abuses of the Communications syllabus in a warm glow.

Juliette used to ride her bicycle through the park that separated the sixth-form from the better side of town to which I had no reason to venture. I lived in the opposite direction, but would nevertheless casually stroll through it at the end of the day, in the hope that Juliette would pass me, and I could momentarily bask in her aura and smell her soapy fragrance before she disappeared amongst the trees.

Over time, a year to be precise, this obsession grew. It was no longer enough to simply gaze at her from afar. I had to make some kind of connection. What my motive was remains a mystery to me now. It was not to form a romantic bond. Nor was it physical. These were both things that belonged to the world of others, and had nothing to do with me. It was something simpler, purer. A desire to share... something. To exist, just for a moment, in a state where everything she was giving was just for me. I cannot be more specific than that.

The desire became an ache, filling the day. Nothing, not even Atom Comics, could hold any meaning as long as my need for connection with Juliette went unfulfilled. Inside I churned with a longing unlike anything I had ever felt before, but the slightest imagining of its end in fulfilment was to bathe in starlit wonder. I was unaware that this was what they called love.

So, a moment had to occur, or I would die, or continue to live, which was worse. The moment had to be special. It could not simply be an exchange along the lines of asking her the time. Anybody could do that. It had to be unique, an occurrence that had never happened to her before, and never would again. But what special moment could I engineer? I had never been special for anyone before, except for Lori, and your own mum doesn't count.

I saw Juliette reading a book in the library. A paperback with impossible scenes on the cover. I comprehended that they were on a higher level to those depicted in Atom Comics. A clever book for clever people, clever in a way I was not. It was a book whose title I dimly recognised. Lori owned a copy, albeit with a different cover. I snuck hers off the shelf, not wanting to give her any indication of the unexplainable thing that was happening to me, but I was sloppy and she caught me reading it. She said she was glad I was reading something besides comics, although she was surprised I had taken an interest in magical realism. I could not resist asking her what that meant. It's a type of writing, she explained, where things you find in dreams are presented as if they were real. I did not understand, and I did not understand the book, not getting past page nineteen.

But I latched onto the word 'dreams'. Juliette was interested in dreams. If I gave her a dream, then that would have to be special. No one could have given her one of their dreams before.

The problem was, my dreams were nonsense, and not in an interesting way. They did not involve men walking with flaming candles on their shoulders, or elephants inside a vase inside a box, as featured on the cover of the novel that engrossed her. Instead, they generally featured newsagent's, store detectives, exploding space hoppers and a trumpet.

I would have to manufacture a dream, just for her. But what could I dream, that would be of particular interest to someone about whom I knew practically nothing? They say that creativity is forming a new point of connection between two pre-existing ideas. That night, lying in bed well past the point where sleep could comfortably come, I created.

It was a crisp late autumn day in the park. Lessons had finished. Other students were already racing past me on their bikes. Of Juliette there was no sign. Perhaps she had gone home early today, or not been in at all or taken a different way with a friend.

I walked as slow as possible. I stood still for several minutes by a bin. But eventually I had to face the fact she was not cycling through the park that day. As the sun got lower in the sky, creating what would be a spectacular backdrop for a much happier occasion, I turned to go.

And there she was, cycling right towards me, her cross dangling from her snood and burning gold in the light of the sunset.

Even though it was inconceivable that I ever would, I nevertheless did. I waved my arm, and called her name.

Puzzled, she slowed down, and came to a stop.

'Juliette...' I said.

'Hang on,' she shouted. 'I've got my headphones on.'

The phones' band got caught up in hair clips, giving me an open window to turn and run. But I did not run.

'Yes?' she said, finally, raising an eyebrow in the manner of a shop assistant dealing with an unwelcome enquiry.

'Juliette,' I said again. And then I said the rest. *'It's your cross. I saw it last night. In a dream.'*

She frowned. Thought for a second. *'That's... rubbish,'* she said.

'No, it isn't.' It was all I could think to say.

'Well, I'm not going to stay here and argue with you,' she said, and pushed down on the pedals of her bike. I watched her disappear into the trees, the glorious sunset mocking me from above.

BROKEN

I never went to another Communications class. I would see Juliette around the college occasionally, but I would avert my gaze as soon as I spotted her. Although I still attended my other classes and did the required work, I sleepwalked through it all, my marks plummeting to incredibly average.

My days achieved a monotony that was notable, even for me. I continued reading Atom Comics and made a mental note of the shifts in DRs, but I took no joy in it, carrying out this function out of habit, as a dog tramples down non-existent grass. I did not talk to anyone, not even Lori. In my head there was the near-constant sound of high-pitched screeching, like metal grinding against metal.

I believed that my classmates saw me, if they saw me at all, as something distasteful, an object that should not have been in the room. Although much of this was simple paranoia, there were occasions when those considered 'good types' – clean and tidy with good grades and the correct number of friends – would, when no one else was in earshot, say unexpectedly cruel things – about my clothes, my hair, my demeanour or my general otherness. It was as if, in my lessened state, I had become a hole in which they could dump the last dregs of their adolescent bile before they turned truly adult. As I was no longer angry, I did not, or perhaps could not, react (it was at this time I became obsessional about washing. The idea of my polluting their space with the slightest odour was intolerable. I nevertheless saw myself as the main pollutant, and dirt itself cannot be cleaned).

I was like this for many months. Tutors showed concern at my dip, and my lack of attendance was questioned. And while it was generally assumed I was not happy, no one, not even Lori, thought to suggest I might be ill.

Perhaps if she had admitted that, then it would have gotten in the way of her hardening plan to get me to university somehow (she no doubt saw I was not heading anywhere else). It was not part of my own plan, but then I had no plans at all. I don't think I wanted to die, but I wasn't that bothered about being alive either. On occasion I did think maybe I should have been hit by that bus.

Somehow, I shuffled on in this state right up until it was time to sit my exams in the early summer. It was suggested I still take the Communications paper, even though I'd missed nearly half the course, in the hope that my natural ability would produce a grade that might be of some use. In my zombie condition I would travel in any direction someone would care to point me in, and so I ended up one day, sitting in the exam hall, taking the paper for a subject I associated only with my own erasure. And behind the desk in front of me was Juliette Cass, still resplendent in tweed, the chain of her cross manifestly visible around the back of her neck.

I looked at the first question. It demanded that I rhapsodise about the role of non-verbal communication in the forming of friendship circles. I did not feel like rhapsodising. I did something else instead.

My system of DR identification was crude in those days. There were many years of Atom Comics back issues I had not read (although much of the early era had been compiled into collector's editions printed on nice paper I received as joint-birthday and Christmas presents) and I still could only study a small sample of those published each month. Nevertheless, the bare bones of a structure for ordering were there. And so I wrote:

> *November 1959:* Astonishing Stories Featuring Ghost Frog #56 *(DR0001)*, Suspenseful Action Comics with the Silent Scissor #64 *(DR0001, DR0002)*, The Trout #1 *(DR0001, DR0003)*.
> *December 1959:* Astonishing Stories Featuring Ghost Frog #57 *(DR0001, DR0004)*, Suspenseful Action Comics with the Silent Scissor #65 *(DR0001, DR0003, DR0005)*, Romantic Adventure for Girls Now Starring Radio Girl #28 *(DR0001, DR00006)*.
> *January 1960...*

During the course of the two-hour exam, I wrote from memory the titles and issue number of all Atom Comics from 1959 to 1976, with the DRs as I understood them (you might be curious as to why not all Atom Comics begin with an issue #1. This is because many Atom Comics heroes make their first appearance in established anthology series launched in the Quality Tales Comics era. Although also majorly written by Joe David, and with art by Ben Hammer and Mo Lightman, the stories in these anthology comics are not considered to occur in any of the differing realities of Atom Comics. Having said this, there is a school of thought, to which I do not subscribe, that all potential existences, including those found in other fictional works and the one we ourselves live in, must inherently be part of the Atom Comics Omniverse. For me to entertain this idea, I would have to admit that the Atom Comics movies are in some sense canon, which they are not. But I digress). I felt a sense of real achievement as our booklets were collected, even if what that achievement actually was was obscure, even to me. For the first time in many months, the metallic sound screeched less harshly.

This slight peace lasted all of three minutes until we were excused to go, and Juliette Cass pulled out her chair, stood up, turned to wave at a friend at the back and looked straight through me. While the moment in the park had etched itself upon me forever, she remembered none of it. A thousand and one things had happened to her since, wiping any trace in her mind of the strange boy from her class who stopped her in the park and said the odd thing. I walked home with the screech once again loud in my ears.

That was my last exam. I retired to my bedroom that was barely a cupboard, amongst the stacks of Atom Comics I had accumulated over the years, and lay. For weeks I stayed there, only leaving to go to the toilet and eat food silently in the kitchen while Lori stared at me, not knowing what to do or say. My exam results came in the post (I declined to go down to the college to clamber through walls of celebrating fellow students to read them from a board). My Communications exam paper effort had failed to gain any marks at all. My other grades in stronger subjects were not good. No university was going to do anything with these. Lori's dream was over. And I didn't have a dream. I went back to bed.

There was an awkward breakfast table conversation between Derek and myself. He tried to cajole me into going down the job centre. Lori made no such demand. Instead, she appeared to be waiting, knowing that somehow it would all fit into place, despite all evidence, if only she had faith.

Then, just as summer was nearly over, and an unwelcome world of benefits claims and worse was about to fall on top of me, Lori gently knocked on my bedroom door. I did not answer, but she came in anyway and handed me a foldout leaflet, like many I had seen before on racks in the college library. It was something to do with one of the universities I definitely wasn't going to. I did not even want to glance at it until Lori took it back out of my hands, turned it over, and handed it back, shaking my shoulders to make me look at the thing. There, gazing back at me, was a classic drawing of the Silent Scissor by Mo Lightman.

Vibratism Studies. A degree in the life, teachings and cultural influence of Micajah Culp. At this time, I had no awareness of Culp or the connection between him, Lightman and Atom Comics in general. I had no real idea why Lori was showing me this, except that she might have thought I'd like the picture.

Although my memories of Lori become more vague with each passing year, I do remember this very well. The way she nervously, hopefully prodded the paper, how she said that she'd talked to them on the phone, and that there was hardly anyone applying to the course and they would take nearly anybody, regardless of how they did in their exams. That they would take me.

And I said yes, right then. I would go to this town I had never heard of to study the work of someone I knew nothing about. Leaving a home I had barely spent a night away from, making a journey longer than any I had ever made, heading into a world for which I wasn't prepared and didn't remotely understand. All of my fears, all at once, but still I said yes. I said it because I knew that by going, I could make Lori happy. Happier than she ever could be if I stayed. But I also did it because for the very first time in my life, I would be in a room where I might be able to talk about Atom Comics, and in that room, there would be someone who would understand what I was saying. I never knew how much I wanted that until the possibility was dangled in front of my eyes. As Lori cried and hugged me, I could feel myself crawling towards what appeared to be the tiniest sparkle of light.

HAPPY

You might think over everything I have mentioned and surmise I had an unhappy childhood. And true enough, it did conclude with a lengthy period of untreated clinical depression. Also, there were many miserable incidents leading up to that, and an air of prevailing sadness over many of its days. But still, I would hesitate to write off my childhood as 'unhappy'. It's just that the happiness was found in little pockets of time, the in-between moments. The afore-mentioned nature walks with Lori, when they weren't too rain-sodden. Late afternoons round friends' houses playing computer games, before they got bored of me. The thrill of a new batch of Atom Comics in the big newsagent's in town. I was happy sometimes. Maybe there were other kids who were only just as happy as I was. But unlike them, when I wasn't, I couldn't fake it.

Coming up out of all that and I've got the bends. Still crouching above the grass, I nearly topple over, and have to steady myself with my hand. The onrushing tingle of a dead leg sets in as I struggle to straighten myself.

I am happy with what I have done. I recognise myself in all my thisness and thatness in these words. Daddy says it's good but what's next? There must be a plan, he says. Can't he just give me a moment, I ask him? He grumbles, worrying away at the problem in spite of me.

Meanwhile, Olly maintains his vigil on Gaskill Towers. There have been several false alarms involving men in caps and men with rucksacks, but never the golden combination of the two. I look at my watch. Somehow, so much of this nonsense has now occurred it has gone half-twelve and even the shade from the sickly tree is not protecting me from the heat. The sky is clear, save for one solitary, near-stationary cloud. I will it to pass in front of the sun. It refuses to budge. My nice new trousers are beginning to stick to the back of my legs. For one blasphemous moment, I yearn for shorts, not that I would ever wear them if they were available. My legs have not seen the sun since the last school sports day. But worse than anything, I think I can smell myself. This is not acceptable. It all has to stop.

'I have to go,' I say, but Olly puts out his open hand as if to put me on pause.

'Wait,' he says, 'he's coming. I can sense it.'

'I don't think you can sense it,' I say.

'He's coming.'

'I've got to go, though.'

'Any minute now, he's going to come out that door.'

'Well, he might do, but I do need to go, so...'

'Right now, he's getting in the lift, and he's going to come down, and go out that door of that tower there, that one. The one nearest us. Any minute now.'

'I don't doubt you, but...'

'Can you not just wait one minute, Fantasticus? You're meant to be a superhero. Help me out here, huh?'

'I'm really not a superhero. I just did one thing that you have construed to be heroic, but that doesn't mean... hang on, is that him?'

Sauntering out of the entrance of the farthest tower is a man, complete with baseball cap and rucksack. I have to admit, he does look a bit criminal.

'Shit, yes! See, I told you I could sense him!'

'You did get the tower wrong.'

'That is a fucking miserable complaint, Fantasticus. Can't believe you just stooped to that. But I don't have time for your bullshit. Get ready for action!'

'I don't want to get ready for action. A stern talking to, at—'

'BUNDLE!' cries Olly, as he charges headfirst at the

approaching figure. The man looks quizzically at the stocky, suited and sweating figure approaching him from too long a way off. 'Give back Ahmet's money, you prick!'

'You what?' shouts back the man.

'That twenty pounds you stole, give it back!'

'Oh, that. Can't. Spent it!'

'I don't believe you!'

'Not bothered, mate.'

By this point, Olly is running out of puff. As he finally reaches the man and attempts to push him to the ground, he has little energy left, and the impact is small. The man, meanwhile, rather deftly knees Olly in the privates at his own leisure, causing him to collapse in a besuited, wailing ball onto the ground.

The man keeps on going in no hurry. As I walk as fast as I can over to Olly (I'm not running, I'm just not), his nemesis passes me on his way out of the Towers grounds. 'Don't try anything, pal,' he says. Obviously, my reputation has not preceded me to the point of reaching him.

Olly looks up at me from the ground, clutching his bruised parts, his breath sounding all the world like an airbed being inflated.

'When I said "bundle",' he wheezes, 'you were meant to bundle.'

'You didn't say that was the plan, and I said I wasn't going to help with violence.'

I stare at him for a moment, waiting for him to continue the argument, but his breathing just gets more squeaky as he lies curled up on the ground.

'Are you going to help me up or what?' he says.

This is the sort of thing I often don't think to do until

prompted. I hold out my hand, and pull him up to a sitting position.

Olly does not say anything for some time, as his inhalations take on the quality of air passing through a flue on a windy day. I begin to worry that he might not be alright, and think about what a hassle it would be if he's not.

'I ran too soon, didn't I?' he says finally. 'Should have walked towards him like I didn't know who he was, then run. Fucked it up.'

He cries. Great big manly sobs.

I know you are meant to say comforting things at moments like this, but no comforting things come to my mind, and so, not for the first time in my life, I stand there, not saying anything while someone breaks down in front of me.

Again, the question of when one thing becomes another arises. A slight pause is acceptable in this situation. It creates the sensation that I am ruminating, conjuring up the precise phrasing that will bring Olly comfort from the benefit of my wisdom. There is a point, however, when that pause will become too long, and the need for me to say something will become overwhelming, for both of us. Needless to say, I pass that point, and we carry on to the sound of his crying for a good extra half minute before I finally come up with something, anything, to address it.

'You ran very well,' is what drops out of my mouth eventually. 'At the start.'

He looks at me in disbelief with one eye, the other pointing at a tower block.

'Is that all you've got to say?' he bellows. But it stops him crying.

I don't try to think of anything else.

111

'Yeah,' he says finally. 'I did. But that's just the problem with me. No stamina. I give it all that, but I can never get anywhere. I was meant to have a job interview this afternoon. Put on my good suit and everything. But like always I let myself get distracted. Was going to be a helpline operator. That's a fucking joke. I can't help anyone.'

'You could still go,' I say.

'Nah, what's the point,' he says, one eye now looking directly at the sun. 'Never even kept a job more than three days. I'm in my mid-thirties and I'm still stuck under my mum and dad's roof. Literally in the fucking attic, for fuck's sake. I'm not like you, mate. You've done loads of stuff.'

'Not really,' I say, genuinely not being able to think of anything I've done that counts as an achievement at that moment.

'What are you talking about?' said Olly, sitting himself up with the force of his own truth. 'Not only are you Fantasticus Autisticus, but your database is legendary. All those kids in the comic shop, they all talk about it. Well, one of them.'

'Not to me they don't.'

'That's because you're so brainy they're frightened of you. They can talk to me because they know I don't know shit.'

'I'm sure that's not true.'

'Well, I am a fuckload more approachable than you, so there's that as well. But that database, that will live on long after you've died. You're already immortal.'

I feel myself blush. I am very bad at taking compliments (although he is wrong. Unless someone takes over the web hosting fees, the database will inevitably disappear a few months after my death).

'Anyways,' says Olly, gradually heaving himself up off the

tarmac, 'you go and do whatever it is you need to do. I'll... I dunno. Go home, I guess.'

There would have been a time when I would be thinking nothing of leaving Olly there to make his own way home in misery. After all, he's just given me permission to leave. And I do want to leave. A little Olly goes a long way. But even I, who habitually learns life lessons and forgets them utterly in the moment when the knowledge may actually be needed, can hear a voice, much tinier than it ideally ought to be, telling me that Olly does not, in fact, want to go straight home to his parents' attic conversion while feeling humiliated and a failure.

'You could walk with me, if you like,' I say. 'Back into town. Stop off at the comic shop.'

'You've got things to do,' he says.

'They can wait,' I say. And they can. The emails can wait forever. If I never answered them it would change practically nothing. And as for the book that Daddy wants me to write... it can wait, can't it? I could do it tomorrow, and it would be just the same as doing it today. No need for any of it, not now. I can just stop, and focus on the here and now and help an actual friend in need like a sensible person (just thinking these thoughts make me feel as if I've killed a dragon).

'Yeah, I'd like that,' says Olly, softly, seeming small and humble to me for the first time.

I pick up the books from the grass, and we walk across the road by the roundabout, narrowly avoiding the vehicles it spits out at high velocity, through the bad part of town and back towards the decaying beginnings of the high street. All the while, I let Olly talk incessantly about the films he's seen and I never will, as I nod along politely with the spew of information I have no use for.

As the high street becomes more acceptable and we pass the charity shops, there is a bus stop.

'You know what?' says Olly. 'I think I will go home. I've had enough for one day.'

'Are you sure?' I say, like a good human. 'I've still got some time to kill.'

'Yeah, I'm sure,' he says. 'Could do with a kip and some zonking-out time.'

'Listen,' I say. 'I'll give you my mobile number, now I've got one.'

'You don't have to,' he says. 'You're a private person. I know you don't want to be bothered. I get that.'

I shrug. 'I don't mind,' I say.

'OK,' he says. When I hand him my scribbled number on the back of an old receipt, he takes it and smiles as if it's the best present anyone's ever given him.

The bus appears round the corner.

'Take care, mate,' he says, as he gets on, and I say something similar in reply.

I wave him off with a spring in my step, only slightly marred by the un-decreasing pain from the rubbing of my shoes. The spirit of good social interaction has flowed unexpectedly through me and my time feels well-spent. I carry on heading for the comic shop, resolving to sit there in the cafe at the back, but not to answer my emails or any other obsessive nonsense. I will simply be there, enjoying the powdered milky coffee paid for with the last of my loose change and the general atmosphere, with open body language that will encourage any potential young disciples to ask their questions.

After a quick freshen up in the bathroom Marcus is obliged to offer to cafe customers, where I find little unpleasing odour emitting from my body (it's amazing what a negative frame of mind can do to your perception), that is what I do. My arms are unfolded and my head is high. I could live like this forever, I think, just before the dragon, undefeated, wakes and slowly moves.

It doesn't take long. A few minutes, if that, before the dragon has wrapped its tail around me, tightened its grip and thrown off its mask. The job is barely half done, Daddy hisses, still half-snake. Follow the system. Keep going, until complete.

I enjoyed a good few minutes without him but I know it's over now. I must do as he says, or he'll be an unscratchable itch at the back of my skull, ruining every moment I have with my daughter (who I hope never has to live a single moment with something like this).

OK, Daddy, you win. But what is the system? The three random books you happened to have on you at the beginning, clearly. Autobiography, children's stories, fragments. No more books, so back to the beginning. Carry on until you run out of life.

I could question whether any more fairy stories, while initially an interesting experiment, would serve any further use describing my adult life, but it's an argument I'd never win. This is the way it always is with Daddy. First he makes a system to help me with a task. Then somewhere along the way everything flips, and the system exists for its own sake, its original purpose lost. It manifests itself through my actions, and I no longer benefit. I should see it coming, but I never do.

So, autobiography again. I am more comfortable with it now that I have established myself better. For the time being, I am onboard with Daddy's plan.

Closing my arms and lowering my head, I make the world shrink tight, like a skin around myself. I cannot stop this. I cannot.

THE EDUCATION OF FANTASTICUS AUTISTICUS

I

A late September day, and I sat on a train on my own for the first time. There was much that could go wrong. I had to change twice, and the backpack that contained all my belongings in the world (except for my Atom Comics collection, which I accepted could not come with me and must wait for my return at Christmas), was unwieldy and already hidden on a rack behind the newer, better-packed bags of strangers. My childhood fear of long-distance travel was taking on new and exciting adult variations. What if I could not get the bag out in time before the train stopped, I thought. Would I have to stay on the train, in which case I would be travelling without a valid ticket, or get off without it, leaving me to continue my journey but no longer owning anything at all?

In the event, the backpack was retrieved and the train vacated successfully at the first change, although who knows what might have happened if I hadn't got ready to disembark three stations before. The next would be at the city that housed the main site of the university I was improbably enrolled in. From there, I would take one more train, a stopping service through its satellites, deep into the surrounding countryside. For the campus where the Vibratism Studies course took place was not in the city at all. Instead, it had its very own site within a small village, some miles away. I had no idea of how universities worked, but this still struck me as odd.

Not that I was dwelling on such things on that long journey. I had minor concerns about my ability to look after myself as I had failed to master any of the simple recipes Lori had tried to drum into me, and a small worry that I had no real idea how much anything cost, but the major problem was where I could purchase Atom Comics. I expected that the main city would have its own big newsagent's, with them all comfortingly displayed on a bulging rack, but how often could I travel there? What if I had to study so much I wouldn't have the time? I must make time, I vowed. If anything was certain at all, now that everything else was up in the air, it was that.

As to the issue of money, Lori's poverty-level income meant that I qualified for a full grant. But that was not all. Several days before I was due to leave, Lori revealed to me that she had been saving, all these years, a little extra to keep me going, in order that I didn't have to supplement my grant with a part-time job (this saving indicated that Lori's university dreams for me went further back than I had realised, and also helped explain why we were always quite so poor). It wasn't much, and I would soon discover how little such an amount could buy you. But even then, back when I understood hardly anything at all, I could tell from the way she handed me the cheque book for the bank account she had set up for me, that giving me that money was important to Lori. Perhaps, in her mind, the most important thing she ever did.

I know that in order to communicate colourfully this period of my life, I will need to use some poetic licence to fill in the gaps in my moth-eaten memory. I will say this person said or did precisely this, when in fact it was perhaps only slightly that way, if at all. What I will not do is fabricate the missing details of my parting with Lori at the train station, and make her suffer the indignity of having words that are not hers placed in her mouth. All I will say is what I remember. That she cried with the most incontestable sadness as she was separated from her only child for the first time, who she had looked after for eighteen years with more diligence than most, but that the same sadness was eclipsed by a forcible determination to make sure I got on that train. And that when I saw her standing on the platform as the train began to speed and she shrunk to toy-figure size, just before disappearing, that despite Derek's now-regular presence by her side, she appeared the most alone person in the world.

But while Lori had seemed so small then, as the second train entered the outskirts of the university city some hours later, I saw that this place was on a scale I had never before experienced. The buildings were taller, the roads wider. Ancient rubbed up alongside the abrasively new. It was as if this city could fold in and collapse on me at any moment. Once I had navigated my backpack through the subways of the train station that led to the last, lonely platform, where the regional service train waited, I already sensed a change of atmosphere. On board, after several hours of sweaty claustrophobic crush, this train was quiet, the air cold from open windows. Just a few others and myself wanted to make the journey to these outer villages. And as the train travelled through suburbs and into countryside under darkening skies, my fellow travellers became fewer and fewer. By the time we reached my station (where the train terminated), I was the only one left.

Stepping out onto the platform, I felt it immediately. A pressing gloom that went beyond the encroaching night. It was in the air, diffusing through my clothes and coming to rest on my skin. This was not the gloom of the inner depression I knew only too well, or the reek of poverty that pervaded the block of flats I had just left that morning, but something else. An attack from outside.

The Centre for Vibratism Studies came with its own little halls of residence building. This was where I would be staying for at least the next year of my life, and to locate it I had been issued with a rudimentary map of the village. My orientation skills were poor, but as the place more or less consisted of one street and several side turnings, even I managed to find the converted Victorian schoolhouse with little trouble.

I did not like the look of it. I could easily imagine ghost children slipping out of the walls in their cloth caps and high socks. But still, the windows were double-glazed and a warm yellow glow came from within. That, at least, was homely.

There was a code you had to enter to get in through a back door. After I began to jab at the awkward buttons, I paused. From inside, I could hear the sounds of kitchen clatter, shouting and music. Could I really live here, in a space I could not remotely control? Derek's morning loitering notwithstanding, I was used to my home being dependably quiet and still. But what could I do? There was nowhere else to go but back. I finished entering the code and the lock clunked. The door was open, the threshold ready to be crossed.

Stepping into the hall, I was hit by the smell of cooking and cigarettes (normal and other). I decided to follow the odours. The cooking was easy enough to locate. A kitchen was not very far down the hall. I looked in as I passed. 'Hi, there,' said a boy about my age (I could still not think of myself as a man), glancing up from his bubbling pot and smiling. I tried my best to smile back but, as often happened with me, it didn't work, the tips of the lips refusing to move that bit far enough. He shrugged and went back to stirring, his dreadlocks swishing from side to side as he swayed to the bass-heavy music he was listening to. I knew I should stay. I should force myself to smile and shout questions over the music that would help me navigate the building and find my room. But the smile still would not come, and the words would not form in my mouth. Sometimes they just don't. And I cannot shout at the best of times. So I carried on.

Another door promised the blue light of a television and tobacco, but I was still reeling at my previous failure at communication. I had no idea how many were in there, or what type of people they might be (and did it matter? I did not get on with any type). The idea of casually introducing myself closed my throat up still further. I skipped past as fast as I could, before anyone inside might see me.

That left on this floor only a staircase leading up, and an office door. On the door was a sign.

Christopher Hillesley
WARDEN

Underneath was a metal slide, meant to reveal whether he was IN or OUT of the office. It hovered between the two states, uncertainly.

I decided to knock. At school, I had always found it a lot easier to talk to teachers than fellow pupils. Anybody with authority still came with the vague promise that they would not put you in a headlock for no reason.

No one answered. Thinking that maybe I wasn't knocking

loud enough with my body constrained by the counterweight of my backpack, I took it off and placed it on the floor. I knocked again. Still silence.

'You won't get anywhere with him right now,' said a voice behind me in a strong, harsh accent I could not place, except that it was very much not that of where I was from.

I turned to find behind me a large man, a good fifteen years older than me, with grey-blue eyes so uncomfortably intense I had to stare at the floor with some rapidity. Eventually once again raising my gaze, I took in a drinker's belly, a beard that had been left to its own devices and the shorts and sandals of someone feeling incredibly at home.

'Is he not in?' I said, the age gap between us allowing my throat to loosen enough to finally get some words out.

'Aye, he's in,' he said. 'But by this time, he'll be… relaxing. But don't you worry, newbie, I'll show you what's what. What room are you?'

I once again unfolded the piece of paper with the details I had been sent.

'Eleven,' I said.

'Ah, you're next to me. I'm Graham, by the way.'

He held out his hand. I completed the social transaction by saying my name and giving him mine. My hand disappeared within his giant grip as he squeezed it like a lemon.

'Christ, your skin's soft,' he said. 'Not a callus on you. Bet you've never done a day of manual labour in your life. Am I right?'

I didn't answer. What did he expect me to have done?

'Me, I've just come off a construction site. Worked all the hours I could to pay this year's fees.'

'You don't get a grant?' I said. Despite his intimidating size and demeanour, I was finding him unusually easy to talk to, by my standards. He was someone who had the authority of age but not of position, meaning that he could potentially teach me things but not then punish me for failing to learn them. There were not many people who would fall into this category, but those who did, such as the school librarian or the woman from the zoo who brought in snakes to show us, I tended to warm to.

'PhD, mate. No grants for postgraduates. Anyway, follow me, and I'll show you where your room is, not that you'll be able to get into it without the key.'

'Where is the key?'

He nodded at the door leaking smoke, before hitching my backpack over his shoulder like he was taking it to market, and heading up the stairs.

'Thank you,' I said.

'Don't mention it,' he replied. 'By the look of you, you're going to need all the help you can get.'

II

After showing me my own impenetrable door, Graham took me inside his own room. It was stacked high with books, mugs and mysterious knickknacks. He had his own personal kettle which he used to make tea with milk just seconds from the turn.

'So what made you decide to apply for this course, then?' he said as he handed me the scalding hot mug. 'Wait, don't tell me. You are absolutely fascinated by the ideas of Micajah Culp, correct? Hang on, I'm telling by your face that I'm on the wrong track here. Wait, wait, I've got it now. Is it that you didn't have the grades to get in anywhere else, and this is the only place that would take you?'

I nodded.

'I've been here seven years, in this hall. And if I can finally wrap up my blasted thesis, this year will be my last. And in that time, I have seen many students come and go. And not one of them, when they arrived, had the faintest fucking idea what Vibratism was. I'm guessing you fall under that description.'

'Yes,' I said. 'But it's something to do with Atom Comics?'

'Ah, with Mo Lightman, yes. They always catch some poor soul with that honeytrap leaflet. Guess you're this year's.'

He offered me biscuits from a jar.

'Take three, for Christ sakes. You need fattening up. You're practically a stickman.'

He watched me demolish the three biscuits. I hadn't eaten since Lori's sparse packed lunch, and that was three trains ago.

'Wow,' said Graham. 'You're hungry. We should get some chips. And if you don't like chips, you're in trouble, because that's the only thing to eat in this place.'

I did like chips, and some minutes later after Graham had exposed himself to me while changing into some long trousers, he led me back down the stairs, my backpack resting safely in his room.

'There's a payphone,' he said. 'You should phone your ma and da, tell them you've arrived safely. You live with them back where you come from, yes?'

I said yes, sort of, and did as I was told. I don't know when it would have occurred to me, left to my own devices. Lori sounded happy to hear from me, even though I'd only been gone several hours. I told her I was there, and there had been no problems with the trains. I didn't know what else to say and hung up. Graham looked unimpressed with the quality of my phone call.

'A man of few words, huh?' he said.

I said nothing. He laughed like I'd made some kind of joke.

'I'll introduce you to the rest of the gang,' he said, as we passed the lounge. There was no getting away from it this time. My fate was out of my hands and into Graham's, a man who would make me eat three biscuits and say hello to people, whether I wanted to or not.

Sprawled over sofas and armchairs that bore the marks of many years of stray cigarettes were a variety selection of young people. Some girls, some boys, some clean-cut, some less so. Graham told me what their names were. He made me announce mine. They waved and half-smiled, acknowledging my existence while indicating I was not as interesting as the large television (I would eventually find out what my favourite programmes looked like in colour).

The dreadlocked boy from the kitchen was there, a plate of bean-based food in front of him. His name was Cam. 'Hello,' he said. 'Again.' This time I managed to squeeze out a hello back. I hoped this satisfied him, but suspected not.

'I wouldn't worry about learning their names too much,' said Graham, as we stepped out into the heavy night air. 'Half of them will have dropped out before Christmas.'

'Why?' I asked.

'Vibratism Studies... it's a calling. And virtually nobody gets called. Me, I was hooked from the first week. It was like an ever-unfolding riddle, reaching into places you could never imagine. That's why I've spent seven years and a hell of a lot of cash for a bricklayer pursuing it. I'll be sorry to get to the end of it and back into the real world. But most of them don't see the mystery. They just see a whole lot of mad shit.'

I was going to ask more questions – about the halls, the course, what Vibratism even is and what it has to do with Mo Lightman – but we were at the chip shop already (nothing was far from anything else in the village).

'Prepare yourself,' said Graham, 'for the finest hospitality.'

The chip shop door creaked and a bell rang. It was empty, save for some flies irresistibly drawn to a crackling zapper, and a woman standing in the middle of the floor – butcher's arms folded, hair up in a bun, red-faced with anger at something we hadn't done yet. She glared at Graham as if she recognised him.

'What do you want?' she said.

I did not know what I wanted. I strained up to look at the board.

'Come on, I haven't got all day,' she said, gesturing at the empty shop.

Graham cleared his throat. 'Paula. My fine woman. I will have a large haddock, large chips, a pot of mushy peas, a saveloy sausage and a can of pop. And my friend will have the same.'

Panicked, I reached for my fake leather market stall wallet, newly purchased to hold my new bank card and new money. At this moment in time, thanks to my not yet having mastered the art of planning ahead, it had little in it.

'I... I don't think I've got enough for that,' I mumbled.

'It's on me, friend,' said Graham. 'I can tell you haven't quite found your feet yet.'

'Thanks,' I said, trying to process the unexpected generosity and the fact he'd called me friend twice. I already knew that word could be used just as a figure of speech, but he really sounded like he meant it, unlike the schoolkids who would call you mate before giving you a Chinese burn.

The woman stomped behind the counter and flung two fish into the bubbling batter mix.

'Service with a smile, Paula,' Graham shouted over the electric sizzle of the chips in oil.

Paula scowled back.

The food was eventually cooked and salt and vinegar sprinkled vigorously, with it all wrapped with a surprisingly delicate precision by Paula.

'Goodbye, Paula,' cried Graham, as we took the bags from the unsmiling woman, 'or should I say *au revoir*?'

She shook her head and scowled, and we stepped out under dusky skies as the door closed behind us with a tinkle of its bell.

'Believe it or not,' said Graham, 'she's one of the friendlier locals.'

We ate our chips in a disused Edwardian bus shelter. 'Possibly the only truly beautiful thing in the village,' according to Graham. Despite them being quite possibly the nicest fish and chips I had ever tasted, I could not remotely finish all that he had bought me. It was without doubt the biggest meal I had been presented with in my life. 'You not having that?' he said, pointing at my half a haddock and leftover chips, finishing them off in no time at all.

'See that?' he said, pointing to a starkly modern white cube of a building on the other side of the road, looking like something that had fallen from space and embedded in the village earth. 'That's the centre. Your lectures will be there. Seminars. Tutorials. It's your one-stop shop for all things Vibratist.'

I recognised the building from the leaflet. The photographer had carefully framed it so its incongruity amongst the brown-grey old houses that surrounded it was hidden. I had imagined that it would be one building of many of this kind, part of some educational utopia in the countryside. But no, it stood antagonistically alone.

Graham stared at it, as if it stirred emotions in him he was not ready to articulate. Only for a moment.

'Right,' he said, standing up suddenly. 'Pub!'

III

I had never been into a pub before. They seemed terrible places, full of noises and people and no Atom Comics at all. And the smell that oozed out of them of spilt beer and cigarette smoke was an unsettling grown-up smell I did not feel ready for. Alcohol itself was something I was an almost stranger to, save for Lori's special Christmas treat of Bucks Fizz. But here I was, in a pub, wobbling unsteadily on a sticky high stool, drinking beer, or trying to.

'Come on,' said Graham, 'take a proper swig. It's not a slow drink. It's a fast one. That way you can drink more of it.'

I took another mouthful. It was not pleasant – not sweet like enjoyable drinks had been up until this point in my life, and not at all milky, like a nice cup of tea.

Graham, meanwhile, was well on his way to the bottom of his pint. I had barely cleared a quarter of mine. But still, I kept forcing myself to drink. Not finishing this huge glass of disgusting liquid, I sensed, would be to fail a crucial life test of far greater importance than any exam I had taken. It was an initiation. What lay on the other side of it, I had no clue, or even any sureness that it was something I might even want. But the test had weight. I could feel it pressing down on me with the force of destiny.

The pub itself was not so offensive. The smell was more of pipe tobacco than of cigarettes, and there was no music. In fact, it was comfortably quiet, except for the sound of locals barking happily at the bartender and a game of pool in a back room. I did not mind being there so much, I supposed.

Graham asked me questions. Where I was from. What I liked. Whether I had a girlfriend. Even the most uncomfortable ones didn't make me wish he wouldn't ask more. I did not realise until that moment how intoxicating it was, even for those of us who instinctively lean towards invisibility, to be an item of genuine interest. At the very least, it proves that you exist.

I did not ask Graham questions, but he told me about himself anyway. How his dad was violent, and getting onto the Vibratism Studies course all those years ago was his way of escape. How he'd always combined study with manual labour, and over the years, as well as building sites, had worked on factories, farms and an oil rig, amongst other things. That he used to have a motorbike which he sold to a friend to pay for fees but once he'd earned his doctorate he was going to buy it back and drive it through the Alps, for a month, or maybe a year. And how over the years he'd discovered some things, but now was not the time to talk about them.

I found that I was on my second pint. Graham was well into his third. And I also found that I was laughing louder. I was talking more. I was rediscovering how to make jokes. I pointed at someone's tiny dog and said it looked like someone had given false teeth to a hamster. I said that some of the men in the pub were so old they must have built the pub around them. And then I found I was not just talking to Graham, who I was making laugh a lot, but also Cam, the boy with dreadlocks from the kitchen.

'Thought you were a right snob when you first got here,' he said. 'I said hello and you totally blanked me. But you're alright. Guess you're just a bit shy. Put it there.'

'I'm not shy!' I shouted as he guided me through some complicated handshake.

And I was on my third pint. And I was singing. And I was shouting some more. And someone put some music on the jukebox and I was dancing. And somehow I wasn't in the pub anymore, and I was pissing in a bush, and I was being sick in a bush, and I was lying on the hard floor of Graham's room with a sleeping bag over me and my head on a cushion but somehow the room was a ship on stormy seas and it stayed that way even though I was asleep.

IV

'Well, that's one thing they'll be taking out of my deposit,' said Graham, sitting me up to remove the sick-encrusted cushion from the floor.

'I'm sorry,' I said. It seemed hopelessly inadequate.

'Don't worry about it,' he said. 'You're not a proper fresher unless you coat something with vomit.'

I thought back over the events of the evening. I felt acutely embarrassed, like someone had stripped me naked in the street. But also, strangely proud. People seemed to like me more when I had absolutely no control over what I was saying or doing. I had jumped over multiple social obstacles that had hemmed me in over the years in one night. And all I had to do was get blinding drunk. I had no idea it could be so easy.

But I was back to the old me now. No singing, dancing or jokes for the time being. Maybe a bit more being sick. Graham brought me a bowl.

An hour or so of that later, and I felt like I could bring myself to get off the floor. I was sitting up, drinking the surprisingly not-instant coffee Graham had made me (a revelatory experience) and not being sick when Cam stuck his head round the door.

'Alright beer-monster, Chris is about, if you want him.'

I dimly remembered that I would have to talk to Christopher Hillesley, the warden, if I was to get the keys to my room. After a much-needed visit to the showers, I gingerly took the stairs down to his office.

This time the metal plaque was slid to IN. I knocked.

'Come in!' said a whisper of a voice, trickling out through the keyhole.

On the other side of the door, sitting behind a desk that seemed too low for his tall frame, was a man I assumed to be Christopher Hillesley. Ageing, but by how much I could not say. His hair was long and flopping and white, a black shirt open one button too many. Pale, papery skin looked like it would turn to powder if you touched it. There was a slight smile on his lips, but it did not seem to be for me.

'I don't know you,' he said. 'Who are you?'

I told him my name and said I needed my keys.

He rummaged in a desk as I took in his office. It was more of a study than you might expect for the warden of a student hall of residence. Books lined the walls, some of them looking remarkably old. The lever-arch folders full of presumably useful documents looked swamped and timid amongst them.

He paused a minute and gazed at me for an uncomfortably long time. I looked at the picture on his calendar of several identical women in mediaeval robes dancing together for a while. Then I stared at his bin.

'Why are you here?' he said, finally.

'My keys,' I said.

'No, why are you on this course? What made you apply?'

That question again. The actual answer of no one else taking me did not seem wise in this situation. 'Because of, um, Mo Lightman and Atom Comics,' I said.

He smiled at this answer.

'Ah, yes,' he said. 'Good, very good.'

He studied me a while longer, and I wondered if he had forgotten about the keys.

'These are yours,' he said suddenly, as if awakening from a trance, and handed them to me.

'Thanks,' I said.

'If you need anything, just knock,' he said. 'I may be in, I may not.'

He looked up at the ceiling and did something rather odd. First he straightened his arms, then splayed out his fingers. I could see that, under the desk, his long legs were also stretched straight either side of him, his slippered feet pointed upwards and hovering some inches above the ground. I waited for him to look down again but when I eventually twigged he wasn't going to, I let myself out.

As I opened my door for the first time, Graham popped his head out from the next room.

'You met Hillesley then,' he said. 'After he talked to you, was he, by any chance. doing something weird?'

'Well... a little bit.'

'Staring at the ceiling? With his fingers and feet all stretched out?'

I nodded.

'Aye, that means he likes you. He's envisioning your potential.'

'My potential what?'

'Your potential for... potential. Your potential as a student of the life and works of Micajah Culp and the influence of Vibratism in art and culture, for starters. He's very good at spotting who's a stayer and who's a quitter, is Hillesley.'

'How does he know?'

'He feels your vibrations, lad. He senses the energy coming to you from other planes.'

'I don't get it.'

Graham grabbed my shoulder. 'You will, you will. Anyway, I'll leave you to get settled in.'

As Graham hauled my backpack onto the landing, I stepped into the room. It was incredibly bare. White walls, a bed, a desk and a chair, a wardrobe, a sink, a radiator. It suited me fine.

At the far end was a window with curtains. Looking out, I could see something I hadn't grasped from the outside. The building was actually built around a small inner courtyard, with windows of other rooms directly facing mine not far away. I could see into them very clearly, so presumably any resident could see well into mine.

The thought filled me with revulsion. What if they could see the shaking... and the flapping. Because I still did it, secretly, after all these years. I'd even hidden it from Lori for some time. She no doubt thought I'd grown out of it years ago. But it still happened, whenever I was particularly excited by something such as a DR shift in an Atom Comic or just an enjoyably repeatable pattern.

I closed the curtains so there was not a gap of a single millimetre. No one could see what I did. Ever.

V

'No, what are you doing? This is food. We don't pull and prod and tear at it. It's... it's food. Don't you understand?'

'I'm sorry. I was just looking for the price.'

'Oh. Let me have a look. Well, it doesn't have a price on it but it's 80p.'

I was in the village shop, trying to buy a Scotch egg. The man who ran it seemed as hostile to any resident of the halls as the chip shop woman, to the point of being scared. No one had ever been scared of me before.

I ate the Scotch egg on the way to the train station. My plan was to head back into the city and buy some food from a supermarket. But more importantly, I needed to locate a big newsagent's.

The city was only somewhat less imposing in the mid-morning sun. The newer buildings glistened more, and the older ones looked that bit less like mausoleums of the Steam Age, but it still felt as if a cog could turn and I would fall into a crack in the pavement and be crushed between slabs at any moment.

The supermarket was easy enough to locate. I had no idea if I was shopping within my means, but Scotch eggs were definitely cheaper here than in the village shop, and the range of frozen meats required to make Lori's recipes was certainly greater. I paid with my first ever cheque.

Wandering round the town afterwards, laden with several bags half-filled with frozen meat, it occurred to me it would have made more sense to go to the supermarket last. As they began to drip, I stumbled upon something far greater than a mere newsagent's. 'Forever People', said the sign. In the window were cardboard cutouts of robots and aliens from films. And comics. Lots of comics. To be inside was very heaven. A whole shop dedicated to sci-fi and fantasy in television, media, and crucially, comics. All the new Atom Comics, months in advance of the ones I had seen just the day before at the newsagent's back home, including titles that they never had. But not only that. Back issues. Boxes and boxes of them, on tables and under. Rare ones I had only ever dreamt of reading sat in protective bags stuck to the wall, the prices of each far more than I had just spent on food. But that didn't matter. Just to see them was something I had never even thought to dream of.

I stood there, paralysed on the shop floor. With the money from my student grant, as well as that saved by Lori all these years, just how much could I buy? How many holes in my collection could be plugged? I thought about what it would be like to own the earliest Atom Comic they had, *Ghost Frog* #8 from 1960. Only the shopping bags pulling my arms down stopped me from flapping and shaking right there.

I had to be realistic. I could not simply buy many hundreds of comics and then return home to Lori, all plans abandoned. No, on this occasion, I would just buy the ones I usually bought, plus a few extra. But in the meantime, I could surely browse a few, as I did in the newsagent's back home…

'Oi, mate! Can you not just stand there reading, getting the floor wet with meat juice?'

A man in a Pummelor T-shirt leant over a till. My first encounter with another Atom Comics reader since the only slightly-remembered ex of Lori's, and they were telling me off.

'Sorry,' I muttered (it was a day of apologies).

I wanted to dart out of the shop in shame and then never come back. But I knew that would not do. This was my own personal pleasure dome, one I had not even known existed, but now could not conceive of giving up. No, I must take the comics I wanted to the counter, pay for them, and come back for more the next week, and more the week after. It could only be this way.

'Fifteen pounds fifty,' said the man, not looking up from the comic he was reading.

I paid with my second cheque, and imagined how many Atom Comics I could buy before I reached the last stub.

VI

My bags of meat also went down badly in the halls kitchen.

'Make sure you keep all that away from my stuff in the fridge,' said Cam. 'I don't want any murder on my food, thanks.'

I didn't know what he meant. I hadn't killed anybody.

'I can't see how you can eat that stuff,' he said, looking at it like it was dirty somehow. 'Quite apart from the slaughter aspect, have you any idea of the effect on the environment of cattle farming?'

I didn't know what to say. Food was food, wasn't it? Food was good. You ate it.

'Listen, I've got a video, yeah. You watch it, I guarantee that you'll never eat meat as long as you live. I can show it to you right now.'

I didn't want to watch a video that would stop me eating the food I'd just bought, or making any of the simple recipes Lori (who, despite her Eastern leanings, would have long absorbed the lesson from her parade of boyfriends that meat was required to please a man) had half-succeeded in teaching me, but on the other hand, I didn't want Cam to think ill of me. I'd already got on the wrong side of him. I'd since made it over to the right side, but it seemed like I was slipping. Staying there was beginning to feel like hard work, but I was willing to put in some effort, so I said yes, I would like to see his video.

He led me into the lounge where the big telly was. Graham was in there, idly smoking a roll-up cigarette.

Cam pushed a tape into the VHS. After half a minute, I resolved never to eat any more meat as long as I lived. Graham, unmoved by Cam's tape, bought my shopping off me (I did, nevertheless, continue to consume dairy. My justification was that Cam also did, and if he was inconsistent in his thinking then I could be too. Also, without dairy products, hot drinks cannot be milky. For similar reasons, I continued to eat fish, as it allowed fish and chips to occur).

Cam let me share some of the beany sludge he made for himself that evening. After we had finished, and Cam insisted that we leave the washing-up 'to air', he invited me to go up to his room. I was not that interested. I had managed to read some of my new Atom Comics on the bus, but still had a lot to get through.

'Come on,' he said. 'I've got something up there, if you know what I mean.'

I didn't, but he was insistent, and as so often in my life, I ended up following someone to do something I did not understand or properly choose.

Cam's room was mostly rugs. Rugs on the floor. On the walls. The bed camouflaged with rugs.

'Take your shoes off,' he said. 'Keep the rugs nice.'

I did as I was told, although I disliked the sensation of my foot touching the floor through nothing but socks, and as I pulled out his one chair, he put on more of his low-end music, this time through big speakers that vibrated everything from the floor to my teeth. He was talking to me as he sat on the bed, unwrapping something in cellophane, but I couldn't hear anything he was saying.

He proceeded to do something that involved origami, tobacco and a naked flame. At the end of it all, he had an enormous cigarette tied up at the end a bit like the skin of the sausages he had persuaded me never again to eat. As he set light to the sausage-end, inhaled from the other, and blew out a significant amount of smoke, I realised this was one of those 'other' cigarettes I had smelt on my arrival.

After he'd taken a few puffs, he held it out to me. I shook my head. Drugs were definitely bad things. I had learnt that in the *Ghost Frog: Fire in Hell's Kitchen* one-shot, in which Ghost Frog's longtime girlfriend Ashley nearly dies of an overdose of street drug Moose.

'Come on,' he said. 'I want you to.'

This did not strike me as a good reason in itself. But then, even I knew this was not a hard drug like Moose, and if I had just a little bit now that may be enough to keep Cam happy, and I would not have to take it again. I took the big cigarette from him and breathed it in, a little bit.

'Nah, nah, that's not going to do anything,' he said, as I briefly felt something like car exhaust fumes in my throat. 'You got to take a big breath. Big. Hold it. Then let it out.'

I wasn't going to get out of this so easy. I remembered how I learnt to take a really big breath before I could make a noise on that cursed trumpet all those years ago, filled my lungs with something less wholesome than air and held on to it, allowing it to do its foul work.

This time, my throat felt how I imagined it would be if I had ever drunk any of the cleaning products with danger warnings Lori kept under the sink. Meanwhile, as I coughed out a smothering fog of smoke, my head floated several feet above the rest of my body and proceeded to bob up and down uncertainly. It was not a pleasant sensation but, on the other hand, there was something about it that made me want to do it again.

'Wow, that was some breath,' said Cam, giggling to himself. 'It's good shit, yeah?'

'Yes,' I said. And it was, I had decided.

The cigarette passed back and forth between us several times. The sensation of floating increased and became less violent in its movement. After a while, I wasn't just floating, but flying.

Cam was saying something. 'I just think people should be free, you know, to do what they fucking want to do. Like smoke what they want, party where they want, without the government or the police stopping them. Fucking hell, I don't think there should even be a government or police. Just let the people do it all themselves, know what I mean?'

I didn't know what he meant. Up until that point, I had never given a single thought about matters of social organisation, or lack of (my views on the matter are vague to this day). So I just nodded at everything he was saying, and idly wondered if people would be free to walk on rugs while wearing shoes in the world he envisioned.

'Hey, we should go into town,' he said. 'There's a big event at the student union. Pound a pint.'

I did not want to go into town. I had just come from there. But as I knew I could not reasonably explain why the answer was no, I said yes.

I found myself on a train after this. Time was now behaving in a strange way, stretches of it disappearing entirely, followed by minutes that would last an hour. The techno-Gothic city of just a few hours earlier was now a fairground of lights in the late evening. I no longer thought it would crush me. Now it was something I could ride.

The student union building was not far from the train station. You could hear it in the distance, throbbing with music that went DOOF DOOF DOOF DOOF. My understanding was that music was meant to have more to it than that, but I didn't mind. One noise is as good as another to my ears, so it may as well have be the same noise over and over again. Meanwhile, the windows turned off and on with rapidly flickering light. This was not my sort of thing, but I was heading straight towards it, and I didn't mind.

Inside was heat, smoke that wasn't smoke really, and people. So many of them, young like me, unlike me dressed like they belonged there, crammed up against walls or against the bar. There was a space in the middle where people packed like sardines danced, somehow not poking each other's eyes out with their movements (I have little idea where my body is in relation to other people's. That most do possess this ability, to the point they can flail their limbs about with abandon while surrounded by many others, never ceases to amaze).

Cam introduced me to several people he knew. He said their names, but I did not hear them because the music was going DOOF DOOF DOOF DOOF. But I nodded and pretended

I had, and everyone seemed friendly and pleased to meet me in a way they never had done before.

Cam followed me into toilets, where the music was still going DOOF DOOF DOOF DOOF, but slightly muffled. He asked me if I wanted to buy some more drugs from a mate of his. Pills. I said no, and stayed firm this time. Partly because I had no idea what these pills would do to me, and also because they were quite expensive and his friend wouldn't take a cheque.

And that was the last I saw of Cam that night. He disappeared amongst the ever-growing mass of bodies, and I suddenly felt very alone. Not the usual loneliness, but the way an alien visitor might, descending on Earth and seeing these new life forms with their strange ways. What were they doing? How does it work? But it wasn't like the machine in the playground. This time, I wasn't frustrated by my lack of understanding. I was curious to know more, and for the first time, that knowledge didn't seem beyond my grasp. I could catch it in my hand, if I just reached out at the right moment, I knew.

At some point, I slipped out, and although the effect of the marijuana cigarette was wearing off, the city still seemed magnificent in the night, and as I ran through the closing doors of the last train, in a beautiful, pure moment, I truly believed a great adventure was beginning. I sat down and laughed at the lights of the city as they streaked by, as if they were telling the most excellent joke. I was still laughing as I crashed down on my bed, tireder than I'd ever been before. I've never laughed like that again.

I look up for a moment. My heart flips over. Past the comic racks, behind Marcus at his counter and through the window, I see Teigan, walking past carrying much washing (even her laundry bag is chic). She must have been home and back in the time it took for me and Olly to achieve nothing at all.

I should hurry after her like I'm in a movie. Olly would. But I am not in a movie, and life does not reward me that way. She is scurrying, as she always does, other pedestrians hazards to be dodged, and it becomes too late in no time at all. I am still sat there, trying to convince myself I made the right choice, feeling the pang of missed opportunity.

What were some of the things she said on that walk, before silence took hold and I could not break it? She lives with her mother but not her father (although she has at least met hers). She was going to do a course, but in the end didn't. What was the course? Something to do with clothes? Or am I just thinking that because she wears nice things? I should take more of an interest in other people, pay more attention. It's hard with Daddy in your ear all the time. No, that's just an excuse.

I wonder if I could get her, or anybody to understand. How sometimes my mouth seizes up. Or how I learn something, like most people prefer talking to not, but then it doesn't stick, and I reset. How I can give someone what they want, socially speaking, on a Monday, and not at all on a Tuesday. It comes and goes, like a faint radio signal. I am tuned in, and then I am not. How people see offence where none was meant (will I now have to spend my life explaining what I am and apologising for any distress it might cause, now I have the vocabulary for it? And will it make any difference if I do?).

Time is ticking. Back. Back.

VII

DOOFDOOFDOOFDOOFDOOFDOOF.

The thud, much faster than the night before, woke me out of the deepest sleep I'd had since some long-ago childhood illness.

I opened one eye. It was very much morning, the sun bashing its way gleefully through the fibres of my curtains.

'Rise and shine! You're late for your first class!'

I recognised the voice. It was Graham's, coming from the other side of the door. The thud was being made by his fist. I bolted upright. I had completely forgotten, with the comics and the meat and the cannabis and the DOOF DOOF music that I was here to study, and the first lecture was tomorrow morning, which was now this morning, which was now.

Checking my watch to see exactly how late I was, which was very, I slid out of bed and ran to the showers down the corridor in my pants, a bundle of clothes in my arms. I was not skipping my morning wash. Although tardiness is unforgivable, dirt is even more so.

Graham was waiting outside with a cup of coffee.

'Here, drink this on the way. Bring the mug back, though, it's one of my favourites.'

The coffee splashed on my hand and onto the stairs carpet

as I tried my best to reach the door without falling over. More splashed on my trousers and on the road as I crossed it with uncharacteristic recklessness, staggering into the white cube with a near-empty mug and no coffee drunk.

The foyer was empty, the welcome desk unmanned and dusty. All I had to go on as to where to head for was the sound of low, muttered talking, like a monk in prayer. I passed a couple of offices then, through a window of a door, I could see a small group of students, each contained within their own desk chair. Cam was there, although only barely awake. There was nothing for it. I gently pulled down on the plastic door handle and walked in.

The murmuring monk broke off.

'Ah, a latecomer,' said a voice like smoke. 'Take a seat, why don't you?'

There, standing in front of the class (starting total: 22), was Christopher Hillesley. Too late, it dawned on me that not only was he the warden of the halls, but also head of the department. Beside him stood a stern-faced young man, dressed in black with a magician's beard. He watched me unforgivingly as I took my place behind Cam. As before, there was a half-smile on Christopher's lips and, as then, I did not know if it was for me or something more intangible.

Various booklets and stapled lists were handed my way. As Christopher began to speak again, and the other students prepared to note down the gist of what he was saying, I saw that although I had a coffee mug, what I did not have was a pen or paper.

The magician handed me a sheet and a nice biro.

'Remember your own next time, please,' he sighed, as if

bored with my existence already. He spoke with an accent I could not place. But I am not good with accents.

Fortunately, it didn't sound like I'd missed much. Christopher was going through various bits of admin that I thought I could pick up from the hand-outs. It would take a while for him to get to the lecture proper, and for me to be introduced to the world of Micajah Culp and his Vibratism, the next staging post in my long crawl to

*

My phone penny-whistles and I dart for it, narrowly avoiding spilling my styrofoam cup of instant coffee over the thing and killing it forever.

It's not what I think it is. Just a message from Olly. It reads, simply, *'Thnxs for today'*, along with a video clip of a martial arts fight involving a man dressed as a dinosaur. I guess it makes sense to him. It would probably make sense to my daughter (who understands all the modern internet jokes and sends me 'memes').

I don't know what to say back. Maybe I shouldn't say anything. Do you have to respond to every text you get sent? No, that attitude won't do. It's all about being reciprocal. That's what people want. But what do I have to give?

My fingers hover over the typepad.

'Go to your job interview,' I type. *'You would be good at answering a helpline.'* I have no idea if that's true. It probably isn't. But it's the sort of thing friends say to each other.

I save his number, ruining the purity of the address book forever.

VIII

What follows is a summary of the life and teachings of Micajah Culp, as taught to me in that initial lecture by Christopher Hillesley, and in subsequent lectures of that first term. The quite exhaustive detail into which he burrowed was delivered in a steady, hypnotic fashion, punctuated by moments when his gentle voice would dissolve to nothing and a silence would emerge, as if he were listening to voices we could not hear, before he picked up the thread he had dropped some moments before.

Micajah Culp was born Samuel Robertson in Edinburgh in 1818, into a Presbyterian merchant family of some wealth. An unremarkable student, he swiftly accrued significant gambling debts in early adulthood, resulting in his short time working for the family firm ending in disgrace when he was caught embezzling funds. His sternly religious father insisted on pressing charges, causing his swift emigration to the United States in 1832 as prosecution loomed.

For the next decade, Robertson's movements are uncertain, although there is evidence to suggest that he lived at various times in New York City, Buffalo, Philadelphia and Richmond under a series of aliases. In 1843 Robertson re-emerged, now under the name of Micajah Culp, travelling the southern states operating as a faith healer and seller of medicinal potions.

It was a couple of years later that Culp's true transformation occurred. Possibly the result of the accidental ingestion of peyote while in Texas, Culp claimed he had been visited by the Archangel Gabriel, who revealed to him via a series of coded visions involving a lion, a she-goat, a snake and an unspecified sea beast that each person's soul vibrates on multiple, and potentially infinite planes of reality, with each individual living many different lives simultaneously. The Archangel went on to explain that through a careful process of meditation, diet (bran-based), enemas and medicinal potions such as those sold by Culp, a person can tune their own earthly vibration to those of a different plane, merging with the self which exists there. In this way they move towards a theoretical state of totality, only achieved when the selves from across all planes, infinite though they may be, are merged. All of this was contained within a series of explanatory pamphlets, also for sale.

It is unclear if Culp believed any of this, or whether he simply saw the moneymaking potential in his hallucinatory experience. Nevertheless, his unique brand of charlatanry, conscious or otherwise, proved successful, attracting a wealthier, more educated clientele who felt themselves above the usual fakery. As time went on, Culp was able to employ others to travel in his place, while he concentrated on establishing the First Church of Vibratism of the Horn of Gabriel in Chattanooga, Tennessee in 1856.

Culp collected his writings in the book, *At Gabriel's Command: Answering the Call Across the Vibrating Planes* in 1858. The book sold well, allowing Culp's message to travel beyond the South and the founding of further churches as far afield as Boston and San Francisco.

It was not to last. Conscripted to fight for the Confederacy in 1864, Culp quickly deserted but was captured and shot by his own side on May 16th of that year. Following the Civil War and the death of its founder, the Church of Vibratism quietly ceased to be, all branches having folded by 1868.

The teachings of Culp did not end there. Copies of *At Gabriel's Command* still circulated, gathering new advocates, often in the creative arts. As the twentieth century dawned, Vibratism refused to die, its influence strongly felt in early abstract art and modern architecture. Culp's work was reprinted regularly, particularly in the 1960s when, due to its hallucinogenic inspiration, it became a text of the counterculture.

Such was the public face of Vibratism. For some time, there have also been rumours of another, secret aspect, known as the Vibratist Assembly. Its origins, if it has ever existed at all, are obscure. It is said that the earliest members were associates of Culp himself, forming a secret society at some point after his death, following an obscure agenda of influence both in the United States and abroad. Although seemingly benign, it has never been concretely established what this alleged society may be trying to achieve. It has been theorised that the Vibratist Assembly is dedicated to the identification and indoctrination of promising individuals, encouraging them in their own Vibratist journey as well as utilising their talents in turn in order to further the organisation's own plan, that of world peace through self-realisation and transcendence. As there is no hard evidence of the Assembly's existence, however, the theory remains just that.

All that can truly be said of Vibratism is that it has, if only in a small way, helped shape the world as we know it, even if the vast majority of its inhabitants remain completely unaware of the movement. That this is the case appears to be little by accident, much more by design.

IX

'Was there a creepy guy at the lecture?' Graham quizzed me in the pub that afternoon, as I mastered the art of leisurely drinking. 'All in black, stupid beard? Stands about like he owns the place?'

'Yes,' I said. 'But I missed the beginning so I don't know who that was.'

'That, my young friend, was Dolf Richter. He is the only other PhD student at the Centre, and Hillesley's teaching assistant and apprentice.'

'Apprentice?'

'Aye. Second choice. Hillesley wanted me, but I said no. You have to keep your independence with that lot, or they'll suck you in.'

'I don't understand.'

'No,' said Graham, downing what remained of his pint, which was a fair amount. 'It won't make sense now. But I'll tell you about it some other time.'

The subject forcibly changed and the afternoon continued. Cam appeared at some point. He asked me what I made of the lecture, as he made a gesture of something flying over his head. I agreed with him that it was hard to understand. What I didn't say was that while the lecture was indeed challenging, there was something about the subject matter that had already gotten under my skin. Culp may have been a con artist, but he had a system. And while I am very particular about what outside systems I entertain, even at a distance, there are some, like Dewey's, that tickle me. Culp's reached for totality (in a way that I now appreciate as being beyond most beliefs' simple divisions between good and bad). I admired that.

But that was not for now. Now was a time for drinking and the afternoon became the evening and by the end I was drunk and stoned in Cam's room again after forgetting to eat as he explained once more his vision of a society absolutely free of rules and I nodded again but Graham was there too telling him 'You're so stupid, you don't even know you're stupid' and I felt like I was on a train heading into a tunnel except the tunnel never came and instead dots appeared in front of my eyes and I ended up on the floor with Graham holding me up as Cam made me sip some water.

And as my first term began, it continued. In lecture after lecture, Christopher outlined the life of Micajah Culp and the central tenets of Vibratism in-depth (we would not even begin to explore the artistic side of Vibratism until after Christmas, and so no hope of Mo Lightman until then). Seminars with Dolf followed, in which we studied written sources, mostly by Culp himself, whose style proved unconducive to being understood by late twentieth century nineteen-year-olds. Dolf would bark out questions about the set readings, and we would as one fail to provide an answer satisfactory to him, causing him to roll his eyes impatiently at our group stupidity. As Graham predicted, the number of students swiftly dwindled as many realised that no amount of undergraduate high-jinks could be worth the strain of wading through page after page of nineteenth century mysticism (mid-term total: 14). I got low marks for my first essays, but enough to pass. Meanwhile, there were nights in the pub, occasional forays to the student union where the music continued to go DOOF DOOF. There Cam introduced me to more of the friends he seemed to make so quickly and effortlessly, and while I wouldn't say I got on with any of them particularly well, they didn't seem to mind me that much either, viewing my awkwardness with amusement but not the contempt I had become accustomed to. I considered this an acceptable state of affairs (one time, after months of incessant badgering from Cam, I finally even did a pill. A pill of what I do not know. All that I do know is that while Cam and his friends were running around hugging each other and claiming they were 'buzzing', I felt nothing at all. While I suspected them of falling victim to whatever the illegal equivalent is to the Placebo Effect, Cam insisted that the problem was at my end. 'There's something wrong with your brain,' he said. 'There must be. Everyone else is off their tits').

And every week I would go and buy Atom Comics. More and more of them, all paid with a cheque. By the end of that term I was well into my second book, with a pile sitting in my room that, while much smaller than my collection back home, was not to be sniffed at either.

When I went home at Christmas, laden down with plastic bags full of them to add to my bedroom collection, Lori met me off the train and cried with joy to see me again. I had not been a good son and had not remembered to phone her regularly. She had phoned me on several occasions, ringing the payphone and hoping someone would answer. Often, no one did. When it was time for me to leave, she was as equally determined as before to see me get on that train and back to the education she had been exiled from all those years before.

There was a field trip near the beginning of the next term, the only one we ever went on, to a university library, in a town some miles away. What was significant about this library is that it housed one of only three surviving copies in the world of the first edition of *At Gabriel's Command*, which had somehow made its way across the Atlantic as part of a private collection, along with various other pamphlets and documents relating to Culp and the early years of Vibratism. The book and some highlights of the collection were on permanent display under glass on the top floor, occasionally visited by Culp scholars but otherwise ignored by students, who would rest their water bottles on the case while using the photocopier. Cam and the other remaining classmates declared the trip a waste of time, causing much seething anger in the face of Dolf and wistful acceptance in that of Christopher. I did not mind the trip. I liked being in libraries.

During this term, we began to look beyond Culp's writings and at his cultural influence, although at this stage still sticking firmly in the nineteenth century. We studied the symbolist poetry of Jean Barbier. The Pre-Raphaelite paintings of Ruth Hutchinson-McDade. The naive pottery of Benjamin Pease. It was while reading extracts of the realist novel, *Katarina Balabanov* by Alexandr Nenashev, in which a farmer's daughter undergoes a series of small but significant spiritual changes while carrying out her duty of placing frogs in casks of milk to keep it fresh (an old Russian folk custom), that I experienced something new.

I don't know how to explain it except that there was

something about the language describing the process of dropping the frogs in the milk, the repetition of the task tuning the titular character in to alternate versions of herself, thus gaining her greater perception (Christopher's interpretation). For the first time, I could honestly say I was moved by art. I saw beauty in the words, in a way I had only before seen in systems and patterns. True, I had been touched by Atom Comics, but for the beauty of their own internal logic far more than their aesthetics. But here, this novel was telling me some truth about the world. About the people in it, and myself. What that was I couldn't have told you. But I was very certain that it was doing it.

After that, the floodgates opened. I could see beauty everywhere. In poems, paintings and pots. In buildings, bridges and viaducts. In films, in playscripts. In cars, trains. In clothes. In rugs. In comic books published by companies other than Atom. Still not in music. But otherwise, an opening of the senses and an expansion of my emotional palette that was both wonderful and overwhelming. I felt old certainties buckle under the weight of all this new information. Something was going to have to give.

X

'So has Hillesley talked about Whitman yet?'

Graham was in my room, flicking through my pile of Atom Comics curiously. My walls were now covered in prints by Ruth Hutchinson-McDade. I had left them bare for five months, until Cam had pointed out that this was odd, and maybe I should hang some rugs. The prints, which I had cut out of an expired calendar I found in the communal bin and remembered hanging in Christopher's office before Christmas, seemed preferable.

'No, he hasn't mentioned him. Who is he?'

'Whitman?' said Graham, gearing up for one of the mini-lectures I had come to expect from him. 'Walt Whitman? *Leaves of Grass*? You've seriously never heard of him? What are they teaching in school these days? Never mind, I know the answer. Shakespeare. Anyway, seeing as you don't know, Walt Whitman was one of the great American poets, and it is inevitable that at some point Hillesley will talk about him in great detail. He's obsessed with the idea that he was influenced by Culp. Problem is, he's got nothing to go on. No hard evidence at all that Whitman had even heard of him. Just a few lines from a really long poem called "Song of Myself". Now, would you like to hear those lines, by any chance? I can see that you would, and they go like this. Ahem.

> *Do I contradict myself?,*
> *Very well then I contradict myself,*
> *(I am large, I contain multitudes).*

'The last line is in parentheses, or brackets, if you don't speak American. Possibly the greatest use of brackets in all literature. Very famous. Joyce quotes it in *Ulysses*, which I'm guessing you also know nothing about. But only Hillesley believes these lines are anything to do with Vibratism. He thinks that when Whitman says "multitudes" he's talking about him tuning into different versions of himself by meditating. And nude sunbathing, which Whitman was into. Hillesley got into a huge argument with another academic over it in a journal the other year. No one else took his side. It was incredibly awkward.'

I knew I wouldn't be receiving Graham's wisdom much longer. He had completed his thesis, and only had to sit his oral exam. Then he would be gone, riding through the Alps on his motorcycle for as long as he could afford before going back to the building sites, or away on an oil rig.

I had only recently enquired as to what his doctoral thesis was about (in fact, I had for the longest time failed to grasp that a thesis, along with an oral exam, was pretty much all that a PhD consisted of. I imagined him going to lectures like mine, but harder). His work was an investigation into the life and work of the Hungarian experimental filmmaker Lajos Kovács (1932-1974). Graham had showed me a grainy videotape of his work. According to him, it was the only copy in Western Europe, which he had paid a pretty penny for from a dubious source. The films were each a few minutes long, and mainly consisted of an intense flickering light in varying colours, not unlike that seen down the student union when the DOOF DOOF music was playing. In the context of Kovaks' practice, this flickering effect had profound Vibratist meaning. Watching the films made my eyes go funny, and the flickering carried on several minutes after the films had ended, even when I closed them.

The pile of Atom Comics Graham was flicking through stared at me accusingly. I had a large backlog of ones I had not read. Although I still bought new ones every Saturday, I no longer felt the urge to devour them as soon as they were in my possession. The amount I was spending on them was less and less. These days, the stubs in my cheque book were written out more to bookshops, art galleries and grocery shops where I would get cashback to pay for student union pints for a pound or to chip in for Cam's drug money (it had been pointed out to me that my introductory rate of free had now well and truly expired. It was also suggested that I learn to roll a joint, but try as I might, my fingers could not work the tobacco and paper in the manner required, and the result was an unsatisfactory fat, flaccid unsmokable slug of a thing).

It was a Saturday that day. I knew I would soon need to go into the city if I was to collect this week's new batch of Atom Comics. But I was enjoying just sitting in the room with Graham, talking about this and that and not even anything in particular. There was no getting away from it, I was enjoying it far more than I had been enjoying reading the comics these days, making a mental note of the DR shifts for the unspecified future project I had been carrying in my head for over ten years. And somehow I didn't go into town that day. And I didn't the week after. The week after I did, but went to the new show at the art gallery and did not visit the comic shop. And next time I happened to pass it, I felt almost revulsed, as if offered food I had already had well more than my fill of. It was over for Atom Comics and me, it seemed. I had somehow fallen out of love, and I wasn't even sad. I was playing the field, and I liked it.

XI

'Ah, my young friend,' said Graham, some time before the end of the summer term, as I passed his door. He pulled me into his room. 'Tonight we drink dragon's fire, for it is over, at last. As of today, I have three letters after my name. P, h and let us not forget a little matter of Mr. D. I passed, is what I'm saying.'

'Um, congratulations,' I said, offering a stiff handshake.

'That's what I like about you, lad. You never hold back.' He gestured at a bottle of whisky and two bulbous glasses. 'I bought this when I began my thesis, four long years ago. I promised myself not to touch a drop until the day I knew I had passed. That day has now arrived, and while tomorrow my great Alpine adventure begins, tonight, with your help, I will be drinking from this bottle of what I will have you know is very nice, very expensive whisky.'

I had never drunk spirits before. From the smell alone, they did not seem to be my type of thing. I did not know how much help I would be.

'Note that I am pouring it neat, as it should be, and not desecrating it with Coke, soda, lemonade or any other ridiculousness. To drink dragon's fire, one must stare into the eye of the beast and inhale it in all its unadulterated glory.'

He gave me one of the little glasses, and chinked it with his.

'I am a doctor,' he cried, 'and I prescribe this medicine!' He took a mouthful, followed by what appeared to be a spasm accompanied by some unsettling gibbering noises, rounded off with a joyful exhalation. I did not want to do this, so took only a little sip. I was used to unfamiliar substances having quite extreme effects on me by this point, so I was not surprised to find it was barely a liquid, more a noxious gas burning its way down my throat and pipework as it searched for my stomach. I coughed uncontrollably for a full minute, then took another sip.

It was after Graham had poured our third glass of this undrinkable substance I was still somehow drinking that he put his face so close to mine, there was no way I could avoid his gaze, or his fumes.

'Tell me something, and I need you to be brutally honest,' he said . 'Don't you think it's weird that a university has a whole centre dedicated to the study of an obscure nineteenth century snake-oil salesman and his crackpot religion, despite minimal interest from students and a ninety-percent dropout rate?'

I nodded. It was odd, now that he mentioned it, not that I was in any state to accurately describe normality at that moment.

'And don't you think it's also weird,' he continued, his nose pressed up against mine in a manner that was very much unsensual, 'that this is just one of many Vibratism Studies centres dotted across the world? You do have to ask yourself why, don't you?'

'It is strange,' I said.

He removed his face from mine to pour himself another and I could breathe again.

'They'll come for you, you know,' he continued. 'To see if you want to join them. They won't force you, mind, but they'll jolly you along. You're the sort they're after, see. Someone serious, with staying power.'

'Who will come for me?' I said. I was not the sort of person people came for.

'Hillesley. That Dolf prick. More after them. My advice, stay close, but stay out of it. Take the benefits, but don't let them take you.'

'I... don't know what you mean.'

'If I told you the whole truth now,' sighed Graham, 'you'd run a mile. And I don't want to take your education away from you. Just be careful. When the gift horse comes, look it in the mouth, understand?'

'Yes,' I said, meaning entirely, no. Words were losing their meaning entirely at this point, and I was somehow on a roundabout in the middle of Graham's room.

Graham rummaged in a drawer and pulled out a videotape without a box. It had 'KOVÁCS' written on the label in thick felt tip.

'Here, I'm giving you this. I'm done with it now. I have a feeling you'll need it in a few years. Comes with a health warning, though. Don't show it to anyone who...'

At least that's how I imagine the conversation went. I had lost consciousness just after he handed me the videotape. I woke up the next morning clutching it on Graham's bed, my head feeling like it had been hit by an avalanche of rubble while I slept. Graham himself was gone, along with as many things that could be carried on his back while riding a motorcycle.

XII

It was the beginning of my second year (student total: 10) and after an uneasy summer back home spent resisting the mutterings of Derek (who seemed to have moved in permanently in my absence) about getting a summer job, I was back in my room at halls (a postcard was waiting for me from Graham in my postal slot. Said he had got as far as Switzerland on his motorbike and fallen in love with a local girl who ran her own whisky bar. He saw no reason to move on from this situation. He reminded me to phone my mother).

Things were not going well. The fresh intake of first years were rowdier than those of the year before. The boy who now had Graham's room played the DOOF DOOF music at two o'clock in the morning, causing me to consider that it might be worse than other music after all, while other students would play racing games outside my door, running up the corridor and down the wooden stairs, banging fire doors on their way. Christopher did tell them to stop on one occasion, but in a voice so soft it registered more as a suggestion than a command.

Cam was the only person I really knew still living there, but things were not so good between the two of us. He would invite me into his room for a joint if he saw me passing, and take me along to the odd thing in the city and meet up with some of his fellow rule-haters, but he clearly found me less entertaining than he once did. Perhaps it was because I had learnt to hold my drink and no longer embarrassed myself on quite such a regular basis that he saw me as not so much fun.

The sum of all this was I was feeling very alone in that place all of a sudden. Maybe it was time to move on.

In the foyer of the Centre, next to the perpetually unmanned welcome desk, was a notice board. It was rarely used, except to advertise the odd bike for sale or student union event, but occasionally there would be postcards announcing rooms for rent in locals' houses. There was one such at this time, so I took the number and a day later followed one of the supernaturally quiet roads that led off from the high street, through the village I had come to find quite homely (despite the oppressive atmosphere and incessant hatred of its residents), down past some large, thatched cottages and a gradual descent into countryside, before I came to an estate of glaring red new-builds at the edge of the village. The house I was looking for was there.

The bell played a little tune and the front door opened. Above me was a tall, red-haired woman, in what I guessed were her early forties. Shoulders broad like a swimmer, wearing what looked to be a silk dressing gown at the quite late time of half-past four. She looked down her hawk nose at me for a moment. Not for the first time, I had the sensation of being evaluated.

'You're here about the room,' she said, and smiled.

'Yes,' I said.

'Come in, come in,' she said, beckoning me in with her finger.

'I'm Fred, by the way', she said. She must have sensed my bafflement from behind her, as she added, 'It's short for Winifred.'

She led me up some stairs, then a few more, past some vases and other ornaments and a well-stocked trophy cabinet.

'Mine,' she said, gesturing proudly. 'Yes, I was quite the athlete in my younger days. Track and field. Nearly made the

Olympic team. But then I got pregnant and that was that. Past my peak by the next one. Still, mustn't dwell on what might have been.' She seemed to be holding back tears. I felt as if I'd been taken on quite an emotional journey at astonishing speed.

The room itself nestled in a cranny, as if it had been bolted on to the rest of the house as an afterthought.

Her face once again composed, Fred knocked on the door.

'Nigel? Nigel. There's another boy come about the room. Can we come in?'

There was the sound of scraping, someone moving something from in front of the door perhaps. Eventually it opened, and inside was a strained-looking young man in glasses, wearing neat clothes he did not know how to tuck in. He seemed nervous to see Fred.

The room was small, but seemed smaller as there were a number of large, boxy computers filling the space between the bed and the wardrobe, along with various items of unspecified electrical equipment slung in collapsing cardboard boxes.

'Nigel is a bit of an electronics whizz, aren't you, Nigel?' said Fred. 'But he's leaving us now after a year-and-a-half. Going to move in with his girlfriend.' I could have sworn she rolled her eyes slightly at this.

I looked round the room a few times, pretending to inspect it. That it was a room with walls and a ceiling was good enough for me, but I knew I had a role to play in this scenario (despite my biological aversion to pretence) and had to make a bit of an effort. I took the time to wonder if it had once been the bedroom of the child whose birth derailed Fred's athletics career all those years before. Where were they now? University, perhaps.

'It's... nice,' I said.

'I'll show you the bathroom, and the kitchen,' said Fred. 'Thank you, Nigel.'

As I headed out the room, struggling to keep up with the brisk pace of Fred's long but still muscular legs that her dressing gown did not remotely cover, Nigel grabbed my arm. He looked at me as intently as someone who evidently disliked eye contact as much as I did possibly could.

'It's great at first,' he said, 'but it wears you out.' He stood there, trying to find the words to clarify his meaning, but they would not come. He simply shook his head in frustration. I knew how he felt.

Fred was waiting for me on the landing.

'This is the bathroom,' she said, pointing past a door decorated with painted shells. I peeped my head round. It was curiously dark, surprisingly large, with the bath somehow in the floor. With yet more large seashells in the places you might usually expect toothpaste and soap, I felt I had reached the border of my understanding, at least as far as bathrooms were concerned.

'Very nice,' I said again.

'And this is our bedroom,' said Fred, opening the door to another room. 'Mine and my husband's, that is.'

I did not know why she was showing me this, and I tried to glance at the room with its curtains drawn, the bed unmade, as quickly as possible. There was an odd smell, almost like sweat, but not quite. I could not help but notice that Fred was standing very close to me in that room. Something touched my leg.

'Very nice,' I whimpered.

'The kitchen's downstairs, obviously,' she said, finally.

In the kitchen, I found a smiling, waving man. 'Hello,' he

said, 'I'm Stuart.' He seemed to be about Fred's age, was much shorter, and wore an identical dressing gown, his hairy bare legs sprouting out of it audaciously.

'You can use this whenever,' said Fred. 'Sometimes we have... dinner parties, but we'd let you know well in advance.'

Stuart gestured proudly at the various devices they had in their kitchen. Besides the toaster and the kettle, I had no idea what you were meant to do with any of them, but I nodded appreciatively anyway.

'You're a student, aren't you?' he continued. 'Down at the Centre? I know some of the villagers have a problem with your lot. They don't like outsiders coming in, doing things they don't understand. But we're not like that at all, are we, Fred?'

'Oh, no,' said Fred. 'We're very open-minded.'

Stuart's face lit up as she said this. It seemed to mean a lot to him.

'Well, I think that's everything,' said Fred. 'Oh, actually. If you don't mind me asking, do you have a girlfriend?'

'Um, no... no I don't,' I said.

'Oh, that's good,' said Fred. This appeared to make Stuart all the happier. They exchanged glances.

'Oh, it's just that sometimes we have lodgers staying here and they have their girlfriends over quite a lot,' said Stuart. 'And it is a single-rent room.'

'So...' said Fred, her gaze uncomfortably sharp all of a sudden, like a bird of prey on a perch. 'What are you thinking?'

I was thinking I wanted to run away for reasons I couldn't explain. But I often felt like that, and had learnt not to trust the sensation.

'Ah... I'll take it!' I said.

XIII

'Well, we'll be sorry to see you go,' said Christopher as I handed back the keys to my room. 'But I do understand. Between you and me the new intake is not quite up to snuff. I do not believe any of them are the serious people we are looking for.'

For some reason, his use of the word 'we' in that moment brought back whisky-soaked almost-memories of that evening with Graham, and something he had said. What that was, however, escaped me.

'I'll give you back your deposit in full, of course,' he said, reaching in his drawer for a cheque book. 'But do feel free to visit, for a chat, if need be.'

'About the course?'

'Oh. Yes. Or... about the course, yes.'

As before, he ended the meeting by looking up at the ceiling, stretching out his fingers and feet, and no longer seeming aware I was present. Just as I turned to go, a door opened, and Dolf stepped out of a room in which I could just about see an unmade bed. He was wearing his polo neck but no trousers.

'Ah, I did not realise...' he said, and closed the door quickly.

'Oh,' spluttered Hillesley. 'I'm... ah, just letting him sleep on the floor, he is in-between places at the moment.'

I happily accepted this information, and it wasn't for some time that I thought it was odd that he didn't just let him sleep in one of the many empty rooms.

In any case, my mind was very much on other things, as less than half an hour later my bag of possessions and myself were situated in the middle of my new room, now completely empty of computers and electronics. What remained – bed, wardrobe, desk, chair, bookcase – I could now see were lovingly crafted items. It struck me as a waste, at first, to give the room to someone whose life was as devoid of style and elegance as mine. Then I remembered that I was now an aesthete, and was in as good a position to appreciate a good wardrobe as anybody.

Stuart, who had let me in this time and helped me with my one bag, was explaining keys. 'This is for the front door. And this is the back. There's no key for this room, I'm afraid, but I don't think you'll need to hide from us!'

He giggled at the thought of it as he handed them to me.

'Anyway, I'll leave you to get settled in,' he said, and slid out the door, as if trying not to disturb me from vital work.

I had mostly finished unpacking when I heard the front door, followed by the sound of Fred's voice, talking to Stuart in low tones. Several minutes later, there was a delicate knock on my door. Stuart's head peeked round it.

'Ah, Fred and I were just wondering if you would like to join us for dinner tonight? Thought it might take the stress out of your first night here.'

I said I would. I had found over the past year that saying yes to things was generally more interesting than saying no to them, and had achieved a level of confidence (or arrogance) that led me to believe I could now handle most social situations to an acceptable standard. Not that I was of a mind to look back, but you would not recognise me as the youth of just a year before, paralysed in awe at the mere presence of Juliette Cass. Now I could hold basic conversations with relative ease, and while it was plain I was not giving everyone everything they wanted, I was not disappointing them at a fundamental level either. And while I had no strong desire to have dinner with a married couple in their forties, I could also see no reason to decline.

Fred's voice called me from below some time later. I noted how easily sound travelled in this house, which explained the deliberate murmuring before. She was waiting for me at the bottom of the stairs. Once again, she was wearing her silk dressing gown, her foot resting one or two steps higher than perhaps necessary.

'This way,' she said, and led me into a room I had not been in before. There, a long candlelit table sat in the middle of a white carpet I was already praying I wouldn't drop anything on, while music that sounded like flutes being played underwater burbled in the background. Fred pulled out a chair at the head of the table and gestured for me to sit. As I did so, she sat herself down to my right, strangely close considering the length of the table. I could feel her knee brushing against mine and I wondered why she didn't just move up a bit.

'I expect you drink wine,' she said. I never had in my life, but nodded as she poured me a glass.

I didn't know what to say as we waited for food, aware that Fred was glancing at me repeatedly, perhaps trying to catch my eye. No chance there, I thought, as I gazed around the room, seeing myself looking very small in the facing mirror that doubled the length of the room. On one wall was a strange picture. I recognised the subject matter from a painting in the local art gallery as being that of Leda and the Swan. This airbrushed modern take included details very much left out of the nineteenth century academic version they had there.

A door from the kitchen opened, and Stuart wheeled in a serving trolley, using oven gloves to place in front of me a fillet of a fish I did not recognise from the village chippy.

The rest of the food was not on the plate. It was in bowls with large spoons in them. It took me a moment as both Stuart and Fred looked at me intently to grasp they were expecting me to serve myself.

I gingerly scooped out a small number of potatoes and various green vegetables, hoping I had not taken too many and appeared greedy.

'Have more than that!' cried Fred. 'Come on, don't be shy.'

'No, don't be shy,' said Stuart, grinning oddly at the idea. He had sat himself down at the other end of the table, directly facing me, leaving a curiously large gap between himself and Fred.

Finally, I had seemed to have dished out enough potatoes and vegetables for their satisfaction.

'Excuse me, dear,' said Stuart, 'would you mind passing me the potatoes?' His voice sounded rehearsed, theatrical even. This struck me as odd, but not significant.

'Certainly,' said Fred, standing up and leaning over me to pick up the bowl. It was then that I noticed that her dressing gown was looser than it had been. So loose, in fact, that as she leaned over me, I thought I might have caught a glimpse of some things round and soft nestled inside. In fact, other than the occasional and inescapable sight of Lori's in such a small flat as ours, I had never seen anything like them at all.

I could see myself blushing, a small red bean, in the wall-length mirror. Even once she had sat down, one was still half-exposed, sitting there in my peripheral vision, my eye darting involuntarily towards it.

I felt excitingly, frighteningly peculiar. I may have felt this way before, during the night when my body had done things I was afraid to ask Lori about, but this was the first time I realised this feeling had something to do with the bodies of others. And while I understood the mechanics of sex from school and television, it had immediately been filed in my mind as being one of the many things that had nothing to do with me. Even the young students wearing little as they danced to DOOF DOOF music had not aroused any excitement. For all that was on display, the crucial areas were always well-contained. There was no passing through borders there, no indefinable movement from the public into the private. But here, suddenly, there was. A breast, to the point of nipple, just to my right, all too graspable. Just a lift of my hand and I could... Something else was lifting. It had to stop. I had to make it stop.

'You said earlier you missed the Olympics when you got pregnant. I was wondering what your son or daughter are doing now?' These words, these strange sentences, were what somehow came out of my mouth. They came out loud, and a full octave higher than my usual speaking voice.

There followed an awful, still hush that the sound of underwater woodwind could not cover.

'Well... you see, the baby, a boy, died,' said Stuart softly. 'Soon after he was born.'

Fred was crying into her hands.

'We've never been able to conceive again,' Stuart continued, 'although we've tried.'

'Yes, we've tried,' Fred croaked.

'I'm sorry,' I said, ashamed and successfully unaroused.

'You weren't to know,' said Fred, dabbing her eyes with her napkin. 'I'm just being silly.'

Stuart reached over the expanse between them and clasped her hand.

'I'll just be a minute,' she said, rising. She slipped out the room and up the stairs.

Stuart smiled at me and asked me polite questions about my course and home for some minutes. I tried my best to answer them and ignore Fred's increasingly glaring absence until Stuart too stood up.

'I'll just see where Fred's got to,' he said, and soon, I was alone, with just too many potatoes to eat. Their murmuring drifted through the floorboards, then stopped. After ten minutes, neither had reappeared. Perhaps the dinner was over, and there was no pudding, I thought. And so I took myself back up the stairs, past the vases, past the trophy cabinet and into my room.

On the floor was a silk dressing gown. On the single bed was Fred, sprawled leisurely and naked, her body a mix of soft and hard, the familiar and the previously unimaginable.

'I'm... I'm sorry,' I said, as if I had wandered in on her in her own room.

'Join me,' she said, dreamily.

I stood still.

'I said, join me.'

I was walking towards her.

'Take your clothes off first,' she laughed, and I did so, not knowing why. It was just something that had to happen, like my first beer with Graham. One of those doors that needed to be walked through, when it appeared.

And things were touched and kissed, clumsily by me, expertly by her, and I knew there was only one more thing to do. An alarm bell rang from a distant point in my mind.

'Shouldn't we...' I said. I knew that some sort of protection was required, but protection from what, and what form it should take or even look like were ideas that were quite absent from my mind.

'Oh, don't worry,' she said. 'There's no chance of my getting pregnant. No chance at all.'

And one moment I was, and the next moment I wasn't. Another border drifted over.

XIV

That was just the first time. Be it late in the evening, in the middle of the night, or during the day when Stuart was at work (Fred did not work, instead spending office hours using a home gym in the garage or else in bed), she would slip into my room, out of her dressing gown, and into my bed, commanding me to join her if I was not already in it. I always did, not just because, like Graham's alcohol or Cam's drugs, the sensation was pleasant, but because Fred was so much older than me, and so much more commanding, the idea that I could simply refuse, due to my being too busy, too tired, it not having been that long since the last time, did not occur.

After the act, she would lie there silently for a few minutes, looking sadder than you might expect, before striding out, often without bothering to put on her dressing gown, which I would leave hanging for her on the bannister, and often back to her own room where Stuart would often be waiting, and I would lie there listening to their whispers.

The activity would usually come in bursts, followed by a lull where Fred would barely acknowledge me when she passed me on the landing. Her mind was elsewhere, and it was as if I had stopped existing for her. During these periods that could last days or even a couple of weeks, I would both yearn for the visits to begin again, while also fearing it, as with them came a whole cornucopia of mixed and contradictory feelings I could not even begin to identify, let alone make sense of.

Yes, my lack of control over this situation left me reeling (I was particularly bothered that Fred did not bother to knock, and so my flapping and shaking could easily have been discovered), but what bothered me the most was that a lot of the time, I wasn't sure we were quite alone. Often, over the sound of the creaking of the bed slats and Fred's deep, almost sorrowful moans, there was another, more distant noise. A frantic slapping, that would get faster and faster, until ending in a cry that was never quite masked by the climactic note let out by Fred.

Sometimes, there would be parties. I would be warned about them in advance, and I would be expected to take myself off somewhere else for much of the night. But once I came back too early, and had to step over a rutting couple on the stairs, while grunts, groans and shrieks came at me from all directions and watching figures moved under ultraviolet light. When I got to my bed, it had clearly been freshly used by others, and not for sleeping. Lying there by myself, listening to an orgasm from below I knew to be Fred's, I decided I did not like living in this place. There was just too much sex.

'Of course we'll be happy to have you back,' said Christopher, as I once again sat in his office, writing out the deposit that he had refunded a couple of months before. 'A lot of the troublemakers from before have gone, and those left have calmed down now they don't have their accomplices. You'll be fine here. Nice and quiet.'

His eyes drifted to the ceiling at the thought of this and I went back to pack my things.

I had no idea what I was going to say to Fred. In fact, as I filled my backpack once again with everything I owned in the world (except comics), the plan coming together in my mind was to simply sneak downstairs and out the door without a word.

It was not to be. I heard a noise on the landing. My door swung open. Fred stepped inside with determination, loosening the tie on her dressing gown.

'I can't!' I cried out, still stuffing a saucepan into my backpack. 'I'm moving out! Right now! To... live with my girlfriend!'

Fred eyed me with a mixture of disbelief and contempt.

'I'm not refunding your deposit at this short notice,' she said coldly, retying her dressing gown tighter than it ever had been. Even though I do not always notice such things, I could tell I had offended her then.

I finished packing my bag with shaking hands and left.

I would see Stuart around the village sometimes. He would give me a friendly, perhaps slightly nervous nod, which I would return. And I would see Fred, less often (she disliked going into the village, and would drive into the city both for necessities and pleasure). She would turn her head as soon as she saw me, and I would do the same. It was almost a race.

And then, I saw her that one last time. She was pushing a pram. This time when she saw me, she did not look away. And despite my aversion to all eye contact, I could not resist the sheer command of her gaze that day.

What was she trying to tell me? I could not make sense of the look in her eyes, that strange mixture of accusation and something else I didn't recognise. I could not make sense of the baby in front of her, other than after years of trying, her and Stuart had managed it after all. That the baby was you, my daughter (can I address her directly? Yes, I must. Surely that is the point of all of this?) did not cross my naive little mind.

And that, from my perspective, is how I came to be your father. I wish there was more to it. But it was as strange and silly as that. I don't know how that makes you feel. But then, what do I know? For all my love of patterns and systems, when it came to it, I couldn't even take a month and count back by nine. And I never saw Fred and her baby again. I thought about Fred only for what she took and gave to me, and the baby not at all. Until twenty years later, that baby sent an email.

*

I check my phone. I know there is no message. There has been no penny-whistle. But still I check it, in the hope the act of observation will change the result. But there is no message.

XV

Back in the halls, life was quieter than it had ever been, and often it seemed as if Christopher and myself were the only residents, the remaining students being few and not keen to spend more time than necessary in the dull, dark village (Cam was rarely seen now, his room silent, his door locked). Well, I say the only residents. I would occasionally spot Dolf Richter furtively slipping in or out of Christopher's office, spending as little time in the corridor as possible, almost as if he didn't want to be seen. It was curious, but still, I thought little of it.

The lectures continued, mostly still given by Christopher, some now by Dolf. For all its prominence in the leaflet, the Vibratist comic book art of Mo Lightman was covered in less than twenty minutes. While Christopher was usually keen to explore everything in exhaustive detail, here he seemed keen to rush through it, and I got little from it, save for clarification of what I already suspected regarding the connection between Atom Comics' differing realities and the multiple planes of Vibratism. It felt strange going back to it for those few minutes, not unlike the sensation of seeing Fred in the street.

Meanwhile, my grades improved, to the point I found myself in the unusual position of regularly being top of the class. It would be Dolf who marked the essays. He would hand them back, wearily, as if their mere existence depressed him. 'Not terrible,' he'd say when giving back my efforts. 'But you could do better.' He did not think anyone else could do better.

There were also more beers drunk, joints smoked and casual friendships made (there were also occasional postcards and letters from Graham, detailing his new life in Switzerland, the swift destruction of the same after his girlfriend went back to her ex, and his continued travels through Italy, Austria and Liechtenstein as his trip across the Alps entered its second year. If there was a return address I would reply, but there rarely was). After another unrepentantly jobless summer, despite the worrying details of my bank account, I returned to the halls for a third year (student total: 5). And it was then, among the latest crop of peace-shattering freshers that I found what I could describe as my first (and not counting the odd brief encounter, my only) girlfriend. Anya was

*

'Excuse me, do you run the Atom Comics DR database?'

A young man, probably as young as I was at the time I have just been reconstructing, is standing in front of me, nervously shuffling from one foot to another. I was not sitting in a welcoming posture. My arms were folded. My head was down. But still he has come.

I nod and wait for him to say what he wants. Even though I had sat down with the express intention of making myself inviting, I do not want to speak to anyone now.

'It's just, uh... I was wondering if I could ask you about the revisions you made for *Atom Warriors* #45–52? I don't understand why you changed DR0890 to 0898, and took out 1401 completely. I know it's to do with the Nexus Event in *Combustible Man: Full Circle*, but I can't see how it cancels them out.'

He looks at me hopefully, waiting for me to answer. I could tell him right away, how in that series it is established that the DR in which Combustible Junior has a red exploding jewel is in fact the same as the one in which he has a green one, with the colour changing depending on the amount of Combustible Energy stored within it, while several key events in this series are now known to have occurred in the imagination of the Sister Radio of DR0300, and so cannot be awarded their own DR number at all. But if I tell him that now, there may be follow-up questions, and more of my time will be taken, and the task I am engaged in undone. I realise now how much I have yearned for my contribution to be recognised in the flesh, my position of authority existing in physical reality and not just the ether of the internet. That is now happening, and I cannot enjoy it.

'Can you send me an email?' I say. 'I don't have my spreadsheets with me.'

'Sure,' he says. He must know I don't need spreadsheets. There are no spreadsheets, and never have been. It's all in my head. Every issue. Every DR. But still he turns to go. He stops himself.

'I can't believe it's ending,' he says.

'It is a shock,' I say. I know he wants more, an elder to help him mourn a death. But I can't be that for him right now. I just can't.

'Can I just shake your hand?' he says. 'That database, man… it changed my life.'

I take his hand and shake it. I even return his gaze very slightly. I wonder what Christopher would make of him. Whether he was the sort he was looking for. I feel strangely warm from his testimony, however much I recoil from its unexpectedly intimate nature. Is this really why I have been doing it all this time?

He smiles shyly and returns to the huddle of youths he emerged from. The glow fades. The task calls. Reconstructing a time of my life when there were few tasks, few systems (Daddy was quiet during those undergraduate years. The more life opened up for me, the less I needed him. But I knew he was always there. I can hear him now, telling me I need to leave autobiography behind soon, that it is becoming time for fairy stories, an idea I like less and less but he won't shut up about. I can put him off for a while longer, but I know he'll never give up). There were people to take their place. People like

*

Anya. She found me in the lounge, late at night, watching a foreign film. I had seen her at a distance from the stairwell earlier, but we had not properly met. I had observed how she walked with an authority that belied her diminutive stature, and heard how her voice could carry into nearly any room in the halls. She was also the most immaculate person I had ever seen. She wore even her most casual clothes like a uniform, her hair tightly constrained in plaits.

'This looks boring,' she said. 'Mind if I turn it off?'

'Do you want to watch something?' I asked.

'No,' she said, 'I just don't want to watch this.'

She turned off the television and sat in the armchair adjacent to my sofa.

'What year are you?' she said.

'Third,' I replied.

'How come you're still in halls?'

'I did try to leave, but it didn't work out,' I said.

'Oh? What went wrong?'

'It was hard to get work done.'

If I had been looking in her direction, I imagine I would have seen her brow furrowing.

'Are you good at this? I mean, do you understand it, this course? Do you think you will get a good degree?'

'Yes,' I said. 'I think. I get 2:1s in my essays.'

I found her sitting next to me.

'I had my first lecture today and I don't think I understand any of it.'

She was sitting very close. She seemed to be waiting for me to say something. As was so often the case, I had no idea what that was.

'Do you think you could help me understand it?' she said. 'Seeing as you're so bright.'

'Um, yes,' I said, as I felt her take my hand.

At some unspecified moment that slipped by without me noticing, I somehow became her boyfriend. Each stage of the relationship was initiated by her, and would always be preceded by a lengthy intervention in her coursework by me. It took some weeks to work our way from hand-holding to kissing to heavy petting, and by that point I was dictating her essays as she wrote them down in her impeccable handwriting (did I know this was cheating? Absolutely, but there was a system in her approach to our relationship that was far more persuasive than that of academia).

At first, Anya seemed very happy with our situation, particularly the 2:1s she was receiving for her work, which eventually elevated to a 1st (something I had never managed under my own name). She liked to do things I liked to do, such as going to art galleries, or the cinema, or the theatre. She did not seem to enjoy anything she saw in them, but she took pride in the act of walking around with me, her hand in mine. She particularly liked it when other students she knew spotted us. She liked it still more, it appeared, if they were female and single, delighting in referring to me as her 'older man' (I still did not feel older than anybody and it seemed like Anya was many years older than me). I could not tempt her down the local pub or the chip shop (the grease made her feel dirty). Instead, she insisted we frequent a restaurant-cum-wine bar at the other end of the village high street. She said we had to go there because it was non-smoking. The drinks were expensive, even their worst beer, and it always seemed to be me who paid. But still, we'd sit on high stools by the window and it looked as if I was making her the happiest girl in the world, although her smile would be more for the room and the street outside as she quizzed me about what sort of job I might be able to get with my degree, how much money, hypothetically speaking, I could potentially make and how soon it would be before I could start saving for a mortgage deposit. Her reasons for asking were not at all clear to me, and the answers I gave were vague. I did not quite tell here there was no plan. I knew enough to grasp she would not like that answer.

It was when she signalled that she wanted to take things to the next level and have a dinner party that dissatisfaction with my performance set in. I did not want to have a dinner party (although I said I did). It seemed a bit odd, cooking a meal in the communal kitchen, then serving it in Anya's pocket of a room, where there was barely enough surfaces available for the number of candles she favoured, let alone our two desks shoved together to make a table for us, plus the one couple and two singletons she had invited. I did not make any attempt to communicate any of this, but I suppose my reluctance must have seeped out of me like a gas.

'If you don't want to spend time with my friends,' she told me as I tried to cover the table with a cloth in a way that did not quite so resemble a draped coffin, 'I wish you would say. But this is really important to me and I'm actually really hurt you would try to sabotage it like this.'

I did not see how I was sabotaging it. I was doing everything I was told. Maybe not with enthusiasm, but that was surely an optional extra?

From my perspective, the dinner party was a success. The guests were present, the food was eaten, and nothing bad happened before they went home. Anya did not see it that way. The singletons had not hit it off. The other couple's chemistry was better than ours. My insistence on having a vegetarian alternative (I could now cook meat-free versions of all the meals Lori had written out the recipes for, plus two more of my own invention) was attention-seeking. I had not said enough. I had looked too sad. And that had made everything else go wrong, for some reason.

No heavy petting occurred that night.

The next morning, I was heading down the Centre corridor for Christopher's next lecture when Dolf stepped out from a door, blocking my way.

'I need to have a word with you,' he said, briskly ushering me into the office he had emerged from.

'Sit, please,' he said. He paced with his back to me for some time, theatrically building up anticipation, before swivelling round suddenly, a familiar-looking essay in his hand.

'This essay,' he bellowed. 'is by a first-year student by the name of Anya. Is that someone with whom you happen to be familiar?'

'Um, a bit,' I said, as a feeling of being heavily slapped ran from the top of my head to my toes.

'A bit,' repeated Dolf. 'This essay is good. Remarkably good. In fact, it's almost as if it were written by someone who has been here nearly three years, and not just a few months. That's very curious, isn't it? That a first-year student would be able to write like that, especially when you consider that her contributions to seminars are so minimal and uninspired? Don't you agree?'

'Yes... yes it is,' I said.

He bent down to my height, his hands on his knees, his beard pointing at me in accusation.

'If...' he said (his voice a murmur), 'I ever!' (now very much not) 'Read! Anything! By this student of this unlikely quality again, I will inform Christopher and you will be removed from the course. Do you understand me?'

I nodded.

'Good.'

I sat there, frozen, having slipped out of time and space and into a state of sheer terror.

'Well?' he said, and gestured with his beard at the door.

I exited at speed and sat through Christopher's lecture, humiliated and absorbing none of it. Although Christopher seemed oblivious to my presence (despite being one of the few students actually there), I had no doubt he was fully aware as to what had just happened. I did not realise how much I cared for Christopher's good opinion of me up until that moment, or how much the course meant, the Centre, all of it. But being with Anya, in a relationship – it's what people did. As long as I was in one, no one would ever suspect me of having once been the child who danced by the railings. I faced a hard decision (always the worst kind).

I went to Anya's room to tell her I couldn't write her essays anymore. She was standing, as if expecting me.

'We need to talk,' she said, with a degree of seriousness that made me feel like I was back in Dolf's office again.

I took a seat. She did not, and began to pace.

'Where do you think this relationship is going?' she asked.

I had absolutely no idea. I sat there in silence to formulate some kind of answer as her pacing got faster and faster.

'Somewhere good!' was the thing I eventually alighted on. Vague, but positive. A perfect response. In my mouth, however, the confident push that such a statement needed did not arrive at the required moment. Instead, the words dribbled out as 'somewhere good?' in the manner of someone taking a wild guess in answer to a maths question. It was hopeless. I can lie without compunction, but I just cannot fake a feeling, however hard I try. Anya did not look impressed. She stopped moving.

'Look, there's no point beating around the bush,' she said. 'You and me, it isn't working out. To be honest, I'm just not sure you're boyfriend material.'

I think she was expecting me to ask why. I did not. Contemplating it all in my room several minutes later, I still did not know how to make sense of it all. What was this feeling washing over me now? Was it sadness? No, it wasn't quite that. It was closer to... relief.

Anya and I would pass each other every day somewhere in the building. At first we would give each other a curt nod and say nothing, but after a while we stopped doing even that. It was not long before she turned up with a new boyfriend, Spencer. Like her, he was well-presented, with skin so clean you could see its shine from a distance. He talked and smiled an acceptable amount, and seemed very dedicated to the relationship project. Anya moved out of halls and in with Spencer after several months, before being thrown off the course at the end of that academic year due to her failing to hand in any more work. I sometimes wonder what she is up to now, whether it worked out for her and Spencer. I would look her up on social media, though I must have once known her surname from the top of the essays I forged for her, I can no longer remember it.

VI

It was shortly after my brief tenure as Anya's boyfriend that the money ran out. Although much of the sum Lori had squirrelled away had gone on essentials, a fair amount had also been spent on beer, culture and soft drugs, with the last dregs being swallowed up by Anya's preference for wine bars. My grant, meanwhile, would barely get me through the next few weeks, let alone until the end of term.

I had taken all the money Lori had to offer. While Cam would regularly phone home for cash top-ups to fund his ruleless lifestyle, I had no family coffers to raid. I had ended up in a compromised position, one that I had been successfully avoiding for nearly five years. I was going to have to get a job.

Of course, the thought still filled me with sickening dread. I was not totally sure that starvation wasn't preferable. But I had just about enough of a survival instinct to recognise its necessity, like having an injection or the putting down of an elderly pet. And so, squirming inside at every step, I began my search.

The village being the size it was, it was no surprise that there were none going there. I would have to go into the city if I were to have any luck at all. I checked the local paper and braved the boards of the job centre, but the positions going were mainly for carers and cleaners, and I had no faith in my ability to care for anybody or wield a satisfactory mop. About to give up and simply stop eating, I passed a small employment agency. I had no idea that such a thing existed, but their sign promised full and part-time warehouse, assembly and clerical positions, available now. Warehouses and assembly sounded far too physical to be considered, but clerical? Clerical sounded like it had something to do with systems. Ordering things. Giving them numbers. I could do that.

After a brief interview with a gruff man who looked like he lived among the filing cabinets in his office, I was on the books. A day later, I was called to the payphone and this same man told me I had a job. I was about to protest when he said it was in a warehouse, but he told me to relax, it was just in the office some evenings, so did I want it or not? I told him I did (I didn't).

Not long after, located on the side of the city that was not fun and where students never went, there I was. After wandering through the warehouse space itself and being nearly crushed by a forklift, I discovered the office I was to work in. One of the few members of the night shift skeleton crew sat me down without a hello and explained the system. He explained it very fast. And then he told me where the drinks machine was and left me to it. I was alone in the office, with only the sound of swearing forklift drivers in the distance for company.

I thought I understood it. There was a roll of stickers with two sets of numbers on them. One set of numbers I had to enter on a computer screen. The other I had to write down in a book. There was a drawer. Sometimes I was meant to open the drawer and take something out. But already I wasn't sure what. Or when. And the numbers in the book had to match up with the numbers… where? And when I'd finished with the stickers I had to put them…

I opened the drawer. I rifled through some pieces of paper covered in numbers that didn't appear to have anything to do with any of the other numbers and closed it again. I went to the drinks machine and came back. None of it had decided to make sense while I was gone. I looked around. There was no one except for the forklift drivers, and I wasn't asking them. But I knew I was expected to clear that roll of stickers before the end of my shift. I started to panic.

And there he was, the voice that was not a voice I had barely heard for some years. He could help me. He could make a system. Maybe not the one I had been shown but a better one. All I had to do was give control over to him and everything would be alright. It would be just like the old days. What else could I do?

I did as I was told. Numbers were entered on the screen. They were entered in the book. Every so often, I would add some up, open the drawer, write the total down on a piece of paper, put the paper in the folder, and close the drawer again. As I went along, I would tear each sticker complete with its backing paper off the roll and put them in piles of twenty.

I carried on in this way for two and a half hours. When the man who had shown me what to do finally reappeared, my desk and the floor surrounding me were covered in little piles of twenty stickers (it would have made more sense to make the number of stickers in the pile substantially higher, but that was not the system).

'Ah,' he said, surveying the empire I had built. 'This is really... wrong.'

Hurriedly, he gathered up as many stickers as he could hold and checked them against the screen and the book. 'Shit, shit, shit,' he said, for some time, and then for a while more as he opened the drawer and flicked through the papers in the folder, frowning in perplexment.

'Do you want to go home early?' he asked me.

I said I would. It seemed for the best (I cursed Daddy, and myself, on the train all the way. How could I have been so stupid to listen to him after all this time? A moment of weakness, a stress reaction. I would never make that mistake again).

The next morning, I was summoned to the communal payphone. It was the man from the agency, telling me I didn't have a job anymore and he wasn't going to get me another one. He hung up. I had no idea how to get paid for the work I'd done, but I wasn't going to phone him back and ask.

This left me with the problem of still being broke. Having

a job had turned out just as badly, if not worse, than I thought it would. But what else was there? As I lay on my bed, staring at the vintage lampshade that had cost me twenty pounds and wondering why I'd wasted so much money on something so basic, a list began to read itself in my head. *Ghost Frog* #292, *Ghost Frog* #293. *All-New Radio Girl Adventures* #17, *Ghost Frog* #294…

Having written down every Atom Comic I still owned back home, I took the train into the city. There, I walked into a certain comic shop and showed a man in a Pummelor T-shirt the inventory of my collection.

'How much for all this?' I said.

He blew out his cheeks and shook his head.

'I can only give you…' And then he quoted a figure that was considerably higher than I was expecting.

XVII

Returning after Christmas with as many Atom Comics that could be carried on the train without breaking my back, I had to face the fact that things were heading towards an end. Soon, lectures would be over, with only a dissertation, an exam, and five months before I would have to do something else with my life. The one night in the warehouse had demonstrated all too clearly that anything other than what I was already doing could lead only to a dead end. It was something of a conundrum I dealt with by not thinking about it at all.

Instead, I threw myself into researching my dissertation.

Although I had initially struggled with modernism, this was something I had recently overcome and was now enamoured with the work of West Coast Vibratist action painters of the 1950s. I asked Christopher and he agreed that it would make an excellent subject for a dissertation. Even Dolf, who was also present and still seemingly sleeping on Christopher's floor, made an approving noise. There was not much to go on in the small library at the Centre (which mostly stocked bound volumes of old Vibratist Studies journals that no one, not even Christopher or Dolf ever read), and nothing at all in the main university library in the city, but a new invention called the internet (accessible via the Centre's one computer) provided me with a few pixelated images and some more titbits of information. If I threw in some critical theory I nearly understood, I had just enough to go on.

Before we broke up for Easter, Christopher gave his final lectures (final student total: 4). Over several sessions, he explained his theories about Walt Whitman in some detail, with further significant focus on his disagreement with the Whitman expert, and why they were wrong. He was not his usual beatific self, and appeared quite emotional as he discussed the pain of being so publicly assaulted by an incorrect opinion. In the corner, Dolf was visibly angry on his behalf, his face turning puce as he quietly punched his own hand.

With the dissertation typed one-fingered and handed in, there was just the exam to sit. Only three of us did, Dolf patrolling up and down beside the very short row to make sure none of us were cheating for the entirety of the time. Cam, whose presence in lectures had become ever more fleeting, but who had managed to hand in something approaching an essay for every assignment and thus stay on the course, was not there. Without sitting the exam he could not pass, and would walk away with nothing. What could have held him back from attending? If he was unwell, I thought, it must be serious to potentially throw away three years of work. Although we spent hardly any time together by then (and the first time he saw me with Anya he had muttered 'Rather you than me, mate', which I sensed crossed some sort of line, although I was not sure which one), I wanted him to be well. I wanted him to pass. His absence preyed on my mind, to the point I walked out of the exam hall without even contemplating how I had just finished my degree.

I found him smoking the most enormous joint back in his room, having already started to pack.

'What do you want?' he said, like we had never been friends.

I told him I was just checking up on him. That I was worried because he hadn't been in the exam hall.

He took a large puff, and sat there, as if weighing up whether to even answer me.

'I just thought, fuck it,' he said, at last. 'I don't want to sit no fucking exam. What do I need a degree for, anyway? It's just a stupid rule you have to have one. Actually, it's not even a rule. Loads of people don't have one. Anyway, I got to do three years of dossing about, which was what I wanted. So I'm good.' He told me that his mum was going to come and pick him up the next day and then he was going on holiday with his uncle in Greece.

'Maybe,' I said, 'if you told Chris you weren't feeling well, you could do a resit—'

'For fuck's sake,' he screamed at me, 'will you stop with your bullshit! You always think you know it all. But you don't, alright?'

I honestly didn't know what he meant. As far as I was aware, I had spent most of my life very clearly not knowing more than everyone else. Up until that point, I had never challenged anything anyone had ever said about me. I had always just taken the hit. But maybe because Cam had been something of a friend once, this time was different.

'I don't think I know it all, Cam. I've never said I did.'

'You don't need to say it. It's all there in the way you stand, always a bit apart. And how you look at people, or don't. Like you're too good to properly look them in the eye. And it's always just take, take, take with you. Yeah, I'll smoke your spliff. Yeah, I'll go to the club night you found out about. But when do you ever turn up with any gear? When do you even learn to roll it? When do you have an idea about anything?'

I didn't know what to say. He sounded right about everything, but somehow also totally wrong at the same time. But why he was wrong was something I could not put into words.

'You know,' he said, the character assassination still somehow not having finished, 'I remember when I first saw you. I was in the kitchen. You walked past. I said hello. You just said nothing. Absolutely nothing. And then you walked on. What a wanker, I thought. But then I spent some time with you and changed my mind because you were funny, for a bit. But I think I was actually right the first time.'

Cam took another puff on his joint. He didn't offer me any. I sensed that he was finished with me, for good. After putting on my shoes and resisting the urge to walk over his rug in them, I left his room.

I sat in my own room, reeling from the blows, crushed and baffled in equal measure. Was that how I was perceived by everybody? Aloof? Superior? Uncaring? I wished Graham was there to talk to. He would help me make sense of it all. I half-considered going into the city to find others I might call my friends to check that they didn't see me the same way. But what if it turned out they did? I couldn't risk it. I stayed in my room (according to his social media account, despite not completing his degree, Cam quickly got a job working for his uncle's scrap metal company, which he now runs. He owns several properties in the UK and abroad and enjoys deep sea diving in the Tropics. Many of his posts rage against regulations and red tape he feels are constraining business growth).

I was not ready to go home, meanwhile. I could still stay at the halls for another month. My strategy of not engaging with the issue of what to do next had been so successful, I still did not have a thought in my head. But now, I saw, as I wandered the corridors of the halls, empty save for a few lingering freshers, waiting for the wounds of Cam's tongue-lashing to heal, I could put it off no longer. I would have to come up with some kind of plan. I resolved to do that the very next day.

That day came and went, and I did not quite get round to doing that. As did another day. And the one after that. A week. Two weeks. A lot of telly watched, cups of tea drank, but no plan. Three weeks. A phone call with Lori where she delicately asked me what my plan might be (Derek had been wondering) but no actual plan. The fourth week was coming. And after that, I would at least have to have the most basic idea about getting out of the halls and back home.

At this point, I was the only student left in the building. Christopher would smile at me if I caught him at his door. Dolf would come and go freely, seemingly no longer bothered by anyone seeing him. Meanwhile, the silence in the corridors was a great big hole where the plan should have been.

And I was just minutes, perhaps seconds away from starting to make my plan when as I walked past Christopher's office, his door opened slightly.

'Ah, there you are,' he said through the crack. 'Are you busy?'

'No, not at all,' I said, as I saw Dolf looming behind him.

'Good,' he said. 'Come in. We have something of a proposition for you.'

XVIII

Inside Christopher's office, I was surprised to hear jaunty pop music emanating from the bedroom. Dolf was wearing a lighter-coloured polo neck than usual and they were both drinking champagne.

'Dolf has completed his doctorate,' said Christopher. 'We are having a little celebration.'

'Congratulations,' I said.

'Yes, I am very happy,' said Dolf, nondemonstrably.

'Please sit,' said Christopher, pointing to a comfortable chair I had not seen before.

'Would you like some wine?' said Dolf, pouring me a glass of red that did not look like it had been bought from the village corner shop before I even had a chance to answer.

'And some of these?' He held out a bowl of what looked

curiously like dry bran flakes. I declined. He seemed disappointed.

'So...' said Christopher, reclining in his own chair behind the desk while Dolf took his usual standing position by his side, 'do you have any thoughts about what you would like to do now you have finished your degree?'

'No,' I said.

'We did not think you had,' said Dolf. I wasn't sure how I was meant to take that.

'You see,' continued Christopher, 'of the three students to see the course through to the end, your marks were consistently higher than the others. Although we haven't released the marks for the dissertations yet, just between us I can tell you that you are looking at a distinction. As well as displaying consistently high academic ability, you also have a grasp of the fundamentals of Vibratism that most students struggle to achieve. So, bearing that in mind, have you ever considered a further career in academia? That is, lecturing and teaching?'

I didn't know what to say. I hadn't, as I had thought about nothing. But I knew that Graham had to fund his postgraduate activities himself through manual labour. And I patently wasn't going to do that.

'I don't think I could afford to continue my studies,' I said, eventually.

'Ah, now that is where we come in,' said Christopher, with a twinkle that quickly faded as a painful thought crossed his mind. 'Due to the stress of the unjustified and sustained public attack on me from a fellow academic who should know better, I am taking a more administrative role and stepping down as undergraduate course leader. Now that he has completed his qualification, Dolf will take my place. This opens up a position for teaching assistant, to be taken by a PhD student during the course of their studies, with fees paid for along with a modest grant for a period of four years. A position we were rather hoping you would accept.'

I sat there, my mouth open but with no sound coming out. I tried to break it down. On the one hand, it was sort of a job, which was a problem. On the other, it was something of a continuation of what I had already been doing, which I had turned out to be rather good at. Perhaps I would continue to be good at it. And it would postpone me having to think of anything else for a full four years.

'Yes,' I said, eventually. 'I would like to do that.'

'That's great to hear!' said Christopher. 'A toast!'

Christopher reached over his desk and chinked my glass. Dolf moved forward. I realised he was waiting for me to chink his. He nodded solemnly as I did so.

'Of course,' said Christopher, once his and Dolf's glasses had also clinked together, 'you will have to submit a proposal for your thesis. I thought your dissertation on the Californian action painters was a superb starting point for further exploration. Is there anything there you think you could investigate in greater depth?'

I gave it a moment's thought.

'Well,' I said, 'I am quite interested in Raymond McGiveny, because he started out as an action painter and went on to other styles, but it's all tied in with his Vibratism.'

Christopher nodded and smiled. Dolf just nodded.

'Well, that all sounds very promising,' said Christopher. 'Dolf will be your supervisor, if you have no objection.' I didn't, other than he scared me a bit, but that did not seem valid. In apparent celebration, Christopher stretched out his fingers and feet and looked up at the ceiling. Dolf raised his head too, his fingers splayed, and in his socked feet, his toes rose. Whatever it was they were up to, I knew by now to leave them to it, and stepped out the door and into what seemed an ocean of possibility.

Daddy says now is the perfect moment to start telling fairy tales. I tell him no, it's a stupid idea. How can I communicate the complexities of a postgraduate degree and lecturing post through the medium of children's stories about frogs and princesses and magic beans? Daddy says it doesn't matter. It's the system that's important. It's up to you to maintain it. But the system only exists to carry out a task, I say. What is the point of the system if it gets in the way of the task? He says that doesn't matter. It's the system that... It's the same old argument. It'll go round however many more times. And then he'll win.

Penny-whistle. Now my daughter (who passed her test and was given her own car at an age at which I had never made a solo rail journey) says she'll be another half hour, sorry. Pile-up on the motorway caused a traffic jam she's still stuck in (I think about motorcycles). If I want to call it off for another day, she understands. I text her back. I tell her no. I will wait. I have nothing but time.

I will not think of any silly fairy stories. I will carry on telling my story the way I want to.

IXX

Inevitably, when I showed Lori the contents of the fateful envelope, she was ecstatic. The letter inside said I had a distinction for my dissertation, reasonable marks for my exam, and with collected coursework, it all added up to a neat 2:1. That I had somehow secured myself a postgraduate place, doubling her dream of a university education for me with yet more university pushed her over the edge into a blissful daze that lasted for the entirety of the summer.

Once again, I saw her look at me with a pride that was overwhelming for both of us as she saw me off at the train station, everything I owned in the world back in my bag, along with the last remaining Atom Comics in my collection ready to be traded for spending money. And soon enough, I was back in my old room at halls as the building filled up with a fresh batch of students I myself would be teaching, at least until they dropped out.

Even the village struggled to achieve its usual gloom in those early autumn days. The air was scented with promise, another chance at life in a new guise. Wandering through the city with my bags of comics, old friends from before called out to me from across the busy street. I detected none of the hostility towards me that Cam had implied was the natural reaction to my being. Shaking off the last scraps from the cloak of shame he had me wear, I could honestly say I was feeling good. About life, about me, about the future. A contract arrived detailing my duties and entitlements that I signed, not reading any of the clauses, the possibility of any complications arising simply not interesting to me. In a fit of optimism, I bought myself my own laptop computer, and very soon I had progressed to typing with two fingers.

Dolf wanted to talk to me about the term ahead, calling a meeting in what was Christopher's warden office which he now treated as his, despite Christopher's continued presence. I could actually hear him moving about in the adjoining bedroom as we talked. Dolf looked natural behind the desk, fully comfortable with his sudden elevation in authority.

'We will start you off leading seminars,' he said. 'It is easy work. Simply guide students through the set readings. They will come in having not understood them. It is your job to ensure that by the end of the seminar they do.'

Up until this point, I had been so infused with excitement, I had not thought about the actuality of standing in front of a roomful of students and talking to them. As an undergraduate, I had spoken out loud in seminars without experiencing too much pain, but this was altogether different. I would be the focus of everyone's attention for nearly an hour. I did not recall being the sole focus of anyone's attention for that long before. But this meeting did not feel like the time to raise doubts. Dolf did not look like he even understood the concept of doubt. I would have to do it, and that was that.

'As to your thesis,' Dolf continued, 'I will leave you alone for the time being to find your way in your subject, but I shall expect a draft of your introduction and plan for the whole project by Christmas. Is that acceptable to you?'

I said yes without thinking about it.

And several days later, wearing an authoritative lecturer's polo neck, I was stood in front of twenty-four unengaged, uncomprehending students, reading from the works of Micajah Culp.

'"The extremities are antennae; vibrations from the realms are transported thus through blood and bone until collected in the gut..." Now, can anyone tell me what that might mean? Anyone? Anyone?'

I counted two asleep on their desks.

'Do any of you know what "extremities" means in this context? Anyone? Anyone...'

Although I didn't come out of those seminars feeling they were in any way a success, the overall result was not all that different from the seminars I had sat in led by Dolf three years earlier. So I was not as disheartened as I otherwise might be, persevering to go in week after week and watch the number of students dwindle.

It was the thesis that bothered me more. The amount of research materials I had at hand was sparse. There seemed to be more available at the British Library, but not enough to sustain four years of work on the subject of the only recently-deceased McGiveny. Most of what would be of use to me (his archive, his journals) were stored in a small private university in Stockton, California. I raised this difficulty with Dolf.

'Well, of course,' he said. 'You will have to organise at least one research trip there. You have your grant for this, so it is not a problem, no?'

I said no, it was not a problem, which was interesting

because it very much was. I had made so many steps forward in the past few years. I had learnt how to use a train, have a conversation, have sex and even maintain a relationship for a period of just over a fortnight. But the idea of getting on a plane, travelling to another country, navigating my way around there without ending up sleeping on a park bench before somehow flying back again... I didn't even own a passport. Everyone has their limit, and at that moment, after several years of previously unimaginable expansion, mine had lunged imposingly into view. I had been frightened of travel as a child, and I was frightened of it now. I couldn't do it. I just couldn't. Maybe in a year or two. But not yet.

And perhaps it was this fear that set it off. A need to draw things out for as long as possible. Or maybe it was only ever a matter of time. But it began then.

It all started when I was going over what little source material I had for the life and work of Raymond McGiveny. What I could establish was this. McGiveny was born in Riverside, California in 1915 into an affluent family whose fortunes would be eroded during the course of the Great Depression. Enrolled as a student at the Chouinard Art Institute in Los Angeles, his family's reduced circumstances, along with the recent acquisition of a wife and child of his own, forced him to abandon his studies, and he eventually found employment through the Works Progress Administration programme, painting murals in a social realist style. Avoiding enrolment in the armed forces during WWII due to a back injury from a fall from a ladder while painting a particularly high mural, McGiveny drifted into commercial illustration, drawing the pictures for a series of popular children's fairy tales as well as advertisements and billboards. This income allowed him to further his studies, whereupon he became influenced by developments in modernism, the arrival of European émigrés in the United States pushing his interest in Surrealist automatism and abstraction. McGiveny's first show at the Wolk Gallery in 1947 showed him on a similar path to his near-contemporary Jackson Pollock, attempting to conjure up fragmentary images from his unconscious through gestural painting.

In 1948, McGiveny discovered Vibratism and everything changed. Firstly, he abandoned his wife and child. Secondly, in his art, the brush marks were not now the agitated exploration of the mind, but serene Zen-like calligraphics, faces emerging out of the dense forest of fluid lines and echoing again and again throughout the painting. Further developments occurred in the following decade. A series of abstract 'window' paintings, not unlike those of Mark Rothko, appeared. Whereas Rothko's paintings evoked a sense of awe, McGiveny's windows (and unlike Rothko's, wider than they were tall) bathed the viewer in incredible light, as if glimpsing Heaven.

The 1960s saw McGiveny's final stylistic shift. Surprisingly influenced by the younger 'finish fetish' West Coast artists of the time, whose work evoked the plastic and metallic surfaces of the industrial age, McGiveny returned to the techniques he learnt as a billboard artist to produce paintings that glowed with luxurious colour and glinted with metal flake paint. McGiveny continued in this vein until his death in 1991, the paintings becoming colossal and wall-sized, not unlike the murals he had painted in the 1930s. Now, however, the subject was not the exterior but the interior world, specifically the spiritual development attained through Vibratism.

Although successful, like many West Coast artists McGiveny was overshadowed by his New York contemporaries.

Consequently, there had never been a major retrospective or monograph. Barring some reviews in art magazines and short interviews, without my getting on a plane, this left me with little to go on.

But more than that, as I went over this information, I became very aware of all I did not know. I only had a scant understanding of what the Works Progress Administration programme was. I did not grasp how they got the flakes into metal flake paint. I did not even know fairy tales (Lori had not read them to me. The violence and preponderance of hereditary power and wealth were not to her taste). Over the next few months, I researched every single aspect of all I didn't understand in McGiveny's life, filling my head with everything from custom car paint jobs to the Brothers Grimm and much in-between. I thought I was in control.

XX

When I got a knock on the door one evening from one of the few remaining freshers, telling me I had a visitor, I was surprised. I did not have visitors, as none of my remaining friends from the city would ever deign to make the train journey to this cursed village. That it turned out to be Graham, therefore, was not as startling as it otherwise might have been, despite not receiving a postcard from him for some months, as he was one of the few people on Earth who knew where to find me.

'I knew you'd still be here!' he said, as soon as he stepped through the door. 'There was no way they weren't going to offer you a post. And...' He leaned in, as if passing on a confidence. '...I knew there was no way you were going to say no.'

Out of his backpack he pulled out a bottle.

'Austrian rum. You're not really meant to drink it neat. It's more for cooking. But let's drink it neat.'

After collecting some glasses from the kitchen, we went up to my room, now decorated with much of the stuff he had left behind several years before. He paused outside his old door for a moment, inhaling memories.

'Sorry I haven't been in touch,' he said. 'I was in an Austrian prison for a month or three.'

'Why? How...' I said, needlessly.

'Just a little matter of a lady's honour. And mine. And some bloke going through a plate glass window. Still, no biggy. Anyway, my tour of the Alps is officially over, a few years behind schedule. Now it's back to hard labour for the foreseeable.'

'Couldn't you use your qualification to get something better?' I said, putting off the moment when I had to take a sip of the rum, the mere fumes from which were making me feel woozy.

'Why do you think that sort of job is better than a building site? Both kill you one way or another, just lunking bricks around does it more honestly. Anyway, a PhD in Vibratism Studies doesn't exactly open doors, except the obvious ones.'

'What are the obvious ones?' I said. Not for the first time, Graham appeared to be leading me towards the edge of a great secret, but not letting me see it.

'Drink your rum,' he said.

I did. It was as if someone had mixed Christmas cake with overly-strong cough mixture. I didn't mind it.

'You really don't see it?' he said.

'See what?'

He sighed. 'Oh well, I guess the time has come for me to let you in on a few home truths.'

He topped up his glass and mine, and settled back on the bed, propping his head up with the pillow and his boots still on. He took a deep breath.

'It started for me the same way it did for you, you know. Always loved Atom Comics as a kid. I got a kick out of the idea of differing realities, and just how the story could flip from one to another, and it was up to you to notice it. No other stories for kids, in books, on TV, wherever, respected a kid's intelligence like that. It was Burroughs-level mindfuck. I was a bright kid, you see, but couldn't hack school. All the teachers were cruel and thick. Left with no qualifications. Dossed on the dole for as long as my mam could stand, then went on the sites. Not a bad life. Enjoyed the company, had a laugh. Until I mashed up my leg on my first motorbike, and I couldn't work for a bit, not on the sites. Mam got sick of me being home again. Me and Dad were always fighting. I mean really fighting. Said do something, she didn't care what. Went down the job centre. They had a load of leaflets to flick through while you waited your turn to be talked to. And there it was. A drawing of the Silent Scissor by Mo Lightman. Maybe even the same drawing you saw. A university course where they'd talk to you about Atom Comics. And they'd take anybody. I said, sign me up.'

He took out a cigarette from a packet and offered me one. I shook my head. He paused for a minute, but it was clear there was more, much more, and he was not to be interrupted.

'And,' he eventually continued, 'when I got here, I was encountered with... absolute fucking gibberish. The teachings of a madman, or a conman. I couldn't be sure then, but let's face it, it's the latter. But the fact these stupid ramblings about vibrations and enemas had led to all these different, incredible works of art, in different media over a period of a hundred and fifty years, that interested me. So, while everybody else dropped out, I stayed the course. And as time went on, I began to think, asking myself the questions I've tried to get you to ask, but clearly to no fucking avail. Do you even know what I'm talking about?'

'Ah, yes... no. I've forgotten, sorry.'

'For Christ's sake. One more time for the slow ones at the back. Why does this centre exist? Why does a university have an entire site dedicated to the study of some obscure figure from the nineteenth century? And more to the point, why isn't it the only one? Why are there so many others throughout the world, full of academics writing about this Vibratist shit for journals that literally no one reads, not even other academics? Why have no entry criteria whatsoever for the courses? And what did Atom Comics have to do with it all anyway? Didn't you think it odd, my friend, that Hillesley skimmed over them, seeing as he goes into such mind-numbing detail about everything else, when they used Mo Lightman as the selling point for the entire fucking course? Almost as if he doesn't want you to think about them too much?'

'Yes,' I said, 'I did think that was strange. But what—'

'Shh! Answers are forthcoming. But back to my story. While I was writing my essays like a good lad, I was also doing a little digging behind the scenes, joining the dots. And then, when I ran out of degree, I worked my arse off now my leg was better so I could fund a doctorate. Because what I'd found was incredible, and I needed to know more.'

He paused in order for me to ask the obvious question.

'What did you find?'

'It's real,' he said, triumphantly.

'What is?'

'The Vibratist Assembly. An actual, genuine honest-to-fuck secret organisation, going back nearly a hundred and fifty years. Dedicated to the locating of promising individuals and guiding them to tune into alternate dimensional versions of themself, achieving higher spiritual consciousness, good bowel movements and eventually, world peace. Now, thanks to the presence of members of some very wealthy families in their ranks, they are not short of cash. They operate by getting said wealthy people to leave educational institutions large sums of money in their will, on the proviso they open a Vibratism Studies centre such as ours, and leave it to operate with as little interference as possible. And then, when they identify a likely target... have they come for you yet?'

'Come for me?' I said. He'd asked me this question before. It still made no sense. 'Are you talking about Christopher and Dolf again? I don't understand...'

'Jesus Christ, man, do I have to spell it out for you?' He leaned forward, glaring at me in a way that I knew there was no looking away from. 'They're both part of it. They're Vibratists! That's why they've kept you here. They want to make you one too!'

XXI

'Hillesley tried to get me in the last year of my first degree,' said Graham, as we made our way through our third glass of the noxious Christmas cake drink, 'when I was having a dissertation tutorial. I told him I was getting a bit stressed, you know, because I'd never written anything that long before. Said he knew some exercises that would help me with my peace of mind. Now, I didn't know everything then, but I was a bit suspicious. So I said no, I was good actually. And he said it again, like making out that there was more to it than he was saying. And I said no again, really firmly this time. And then he gives me this funny look, like he knows that I know what he's really saying and he knows if he keeps on asking I'm going to lamp him one, so he stops and moves on like he's never said anything.'

'Weren't you tempted?' I asked, as the familiar drunken feeling of the floor sloping away from me began to take hold.

'What, tapping into different versions of me from other dimensions so I can achieve enlightenment and help bring about world peace? Not really, because it's all bollocks, isn't it? And besides, look at Hillesley. He's a nice enough guy, but he's been doing this shit for years and he's not exactly the Dalai Lama is he?'

'He is still very stressed about the Whitman argument,' I said.

'Exactly. If Vibratism did anything he'd be over that by now. It was five years ago for fuck's sake. And look at Dolf. Utter prick. But anyway, all that's just my opinion. I can't tell you what to do if they offer. What are you going to do?'

It was a good question, but one I was becoming too inebriated to give sensible thought to. I didn't feel the need for any particular spiritual development, or indeed of having a spirit to develop. On the other, I did not want to make Christopher or Dolf angry.

'If I said no,' I said, my rum-soaked tongue starting to fail me, 'would there be conse… conse… bad things?'

'Don't worry,' he said. 'There won't be. That's not the Vibratist way. They offered me the teaching assistantship anyway. Think about it. They need research. If all the investigation of Vibratism is happening in their own centres and journals, then nobody else is going to do it. And if loads of people are writing about it already, no one's going to think there's even a mystery to solve. That way, they control the narrative, and no one's asking awkward questions.'

'That is very, very clever of them.'

'It is. Why do you think Hillesley even talks about the Vibratist Assembly in lectures? To get the word out it doesn't exist.'

I was struggling now. Graham sounded like he was saying sensible things, but the responses forming in my head were beginning not to be. From this point on, my memory of the conversation gets a bit hazy. I remember we moved on to lighter matters, and I told him about Anya ('Nice one!' he said) and Cam ('Always thought he was a faux-anarchist wanker'), although I don't think I said anything about Stuart and Fred (I never told anybody else). I must have told Graham about the odd thing of Dolf sleeping on Christopher's floor because he rocked backwards and forwards with joy.

'Ho, ho! I knew it! I knew it!'

'What... what did you know?' I said, half-forgetting the subject of the conversation I had just started.

'Dolf and Hillesley, sitting in a tree...'

'Oh,' I said, the floor coming up to meet me and then down again.

'Listen, if you ever have trouble with either of them, you can use this. Hillesley was Dolf's PhD supervisor, and if they were in an undeclared relationship, that could invalidate his qualification. At the very least, they would do anything not to draw any attention to it. What you've got there is solid gold. Use it wisely, my friend.'

And then things get very murky. Graham was saying something about Atom Comics, about how they were like flypaper and us being in that room right then was the entire point of them, and then maybe he might have asked me if I still had the tape and perhaps I said yes and possibly he said I should show it in a lecture because it was so rare no one would ever see it anywhere else but to be careful because... and after that I guess I must have passed out and he must have slept on the floor, but when I woke up he was gone again just like the last time, leaving behind what was left of the bottle of rum which I poured down the sink as soon as I'd stopped being sick in the toilet.

XXII

'Is this it?' said Dolf, waving the printout of my thesis introduction at me. 'Is this really all you have done?'

'Um… I've done a lot of research as well.'

'Yes, well. At this level, you are meant to be able to do both at the same time.'

'It's just hard to —'

'It's not meant to be easy, is it? That is why they give you a doctorate at the end. Have you arranged your research trip yet?'

'No, I'm not quite ready yet. There are still a few things I want to look into before —'

'Everything that is of interest to your subject is in California. You're wasting your time and mine if you do not go soon. Sort it, please.'

I said I would, but I knew I was not ready. It had occurred to me that I could not possibly go to California before I understood California. I did not understand its history, its geography, or its economy. And until I understood all those things and more, I could not understand McGiveny as a Californian artist. I knew this was not something I could explain to Dolf, but I was most certainly right (I had this thought not long after Christopher came to my door and said there was bad news. Bad news about a bike and a car and a motorway).

Meanwhile, Dolf was moving on to other matters.

'I want you to do two lectures this term,' he said. 'Nineteenth century Vibratist art and culture. You may choose the subject matter.'

I gulped inwardly. I knew it was coming, but I was still emotionally unprepared. The seminars I had been giving recently had been going well, in the sense that time had passed and I had filled it. But nearly a whole hour of just me talking was a step further into the unknown. Not quite getting on a plane and flying to America, but still enough to unnerve. It was almost like putting on a show. But it could not be that. I was not here to entertain. I was here to educate. If anything, a lecture should be as non-entertaining as possible.

I selected the things that had moved me most when I was on the receiving end – *Katarina Balabanov* by Alexandr Nenashev, and the paintings of Ruth Hutchinson-McDade. Dolf pencilled them in mid-term, either side of Reading Week. I could put off thinking about them for a while, at least.

Shortly after, it occurred to me that there was little point trying to understand the state of California when I did not yet understand the United States of America (I don't know anything about cars and bikes and motorways. But apparently there is a good way to overtake and a bad way. The car did it the bad way). I would have to study the whole country's history, from the Founding Fathers on - no, from the first known settlements on, before I could even hope to comprehend California's place within it. Although Dolf was expecting a new version of the introduction, better this time, and a first chapter, I simply could not start working on them until I had got my head round this.

Meanwhile, I was spending less and less time doing anything other than studying. It would not do to hang about the union any more now that I was a lecturer, even though I was also still a student, and although I had picked up some of my friendships from my undergraduate days, it was getting harder to meet up. I was busy, and they seemed more so, with their new jobs in offices that they needed to get up in the morning for and put on their ironed shirts and trousers and skirts. Over the course of a few months, we once again lost touch (was it this lack of release in any form that led to what happened? Or was it inevitable? That which is repressed always returns).

'Chris wants to see you,' said a fresher as I unpacked my shopping one early evening.

'Now?' I said. I had a lot of frozen things to put away in the freezer and I was having trouble making them fit.

'I dunno,' said the fresher, wandering away and forgetting I existed.

I finished jamming frozen vegetarian sausages and pies in the ice cave of a freezer as quickly as I could, and knocked on the door of the office that was Christopher's but also somehow Dolf's.

The door seemed to open of its own volition. Behind his old desk was Christopher, Dolf by his shoulder in their usual arrangement. The comfy chair from the previous meeting of the three of us was once again present. As before, I was invited to sit in it and offered the curious bran snack by Dolf, which I once again refused.

Christopher smiled. Dolf tried to.

'It's nothing to worry about,' said Christopher, 'in fact it's quite the opposite. We have noticed, the two of us, and it's quite understandable, after... well... you know what happened... What I am saying is that we have both noticed that you have been appearing slightly tense, of late.'

I shook my head, despite the obvious truth of the statement.

'How do you think you are coping,' said Dolf, 'with the demands of the teaching, and the research?' He said it as soft as it was possible for him to speak, as if it were not him personally that was putting much of the pressure on.

'Fine,' I peeped.

'Well, just in case it's ever not fine,' continued Christopher, 'we would like to share something with you. It's, ah... a relaxation technique that we find works very well and can alleviate any stress you might be feeling.'

Relaxation? No one had ever asked me to relax before that I could remember. It had been taken as a given by all who encountered me that a state of perpetual tenseness was my natural condition, and not to be interfered with. I wasn't sure if I liked the idea.

'It's quite easy,' said Christopher. 'You may have seen us do it before and wondered what we were up to.'

'You must have thought we were crazy people!' said Dolf, chuckling surprisingly.

'Yes, there's nothing much to it,' continued Christopher. 'All it involves is, that you stretch out your arms like this, spread your fingers, like so, and straighten and spread out your legs and lift your legs...'

'If you're standing you can just lift your toes,' interjected Dolf.

'And then, you simply lift your head...' said Christopher, 'and look up.'

He demonstrated, as did Dolf. I watched them until the younger man's head sunk downwards again and he glared at me in puzzlement. Only then did I realise they wanted me to join in.

I did not want to do it. It reminded me of music and movement in school. But Dolf would not stop staring at me with his splayed fingers and his toes raised, and simply to avoid the deep discomfort of his relentless gaze, with some reluctance, my arms spread slightly, my fingers splayed a bit, my legs raised just an inch or two, and my head rolled ever such a tiny amount back.

This was not the first time I had been led into something that was not really my idea. But before when I was boozing with Graham, smoking with Cam, having sex with Fred and relationshipping with Anya, I went along with it because I always sensed that there was something beyond it I wanted, or needed. It was always my choice, really. But this did not feel so good. It was not that sitting in that odd manner was totally unpleasant, but whereas drunk was drunk, stoned was stoned and sex was sex, this was a trick. This was the door to something I'd never signed up for. I felt messed about, violated even. And, just as a strange vibration began to tingle in my fingers and toes (and out of the corner of my eye I could have sworn I saw Dolf hovering a few inches off the ground although of course I didn't), with all my will I pulled myself out of whatever was sucking me in, sat up with a jolt, and ejected myself out of the chair.

'I'm sorry, I've got to go,' I said.

The pair of them looked confused as I headed for the door.

'Did you not feel relaxed?' said Dolf.

'Yes,' I said, the doorknob slipping in my sweaty hand, 'very relaxed. I'm just... busy.'

'We can try it again another time, perhaps,' said Christopher.

'I don't want to!' I cried, as I finally managed to get the door open.

'Do you think he'd try an enema?' I might have heard Dolf say as I ran up the corridor as fast as I could.

XXIII

I hid in my room for as many days as possible before it interfered with my work. When I inevitably passed Dolf in the hallway, he nodded as if nothing untoward had happened, as did Christopher when I saw him some hours later (he even half-smiled).

I continued my research. Studying the history of the United States of America seemed inadequate. Surely I would have to go much further back in order to fully appreciate the founding of the United States in the first place, But how much further? The Renaissance? Yes, but to understand that, the Middle Ages. And to understand that… (Christopher said that he wouldn't have suffered much. That he understood that it was a bit of a shock. It was a shock for him too. He had taught him for seven years, after all. That he would be there if I ever needed to chat).

The first lecture I had to give crept up on me. I ended up staying up most of the night before writing it. In the event, I had a lot to say. I was worried that I would overrun, which would have been most disorderly. Still, I was happy with what I had written. I felt I had explored the main themes of Alexandr Nenashev's *Katarina Balabanov* and how they connected to the Vibratist teachings of Micajah Culp, only recently translated into Russian at the time of the novel's writing.

The next morning, I stood in front of the class, which had already dropped to just twelve in record time, and gave my lecture. I read from my typed notes at quite a brisk pace to make sure I fitted it all in. As I progressed, I suppose it's possible I might have speeded up still further, excited by my clarity of thought and compositional skills, because when I finished and looked up past the class of not-quite-rapt faces and to the clock on the wall, only twenty-four minutes had passed. At some point, Dolf had crept into the room without my noticing. He stood under the clock now. It was dark, because I had been using the slide projector to show the few photographs in existence of the folk custom of putting frogs in milk that was the book's ostensible subject matter, but even so, I think I caught the whites of his eyes as he rolled them.

The class evacuated and Dolf wearily glided towards me. I had the feeling he would have some criticisms.

'Do you know what the problem was with that?' he said.

Perhaps he wasn't going to say it was too fast. Perhaps it was something to do with the structure, or the conclusion, or…

'It was too fast,' he said. 'Much too fast. None of the students could have understood it. I didn't understand it. Go slower next time. Much slower. And don't rely on your notes so much. Don't just read. Have… fun with it.'

I nodded in defeat and collected my slides from the carousel.

A fortnight later, there I was again, standing in front of the class (now minus two), my notes from the night before, which had ended just four hours ago and followed by two hours sleep, on the lectern in front of me. I opened my mouth to speak. But to say what? I was to give a lecture (something that I had written), but Dolf had instructed me to not rely too much on the written notes. To have 'fun' with it. How was I to read but also not read? The contradiction paralysed me. But still, I had to do at least something now that I was there.

I put my notes on the floor where I could not see them. To my surprise, the words that then came out of my mouth on the subject of the minor Pre-Raphaelite painter and Vibratist Ruth Hutchinson-McDade were precisely the same ones I had typed out the night before. All those years of memorising Atom Comics issue numbers and DR shifts had unknowingly trained my mind, it turned out, to recollect anything I had given my laser-focus attention to (it is for this reason that I know that when I sit down to write all these words that have been churning in my head the past few hours, that it will be precisely they that end up on the page, and not something vaguely like them).

The lecture lasted twenty-seven minutes, the words tumbling out at the same rate as if I had read them from the paper (as it was a visual subject, I had more slides, which added several minutes).

'A bit better,' sighed Dolf, afterwards. 'You could still have more… fun with it.'

Since when was I meant to be having fun? I wondered, as I picked my notes off the floor and dumped them in the bin.

I did not see that Dolf was still watching me from the door.

'If only you could learn to relax,' he said, before striding away, leaving me alone.

XXIV

The end of the spring term rushed towards me. My research took up more and more of my time, as I reasoned that it was worthless understanding the tectonic plates of the Earth's crust if I did not comprehend the formation of the Earth itself.

And that could not be understood until I grasped the origins of the Solar System, and beyond that the creation of the Sun (although Christopher had said he couldn't have suffered that much, he was still alive when they got to him. Before he went, he would have felt the landing on tarmac, the coldness as the blood left him).

I handed in a barely revised version of my introduction and a ghost of a first chapter. I knew Dolf would hate it. I hated it. But then none of my research so far fed into it at all. Until it was absolutely completely finished, none of it could.

Maybe it would have turned out differently if Dolf hadn't had a cold that day. Maybe I would have noticed, as I looked back to the very origins of the stars, the galaxies, time and the universe itself in the moment of the Big Bang in order to understand the art of a minor abstract painter from Los Angeles, that I was not being rational. Maybe I could have dragged myself out of this nosedive. Maybe I would have recognised, at last, the voice that was demanding this of me. But the facts of it are that Dolf did bang on my door in his dressing gown one morning, his nose red and sneezing, waking me up after a night spent studying until my eyes no longer worked.

'I can't do the lecture today,' he'd said. 'I am sick. Christopher is also sick. You'll have to do something.'

'But I don't have anything prepared,' I'd replied.

'Oh, don't worry about that,' he'd said. 'Just show them a video or something. They love that. You have fifteen minutes.'

'I... I'll have to have a shower.'

'There's no time for that! You are perfectly clean. Just get down there.'

Dolf retired to his sickbed, his sneezes on the way echoing

around the landing. I reluctantly sprayed my entire body in deodorant and stood there, bleary-eyed, without an idea in my head. The Centre's video collection only consisted of several tapes, and they had been shown so many times the image could only be viewed through a permanent fuzz, sound distorted to the point of unintelligibility. It did not seem fair to show these to the students. And then (he would have seen his legs. He would have seen the blood) I thought (lying there on the side of the motorway, would he have seen the sky) about Graham's tape. It was quite challenging and avant-garde, and not what the students were used to (I will die too and I have no religion to save me), but I was sure they were bright enough (just do what Daddy says and the moments will be filled with patterns and systems and you won't have to think about it and you won't even notice it when it comes) to cope.

I opened a drawer and pulled out the tape marked 'KOVÁCS'.

Daddy brings me out of it. He is really nagging now. He wants a fairy story. Says he's waited long enough. Change to fairy stories, he says. It's the system.

Maybe it would be easier if I did. It would make it less painful if it were all in code. But the point of the exercise is not to avoid pain. I wish it were.

More figures I recognise distract me, standing outside the window. I don't want to believe it's them, but it unmistakably is. Ahmet, hidden away in the armour of his hood, and a man, who I have seen not long before exiting a tower block, in his baseball cap, rucksack on his back.

The man is gesturing and smiling, explaining something, tapping Ahmet on the shoulder in a display of comradeship. Ahmet smiles back, no longer upset about his missing money or the con played on him the day before. The man slaps him on the back as they share a bigger joke, and then the man is asking him something. And Ahmet nods, and reaches into his pocket, and from a bundle of loose change and used bus tickets, he pulls out another note and hands it to the man.

Right now, it is happening. Very soon, the man will

walk away, smiling, laughing at Ahmet's gullibility, the con complete. The only thing that will stop him is me. And, like always, the moment where that is possible is slipping away as I sit here, bit by tiny bit, until it is not that moment anymore, but instead the moment when it is too late. If I stand up now, I can stop it. If I can stand up now, I can... And now I cannot.

I try to justify it to myself, as I watch the thief head one way, smiling at his own success, just as I thought he would, and Ahmet take the other, the penny not yet having dropped as to what he has done. It's not my place to tell Ahmet what to do with his money, I say. To interfere would be patronising, taking away his autonomy. Maybe there are layers to this situation about which I know nothing. But I know it's all drivel, and I just sat there as a vulnerable person got exploited in front of me. Because I was watching the process by which one moment becomes another. Because when it comes to other people, I don't do anything.

Everything Cam said is right about me. He's the only one who's ever truly seen it. Alright, Daddy, you'll get your fairy story. I'll stick to the system. It's all I deserve.

THE WIZARD BOY AND THE MAGIC SHOW

There once was a little boy who lived with his mother in a very small cottage in a faraway land. They were very poor, so when some wizards passed their way and asked the boy if he wanted to live with them and learn how to be a wizard too, his mother told him he should. The little boy lived with the wizards for four years, learning how to do magic so that someday he would be a wizard just like them. But some of the magic they told him to do was too strong, and he did not want to do it.

Then, one day, the wizards said to him, 'Put on a show for the children of our village, so they know what magic we can do and be happy.' The boy still did not know much magic. But he did know one spell. A special spell that lit up the sky with different colours that changed very fast. And so, he sat all the children of the village down, stood before them, and waved his magic wand.

Wonderful lights appeared in the sky! Green and blue and yellow and orange and red and pink and all the colours in between! But the lights changed too fast, and one of the children

No. I'm not doing it. I am embarrassing myself with this.

Daddy can scream and shout at me all he wants about following the system, but I am not carrying on. But what else can I do? I lost the right to tell my own story, my way, when I let Ahmet get conned by the baseball cap man right in front of me. If I am to proceed, I must earn that right back.

Stepping out of the comic shop, I look in the direction where the thief was headed. There's no sign of him, obviously. His walk is brisk, taking him to new locations where he can cause upset. I've waited for too long, making up stupid fairy stories in my head. And anyway, what would I do? Demand the money back and challenge him to a fight? He will get away. He will keep his money and he will win, because Ahmet and I are weak and he is strong.

Ahmet moves at a sedate pace, on the other hand, and as an orbiter is a creature of most extreme habit. Finding him will not be too much of a challenge. But first I pull out my wallet from my front pocket, and add up the value of the notes. Just enough. Maybe.

I walk briskly. I jog. I look this way and that for Ahmet. The sun is hotter than ever, and the top of my unprotected head begins to bake. It is not long before my breath resembles the wheezing of Olly, and I can feel sweat breaking out of my forehead, armpits and other areas. I will be a disgusting mess when I meet my daughter. But unless I find Ahmet now, I will not be a person worth meeting. And so, although everything within me fights it, I dump the two books I am still carrying, along with the satchel that bangs against my leg and hampers my movement, into the first available rubbish bin, wincing as I let go of the expensive *Radio Girl* omnibus, and I run.

I try to remember the stations of Ahmet's orbit that I know of. The charity shops he loves are in the opposite direction, so he would not be going to them. What did he say he had the five pounds for? Soup, for his brother, but that would be from the cheap shop, and he would have no reason to go there now that he had given the five pounds away to his exploiter. There are only two places he might be going at the other end of town, where the shops and coffee shops are nicer and not normally for the likes of us. One is the expensive bookshop, where he would go just to look at the covers, or, the old crumbling Methodist church, with its stalls of bric-a-brac and chutney and books in the vestibule. I know I have seen Ahmet there before. That must be where he is headed.

I have a stitch. I want to stop more than anything. But I do not stop (I will not prove my old PE teacher wrong now.)

In the far distance, the spire, then the rest. A redbrick recreation of the Gothic. Not much further now. But so much further. I try and trick myself by only concentrating on making it to the next lamppost, and the next, and the next. It does not work.

Now I am not running. I am hobbling at speed, my new shoes shredding the backs of my ankles. But I still keep going. And going. And going. Until…

I see him. His puffer-jacketed head bobbing, about to be swallowed by the darkness of the church. There are steps to climb. One, two… And just as my leg seizes, and crawling becomes a serious option, I am through the open, welcoming doors. I am staggering towards him, grabbing him by the shoulder and nearly pulling him down on the ground with me.

'Ahmet,' I don't say, and simply cough at him instead. I had a whole story worked out in my head, about how I had confronted the cap and bag man, and persuaded him to give me

Ahmet's money back. But none of that is communicable right now, so instead, I take out two ten pound notes and a five from my wallet and wave them at him until he gets the hint.

'Thank you so much!' he says, gratitude oozing out of him embarrassingly. 'My brother was so angry with me when I came back with nothing yesterday, and then today I was so stupid. I fell for it all again. It was only when I got down the road I realised what I'd done. He has a smooth tongue, that fellow. He can talk you into anything. Thank you again for getting it back, my friend!'

I try to speak again, but I feel dizzy and my vision is breaking up into dots. I've already lost Ahmet's attention to a box of crumbling paperbacks. The last time I felt like this was when I'd taken too big a drag on one of Cam's joints. I should not be in this state. I have not covered a great distance. But I have not run in nearly a quarter of a century, and my body is in revolt (and revolting). I wish there was a bed for me to fall on but there is not. Instead all I see is a stack of orange plastic chairs. Somehow I make it over, and perch precariously on the top of this awkward tower. It is not comfortable, but I am at rest, at least until I fall off.

'Are you alright?' asks a kindly voice. 'Would you like some squash?'

I nod, and soon I am draining a little plastic cup. Eventually, the dots subside, and I am also being offered biscuits.

I did it, Daddy, I say, maybe out loud, maybe not, as various elderly women make a fuss of me. I made the sacrifice. I fixed the problem. Now I get to tell my story, my way.

Daddy is silent. He is not happy, but he will let me have my little victory. He knows he'll be back in the driver's seat soon enough.

XXV

I got to the lecture hall as fast as I could, videotape in hand. The students, those that were left and had bothered to turn up that day, were already discussing among themselves whether to leave. As I walked in, they hushed slightly as I explained that as Dolf was ill, I would be taking the lecture, but there was no lecture really and we were just going to watch a video as soon as I found the key to the A/V cupboard.

Some minutes later, and with a few more of them having drifted away, I had everything set up and ready to begin.

'Can I... can I have your attention, please?' I asked. After several more attempts and a bit of shushing among themselves, I eventually got it. 'The video I'm going to show you is of the work of the filmmaker Laslo Kovács. He worked in Hungary in the nineteen sixties and seventies. It's quite avant-garde, and not really what we've been looking at this term, but I think you'll find it interesting and see lots of the Vibratist ideas we've discussed reflected in it.'

I dimmed the lights, bent over and pressed play on the video recorder. After a few seconds of the usual video fuzz, the quintessential colour flickering of Kovács' work appeared, bouncing off any reflective surface in the room.

'Has it started?' said one student, getting a laugh.

'Yes,' I said. I found the question and the attitude behind it surprisingly annoying.

The film continued. One minute. The silence filled by stereo coughing. After a minute and a half, nervous laughter.

'Is there any sound?' said the mouthy student from before.

'No,' I said.

'Does anything else happen?' asked another.

'There's always something happening,' I said.

Three minutes in, conversation had broken out in several groups. A few weren't looking at the screen at all. Someone stood up and left.

'Do we have to watch this?' said the mouthy student.

'No, I just thought you would be interested.'

'I don't think we are, mate,' he said, and got another big laugh.

Ungrateful louts, I thought to myself. Graham was dead and the least they could do was watch his tape. It's all that's left of him.

'It's making my head funny,' said another. It's meant to make your head feel funny, I stopped myself from saying, as my own head began to noticeably throb.

'Shall we go?' said one of them.

There was a mass agreement from the student body that they should. I wasn't annoyed anymore. I was angry. A similar anger that had come over me after Juliette Cass rode off under the brilliant sunset all those years before. Anger at myself for putting the stupid thing on. Anger at them for having no patience. Anger at Lazlo Kovács for making his ridiculous films with nothing in them but flashing lights. Anger at Graham for giving me the tape I never asked for in the first place and then...

Chairs squeaked back as they stood. Except one of them didn't stand. A boy was sat stiff in his chair, not showing any sign of going. In the dark, I couldn't see which one it was. This may be even more awkward than I thought. Just me stuck in a room with one dutiful student. It somehow magnified the failure by providing it with an audience. It would be better to let the video play to the end in an empty room.

'Hey, Bren,' said the mouthy student to his stationary friend. 'You coming mate?'

He shook him gently. Then harder.

'Turn it off, mate!' he shouted at me. 'He's having a fit. Turn it off!'

And that's exactly what I should have done. I should have walked over to the video recorder, bent down, pressed stop and somehow attended to the situation (not that the Centre had thought to supply me with any first aid training.)

But I did not. I stood there, frozen and stupid in my polo neck, letting the video play as the boy's friends crowded round as he spasmed and applied whatever scraps of information they had about dealing with someone having a seizure. Why? Because the video had started, so it must be played to the end. That was the task. That was the system. And that is more important than everything, said Daddy. More important than life or death. More important than yours. More important than theirs.

He was back. And he had been for months, picking up the slack as I struggled with rising up a level and finding myself out of my depth. But only now was he speaking in his own voice instead of mine.

I barely heard them screaming. 'Turn it off! What's wrong with you? You'll kill him!'

The light from the television flickered throughout the room. But still I did not move.

Someone turned it off for me. A spell broke. And I was standing in front of a boy in a chair, slowly returning to life while accusing faces stared at me. They can tell I didn't have a shower this morning, was all I could think.

'You nearly killed him, you freak! What the fuck were you playing at?'

What could I tell them? How could I possibly make them understand? There was no language.

XXVI

'I don't think I need to tell you the purpose of this meeting,' sighed Christopher, his thin voice weighed down with forced authority and genuine illness. He had taken charge of the shared desk, a man clearly about to perform the side of his job he enjoyed the least. Dolf stood behind, managing to look still more severe than usual and enjoying it slightly, despite blowing his nose with frequency. There was no comfortable chair in sight.

I said nothing. I did not think they were expecting me to.

'Are you not going to ask how the student is?' said Dolf.

'Um... yes. How is he?'

'He is OK,' said Dolf. 'Fortunately that kind of seizure rarely leads to permanent injury or death. But what if it had? What then? As it is, you caused a parent to complain. A parent!'

His words ripped me as he blew his nose again. Meanwhile, Christopher inhaled. He looked like a man with a lot to say.

'While the Centre enjoys a certain amount of autonomy from the rest of the university,' he began, face fully drained of its usual wistfulness, 'there are some rules we nevertheless have to abide by. One of these is a basic maintenance of students' welfare. When you saw that young man in obvious medical distress and for some reason that I cannot fathom refused to intervene, as the individual in charge of the lecture you failed to provide this, putting you in direct breach of a clause in your contract. Because of this, I am afraid we have no choice but to remove you of your position as teaching assistant and end the provision of the associated grant.'

I knew it was coming. There was no way the events of the previous morning could have led to anywhere good. But I still had some silly hope that it would all pass as if nothing had happened, refusing even then to read my contract in order to keep that fancy alive. Still, to feel it die there in that office was a heavy, dull blow.

'You may, of course, continue as a student, providing you pay your tuition fees. As to your room at the halls, you have paid up until the end of the year, so may stay until then, after which you must renew or leave. I am sorry it has come to this, but there is no meaningful way we could move forward with you in a teaching capacity. I hope you understand.'

I did understand. How could I ever put myself in front of those students again, all of them younger than me, but seeming so much older, and declare that I had knowledge to share with them, when they were aware I knew so little, I couldn't press stop on a video that was injuring one of them in front of my eyes? What miserable dribble of authority I may have possessed had evaporated.

The meeting was over. Dolf glanced at the door impatiently, expecting me to follow his gaze and exit. I did what his eyes told me and stood to leave. I could not think of any departing words that held any merit. As my feet crossed the floor, I remembered what Graham had said. About how their relationship, whatever it was, could wipe out Dolf's qualification. That I should use it, if I ever got into trouble with them.

Maybe I should have turned around. Maybe I should have made some wicked speech about what I knew and what the consequences would be.

But I did not. The words would have sounded foreign in my mouth. They would not have convinced and fallen dead on the floor.

So I walked out that door. Once again, the future was open, terrifyingly so, and I belonged nowhere. I felt like I was tumbling through space, my shame the only thing to hold on to. I lay on my bed once more and, maybe for the first time since the vague uncle stole my nose, I cried, and there was no comfort to be found, from anyone, or anything.

XXVII

When I finally told Lori I was coming home, using a payphone in the village (I dared not use the one so close to Christopher and Dolf's door) and making up some version of events in which I was not monstrous, she was sad for me, but not for herself as I had feared. Her dream of her child going to university and getting a degree had been more than realised. This was just a bump in the road. Something else would turn up soon enough. She still did not understand quite how unsuitable I was for all other known activities and locations. Even the best option had ended in my expulsion.

After I had made the call, I had to slip into the halls as unobserved as I could, as all my movements had to be now. The boy who I nearly killed did not live there, but many of his friends did. Accusing eyes caught me once or twice on the stairs, but so far no one had thought me worthy even of insult.

So much of me wanted to leave all my things and run. It was like living in a haunted house, in that room, hearing the movements of malevolent forces outside, feeling constantly sick. But I knew once I stepped out that door for the last time, I would be thrown back out in the world, needing a thing to do, a place to be. Nightmarish though my life now was, the thought of going back to a place like that warehouse office, working with systems I did not devise and could not comprehend, kept me in that room for several days, hating myself, hating the part of me that was Daddy, and seething at the injustice of it all (it was Dolf's lecture after all. Wasn't he in some way responsible for sending me in there unprepared?).

It had all been for nothing, the past four years. Not only were my studies now pointing to nowhere (as Graham had said, what could a degree in Vibratist Studies actually get you, besides the opportunity I had now lost?), but everything else I had learned felt like it was slipping away. I could no longer imagine being able to have a friendly conversation, or to look even in the vicinity of someone's face, or to ever connect with anybody on any level ever again. I had reset to my adolescent form, as likely to tell someone I saw their cross in a dream as anything else. But mostly likely say nothing at all.

It could not go on, and by the end of the week I had resolved to fill up my backpack one final time and head back to the faraway flat where Lori was waiting, warm milky drink in hand. There I would hide from the world as long as possible, before the incumbent Derek or poverty forced my hand, at which point I would jump in the nearest river. It wasn't the best plan, but no other options were making themselves apparent to me at that time, there in the miserable room, alone with my failure.

I was creeping out the building one last time to stock up on supplies from the corner shop. The owner was just as suspicious of me as he was when I first arrived, as was the similarly uncharmed Paula (who had transferred Graham's many transgressions of manners onto my tab). Right then, the villagers' distrust felt justified, both of the Centre – an alien structure housing strange ideas that squatted in their space – and of myself, who was, it turned out, a bad element after all. As I teased open the back door, a hand gently clasped my shoulder. I jumped several feet in the air.

'Ah, I'm sorry,' said Christopher's voice from behind me, 'I did not mean to surprise you.'

I turned around. Dolf was there too, in his customary position of slightly behind. They were both wearing dressing gowns. I got the impression they had been waiting for me to walk down the hall for some time and decided to get comfortable while they did it.

'It looks like you're on your way out,' continued Christopher, 'but before you go, there's something we'd like to discuss with you.'

Once again, the open door of the office beckoned. I did not want to step through it again. Nothing good ever seemed to come of it.

'I'm going tomorrow,' I said, hoping that would discourage them.

'Please,' said Christopher, 'it is important.'

Dolf's expression was softer than normal. For some reason, that persuaded me to follow them in.

They sat me down in the only intermittently present comfortable chair. Dolf offered me a cup of tea which I declined, in case they wanted me to relax again and I had to make a quick getaway.

'I get the impression you will not be seeking to finish your PhD,' said Christopher.

'No,' I muttered. There was no money, and without actually being an active part of the Centre, there was no place for me to be, and therefore no point.

'I can see this has hit you hard,' said Christopher, 'and you were not expecting to be moving on so soon. There's not much we can do for you from this point on, except... There is an opening, at a library. A library which the Centre has some connections to. I believe you may have even visited it on a field trip, when you were an undergraduate here. Do I remember correctly?'

I nodded as I recalled the coach trip to the town some way away, looking at the first edition of Micajah Culp's *At Gabriel's Command* behind glass for a few minutes, then killing time in the library for some hours before getting back on the coach and returning.

'Yes, well,' said Christopher. 'Like I said, it's not much. I wish it were more. But they do need someone. It's only a little job. Shelf-tidying, or some such. Not very taxing. But maybe it's something you could do for just a little while, give you a chance to take stock before moving on to the next thing. Is that something you might be interested in?'

A library. Several storeys high. Books out of order. Being put in order. The very idea was beautiful. Why had it never occurred to me before? The thought of it made me want to flap and shake with excitement.

'Yes,' I said, trying to maintain my composure, 'I want to do that.'

'Good, good,' said Christopher. 'I'll let them know. The money isn't very much, but they should be able to help you a little bit with accommodation.'

I stood to go before they could even look at the ceiling, I wanted to flap so much.

Dolf held out his stiff hand.

'Perhaps things could have been different,' he said, 'if only…'

Christopher shot him an unusually stern look, quietening him..

'You are a bright and unique young man,' he said, taking over the handshake. 'No doubt there is something unexpected on the horizon.'

I hoped not. I'd had enough of the unexpected. Enough of change. I only wanted expected things now.

XXVIII

When I arrived back home, I slept for what must have been a week. I did not realise that after all the teaching, the obsessive and pointless researching, the nearly killing someone and everything else, I had burned myself out so absolutely.

Derek tried to press me on what had gone wrong, but Lori shushed him. She knew how much pain it had caused me, whatever it was, and my going over it would do no good at all. Still, the fact I had more paid work lined up kept Derek happy enough.

Weeks passed. I slept. I watched television, but only bad programmes. I did not read. I did not look at a painting, or view a clever film. The pursuit of beauty had led to my near-destruction. I'd had enough for one lifetime. The emptiness of it all, the sheer nothingness... it was a relief.

And the nothingness continued, punctuated only by occasional large envelopes in the post containing information to be absorbed and contracts to be signed. This time I read all the clauses. With the last of the grant money in my account, I replenished my wardrobe, removing my polo necks and any other pretences to authority that may have been inferred by my appearance. The past four years had not happened. I had just left school, and I was getting ready for my very first job. I was practically a new-born.

Then, it was time. Another train, another town. As I saw her disappear out the window once more, I knew that I would never live with Lori again. Seeing me go did not break her up in the way it used to. Derek had his feet too well under the table now. Whatever was waiting for me on the other side of the journey, that was my home. It would have to be.

There is little else to tell now, except of the unlikely moment I was briefly transformed into Fantasticus Autisticus, and how I filled the long, slow years in which I crawled, inch by inch, towards it. Of course, as events look set to proceed, the book will never be written. I will barely have a chance to speak to my daughter (who is always pristine in her photos, eyebrows shaped with an exactness that impresses even me) when she sees me in my nice shirt and new trousers, drenched in my own sweat, wheezing and stinking, and turns away in disgust. A more usual mind would rearrange the meeting for another day, but needless to say that's not going to happen.

I have wandered away from the church vestibule and the stack of plastic chairs. After a couple of meagre cups of watery squash, no one is fussing over me anymore and I leave unnoticed. The most expensive coffee shop in town, where I am due to meet my daughter in one hour's time, is not too far away. There is a solution to this mess that I am in, with my dirty clothes and my cooking skin and no money but I can't see it.

Now I find I am walking in the opposite direction to the

coffee shop. If I walk in the opposite direction, I tell myself, the problem will get fixed. The solution is here, I've seen it, although I can't think of it.

Daddy says it doesn't make sense. Tells me to stop messing about and let him take control.

I tell him no, and carry on walking.

XXIX

As I sat on that train, I cannot pretend I was happy about every aspect of my imminent situation. It was probably unusual, I thought, for a basic library shelf-stacking job to come with its own flat, the rent at a suspiciously nominal level. Although the discount would undoubtedly make my life easier, I sensed the hand of the mysterious and apparently non-existent Vibratist Assembly. In my short time away from the Centre, the very idea of Vibratism, too linked to past failures and uncomfortable situations, had become something I wanted rid of. As much as I yearned for a fresh start, I knew that my new place of work containing one of the few remaining first editions of Micajah Culp's magnum opus (along with a collection of other rare Vibratist texts) meant that would not be entirely possible. Still, the sensation of being prodded by unseen forces weighed heavy on me. They wanted to keep an eye on me (were they keeping an eye on Graham? Christopher seemed to have a surprising number of details about his death), when washing their hands of me completely would surely have been the better option for them. It didn't make sense, but it wasn't a puzzle I was in the mood for unlocking.

All that I was focused on by the time I arrived was finding the location of my new flat, following the photocopied map I had been sent. It was a long walk, but I was not in the habit of taking taxis, while tackling an unfamiliar bus service on my first day was not something to be entertained. And so I walked in that late spring day with my backpack full of everything, pleasingly passing a comic shop and several coffee shops before taking the turning that would eventually get me to my destination.

Forty minutes later, I arrived outside the smallish property, wishing I'd taken a taxi after all. There was a gentle elderly man with thin, cobweb hair and clothes too tight for him waiting for me. He would turn out to be my landlord, and lived on the bottom floor along with his colossal dog, an unlikely cross between a St. Bernard and a Dalmatian. The dog ran up the stairs ahead of us, the man nearly tripping over it more than once as it bounded about excitedly. As he showed me round the studio flat (which did not take long) while in a state of perpetual exasperation at his own dog, I wondered if his slight air of eccentricity was a sign that he too was a member of the Vibratist Assembly. I decided it was impossible to tell one way or the other, but for the sake of my own sanity I would presume that he wasn't (all the while keeping an eye out for any mysterious shenanigans on his part).

Now established in my new abode, by which I mean I placed my backpack on the bed, I set upon the urgent business of locating the nearest fish and chip shop. It was not far to walk (you can only ever be so far away from one), and I was relieved to find it was considerably more welcoming than that run by Paula. The fish and chips, however, were not as good. It was the contempt that had provided the extra flavour all along, it seemed.

After a restless night trying to get used to my new bed and

the area's particular level of nocturnal traffic noise, I set out to find the library where I was to work. I was not expected for several days, but I wanted to get a feel for how long it would take to walk. It was in the vicinity of the train station, but I hoped the journey would be less arduous without a backpack. Still, it took too long for comfort, and I resolved to get my head round the bus route for when my job began. Standing in front of the closed library, a tall antique building in school-red brick and carved stone arches over modern regulation fire doors, I counted the floors (four) and tried to remember the interior, the thought of all those rows of shelves giving me a little tingle of excitement right there in the street.

Several days later, as the library assistant who greeted me on my first day led me through the ground floor where oversized books were kept, I saw that, if anything, I had remembered the collection as being smaller than it was. Just in this first layer of the building, designed for another, more orderly time, there were books upon books, spilling out onto the floor, begging to be sorted and placed.

'There are really just two parts to your job,' said the breezy young man as we passed students battling with the photocopiers, swearing as they lost the fight. 'First is putting returned books back. That means pushing the trolley. Don't worry, there's a service lift, well, for the trolley, anyway. You'll have to use the stairs, I'm afraid. Very old and hard on the legs. But besides that, your job is tidying what's on the shelves already. You start at the bottom, here, and gradually work your way up to the top. By the time you get there, the shelves down here will be a mess again and you start again. It's simple, really.'

Yes, it was simple. Simple and utterly beautiful.

'Do you have any questions, by the way?' he asked, heading towards the main desk and into an office area behind it.

'Yes,' I said. 'What is the cataloguing system?'

'Dewey.'

Perfect, I thought.

In the office was an elegant older woman, wearing pearls, somewhat tall hair and an aroma of perfume and cigarettes. She smiled broadly and introduced herself as the head librarian. I understood that this meant she was my boss. 'It's lovely to meet you,' she said, lightly shaking my hand with a clank of chunky bracelets. 'I do hope you will be happy here.' Immediately my mind pulled this last statement apart. Was she inferring I had been unhappy somewhere else? She must know my story. How could she not, seeing as I had somehow ended up on her payroll without even having been subjected to an interview? The Ruth Hutchinson-McDade print on the wall gave the game away. I knew I had to be careful, and not agree to anything that wasn't in my very limited job description.

And with that, for the first time, I got to work, pushing a trolley round, putting the books on it in their allocated place on the shelves according to the Dewey System until there were no more left, and tidying, straightening, reordering from the ground floor, with the large atlases and encyclopaedias, to the top where, under glass, sat a first edition of *At Gabriel's Command* by Micajah Culp. As this wonderful system manifested itself through me, I felt somewhat lighter. I remembered, I think, what it was to be happy.

XXX

For the longest time, the books and the shelves were all that there was. The ritual of the sorting and the placing and the checking and the tidying felt as if it was pulling the fractured parts of me back together, kneading me into something resembling a whole. I did not mind living a life otherwise so barren. Filling the space with people and things and challenges had made everything worse. But there in the library, no one expected me to have an opinion, or do something they could not. No one expected me to look at them, or smile, or speak. I could just be what I was. A moving body, pushing a trolley, ordering, tidying. Robotic almost, and not an issue for anybody.

But gradually, very gradually over time, other aspects began to accumulate in my life, like barnacles. The library staff would give a polite greeting when I arrived every morning, and I found I could once again withstand a brief conversation about nothing. Local shopkeepers would recognise me as a regular, and I would do the same for them. The barber began to recognise me, commenting on my punctuality. I began to rebuild, using only the most basic blocks (some things, like the drinking, the smoking and the DOOF DOOF music never came back).

It was when I decided to connect my laptop to the internet, however (a whim, barely a conscious thought, that must have been fired by some basic desire to once again connect to something), that things began to open up. It was early days, back then, and paying by the minute made me cagey about this invasion into the silent world I had made for myself. But bit by bit, and inevitably for a mind such as mine, I was soon living there as much as I lived in my flat, my wages feeding an ever-growing phone bill.

Here was the whole world, safely contained within a small screen on my desk. Anything I wanted to know, see or (hypothetically) talk about, I could find it, or at least a door that might lead there. The barrier made it all easier, less scary.

But what did I want to know about, seeing as I was, after all, a man with no interests? There was only one question that had been left hanging at the end of it all. The one Christopher was very keen not to address, despite using it as bait to reel impressionable youths such as Graham and myself in for years. That being, what was the true relationship between Atom Comics and Vibratism? It couldn't just be a simple question of influence. There was more, I knew.

Growing up, I had yearned for there to be one other person I could talk to about Atom Comics. Logging onto the internet, some years after that urge had subsided, I found thousands of them, scattered across the world. Some of them enthused about particular characters. Others acted as cheerleaders for their favourite writers and artists, while others ripped them apart. But what most of them were talking about on their message boards and chatrooms, more than anything, were differing realities. Granted, everything they said about them was hopelessly misguided, and their numbering systems quite wrong, but to see so many engaging with this thing that for so long had only been of interest to me was exhilarating.

I could not stay to correct them. Right now, this was not what I was looking for. The conversations I sought were hidden away, a subsection within a subsection. Still, I found them.

If the Vibratist Assembly had hoped to hide their existence

through misdirection, they had not counted on the World Wide Web. While some clung to the most obvious interpretation, that Joe David simply made flippant use of his artist Mo Lightman's Vibratist beliefs to cover up obvious continuity errors, others took a different, more conspiratorial view. They argued that the DR aspect of Atom Comics was always very deliberate, planned from the moment they changed their name from Quality Tales Comics and launched their new range of characters with interlocking stories in 1959. More than that, they posited that presenting the readership with the idea of differing realities was the very reason Atom Comics existed in the first place.

There were, they said, several clues pointing in this direction. Number one, financially it made no sense to switch a successful brand's name, along with the entirety of their product from one thing to another over a period of a few months. The Quality Tales mystery titles were selling, so why ditch all of them in favour of unproven superhero comics? It was a reckless move for an astute and previously cautious editor such as David. Number two, the growing complexity of the DR element in the stories was a bad business model. Whereas Atom Comics' competitors succeeded in licensing their characters for cartoons, TV series, films and merchandising (the short-lived *Trout* TV show notwithstanding), this was something they themselves had failed to do, as only Atom Comics fanatics could follow the stories well enough to warm to the characters. Casual readers and younger children were generally left baffled.

This invariably led to the third and most tantalising point. Atom Comics rarely, if ever, made a profit. Most copies were returned from sellers and pulped, making those that survived collectors' items. Indeed, they should have, by the rules of the market, ceased publishing entirely at some point in the early sixties. And yet, despite their comics being consistently unpopular, the company kept going, money being pumped in from somewhere. Not only that, they had an unnaturally strong presence on newsstand and newsagent shelves, as if their placement was being bought by an unseen hand.

This unseen hand being, of course, the Vibratist Assembly. According to this theory, not only did Atom Comics exist to attract the attention of a particular type of young person and introduce them to the idea of multiple realms and versions of themselves, but these same youngsters would then be targeted to study academically at the various Vibratist Centres all over the world. Only a few would make it, but those who did, it was believed, were ones particularly in tune with the core Vibratist ideas, and therefore likely to respond to indoctrination, leading ultimately to their spiritual development as they tuned in to their other selves, working all the while to bring peace to the planet behind the scenes as part of the Assembly.

It seemed a high-risk strategy. Both Graham and myself had rejected our invitations to share in the Vibratist secret. Nevertheless, the proponents of this theory argued, it is not unheard of for a fringe group to employ an expensive and relatively ineffective recruitment strategy (such as the mysterious religious reading room next to the launderette, inhabiting a prime high street location while generating no income at all).

And this theory did make many of the pieces in my odd life story fit together. But how many? Was the mysterious boyfriend of Lori's who came, introduced me to Atom Comics and swiftly left again part of it? Had I been headhunted by a

Vibratist at such a tender age? I felt seasick. Nothing seemed stable or even solid anymore.

I talked to people from all over the world with similar experiences to mine. How, floundering around for something to do with their lives, a leaflet had come into their orbit that sent them in the direction of a Vibratist Studies Centre with suspiciously affordable fees and no entry requirements. And then at some point, an authority figure had invited them to learn how to 'relax'. Some, like Graham, had said no before it had even begun. Others, like me, jumped ship very quickly, not enjoying the experience or feeling at least there was something not quite right about it. But a few had stayed on, learning more and more sophisticated ways to 'relax' until, before they knew it, they were mere steps away from being inducted into the Vibratist Assembly itself, all of its secrets within grasping distance, only at the last minute for doubts to creep in, leading to their abrupt departure.

Still, I had suspicions. How did I know they were all telling the truth? Could it be, perhaps, that we were all joining the dots, but to form the wrong shape? It was when I proposed this that another message board user, one who claimed to have travelled the furthest along this path, sent me something it had never occurred to me even existed. An email address. For Mo Lightman.

Up until that point, I was not sure he was still alive. Ben Hammer had been dead for some years. Joe David was retired, batting away any attempts to gain an honest explanation from him about it all with corny jokes. And Mo Lightman himself had not published a comic book or issued any public statement since the early seventies. And yet, here it was, on my computer screen. His personal home email address.

I spent some hours crafting a long and quite meticulous email, asking him to explain his relationship with Vibratism, and any relationship between the Vibratist Assembly and Atom Comics itself. Was he someone whose sincere beliefs were hijacked by his employer for cynical ends? Or was his self-outing as a Vibratist designed to distract from the much deeper-rooted alignment in the company? I made a point of thanking him for his years of service and waited for a reply.

Nothing came for some time. Weeks passed, and I moved from hoping I would get a reply, to accepting I probably wouldn't, to forgetting I even sent the message in the first place. And then, there in my inbox, an email for me from legendary Silver Age comic book artist Mo Lightman.

Considering the length of my original query, there was not much to it. It came in the form of some sort of free verse poem, and read, in full:

> *When you boil it down*
> *What yr asking*
> *Over and over*
> *(and over and over)*
> *Is one thing.*
> *Who am i?*
> *What am i*
> *And what bed do I sleep in?*
> *Maybe im all of the above*
> *(See below).*
> *A patsy*
> *Or plotter*
> *An artist*
> *Of the con variety*

Or otherwise.
Maybe i was
Just one then the other
Or maybe all together.
Maybe not until tomorrow.
Wheres the point
Ye cant pin me.
And who are ye
If you dont mind me?
Who ye say?
Who i say?
Both and neither and in-between?
What it all comes down to is
Yr too uptight kid

I wrote back immediately, thanking him for his reply but wondering if he could clarify a few key points. I never heard anything else from him, and several months later, his obituary was in the papers.

After all this talk about Atom Comics, the inevitable happened. Passing the comic shop in the high street, I caught a glimpse of the latest releases in the window. Old characters in new stories, their outfits changed and exciting developments hinted at. New characters I did not recognise. Would it hurt, I thought to myself, just to see what was going on now, even if the whole thing was just a front for a crank belief system?

After an awkward conversation with the store owner in his vintage Radio Girl T-shirt (I was reluctant to give too much of myself away at that moment, in case my potential relationship with the comics did not work out), I was on the bus, unable to wait to get home before I slid my new comics out of their plastic wallets. It was all the same. The way the paper felt. Their own distinct smell. The thrill of spotting a subtle DR shift between one panel and another. I missed my stop.

My collection grew. The gnawing sense that I had to do something with all the information stored in my head returned. Being a regular in the comics shop to the point of learning the owner's name, I inevitably began to recognise some of the faces that would reappear in the cafe at the back. One of them belonged to a big, loud man, often in a suit. Despite my best efforts, we got talking. He told me about all the illegal things he had stored on a collection of hard drives in the attic bedroom of his parents' house.

''Ere,' he then said, 'you're into that Atom Comics shit, aren't you? Can't be fucked with them myself, mind.' The very first Atom Comics film, *Silent Scissor*, had just been released, and they were on many people's radar for the very first time.

I said I did know a thing or two about them.

'Yeah, but did you know you can download scans of every single Atom Comic ever, for free? Some twat was wanging on about it to me in a forum, like I give a fuck. Anyway, do you want me to show you how to do that, torrents and shit? Cos I can.'

Every single issue. My DR numbers would no longer be provisional. They would be absolutely, irrefutably accurate. Totality, completion. It was all that I ever wanted from life.

The database began. And with it a sense that my life once again had purpose as hundreds, then thousands, then tens of thousands of Atom Comics fans embraced it both as a resource and as something to get angry about on the internet.

Eventually that feeling wore off, but work on the database

continued. Daddy helped me out with it a lot, and there's no quitting on his watch.

Life grew, slightly, in other areas. Inevitably, being online forced me to take a basic interest in politics and world affairs. It was all very confusing and not really for me, but I recognised the importance of being slightly informed. Access to such a large library meant I could expand my knowledge in other ways, although I never returned to the world of paintings, plays and poems (I nearly took out a copy of *Leaves of Grass* by Walt Whitman, but baulked at the last minute). Beauty still hurt a bit too much.

I became aware of the orbiter community, and found my own little nook within it, maintaining a few slight friendships, just enough to keep the loneliness wolf from breaking down my door.

Romantically, I looked further afield. I was an early adopter of internet dating. It took me a while to get it right. At first, the women I spoke to were too far away. Eventually I had to accept that it probably wasn't going to lead anywhere if I couldn't afford the train fare to ever see them. Shrinking my radius of interest to easy commuting distance, I did eventually meet up with some in real life. Some dates went well, others less so. A few led on to something else ('bases' were reached, to use sporting terminology I don't understand), and some almost qualified as actual relationships. But nothing stuck, and after a while I got discouraged and fell out of the habit. Now, it feels like it's been too long.

And in this way, time was filled. One year would bleed into another and it looked like I could make it through the remainder of my life, however many decades of it that were left, without too much incident or upset. And then Derek called about Lori.

XXXI

I went back to what used to be my home twice a year, without fail, at Christmas and summer, when there were few students in the library and less mess to tidy. I considered this my holiday. And every time I went back, Derek would be Derek, and Lori would be Lori. And I would be me. None of us would change, except Derek got fatter and my hair began to thin. But Lori was exactly as she had always been in my mind. Always young, always busy, finally getting her degree with the Open University. I did not see what must have been there. The white hairs hidden by dye. The lines round the eyes. The loosening of the skin.

But one summer, she was different. Slower, more distant somehow. Sometimes her speech was not clear. She dropped one thing, maybe two. Said she had a headache more than once, and she took a herbal remedy to deal with it. But people have headaches and drop things, and there was a lot of work waiting for me on the database, and so I forgot about any worries I may have had about Lori entirely the moment I was on the train back.

I had not spoken to her for some weeks when my landline rang. It was usually Lori who phoned me. I thought it would be her. It was always her.

But it was not. It was Derek, his voice shaky, willing himself to keep control. An awful collection of words, crashing into each other. Stroke. Collapse. Clot. Brain dead. Dead.

I went back there immediately, because that was the thing to do, to witness a man I did not know that well and did not know how to comfort crying on the now half-empty sofa.

I went back again for the funeral, and stood a foot away from Derek, knowing I was meant to reach out and touch his shoulder or his arm, but still I did not.

Don't think I did not feel the loss as badly. It clawed at me during sleepless nights for weeks. But I had already learnt the lesson from Graham's death. They all slip away eventually. It all goes, and then you do. Derek was a man who had lost his world. My world at least was still there, although now well and truly ripped away from its foundation, spinning in space, tied to nothing.

As next-of-kin, all that was hers was now mine. But barring a few keepsakes from the pre-Derek years, I told him to keep all of it. He needed it more than I did.

And then back on the train. Back to books and shelves and comics and orbits and barbers and systems and…

Derek phoned me that Christmas to see how I was. We had a chat. It can't have felt right for either of us. He did not call again.

I know he has Lori's ashes on a shelf in that flat. I have some photos of us in a bird sanctuary, wearing pacamacs in the rain. We both look so young.

XXXII

With Lori gone, Daddy stepped in to help. Despite his sabotaging of my previous life, I did not resist. I guess I realised that he usually shows up when I'm about to crash the car I can't even drive. He keeps me anchored, stops me from reeling. He may not make things better, he might well make things worse, but at least with him I know where I am.

He saw there was too much disorder in this new life I had carved out for myself. He made me sharpen my orbit, taking out the flab and the randomness so that, unless dire circumstances arose, such as the rare purchase of some particular cooking utensil, every visit to the high street was exactly the same. My schedule became more and more regimented, with each activity outside work – washing, dressing, eating, cleaning, reading, watching, sleeping, waking and other habits – given its own time slot, to the point that each day would become more and more identical to the ones before and after, with slight weekend variations allowed.

It was at work that he made what would prove to be the most significant adjustments. Although the system inherent in my job pleased Daddy, he felt it was a little rough around the edges. Specifically, he did not like the fact that when I was tidying and it came time for me to take a break or go home, I would just stop what I was doing and go, regardless of where I happened to be, picking it up at the same place when I came back to it. He felt this was messy. In Daddy's revised system, I would have to make it to the end of the shelf I was working on before I was allowed to leave, even if that meant losing some of my break or going home a few minutes late. He was very insistent on this.

And although it could not have been his intention, this would change things significantly. Because of this, the long crawl finally ended (and in retrospect, I can see I was always heaving myself onward to this point, even when I was standing still). Fantasticus Autisticus was on the horizon.

Further on down the high street, beyond my second-favourite coffee shop, back past the comic shop, taking my time as I can no longer move fast. The sun still high in the sky, burning my face and neck. With a bit of luck I will only be slightly pink when I see my daughter, with my face not beginning to blister until after she's gone (which will be after two minutes, I am sure).

But I need to get in the shade. Daddy says this shop or that, all of them part of my usual orbit, but I am not listening. The answer I am looking for is not in the orbit. I must avoid all systems. Abandon all reason. Do the thing I never do. Follow my instinct. Feel my way out (an act of faith? I wouldn't go that far).

There is a place I have never been. Somewhere no one I know has ever entered. Somewhere that looks quiet and cool. Next to the launderette, the reading room of indeterminate religion. If I go in there and wait, a solution will present itself, I know this. I have no reason for thinking this. And yet I still do.

The door opens silently. Inside, the luxuriously conditioned air licks me like a cat and soothes my burns as I look around.

The walls are the blue of a sky from a dream. There are tables, there are magazines. There is a nice carpet, plump chairs. There does not seem to be anybody here. I pull up a seat and regret throwing away my *Radio Girl: Secret Signals* omnibus. Still, there is plenty to read here. Flicking through one of the magazines, I see the usual photos you find in these things, of sunsets and cornfields and women in white dresses holding babies. The text bounces off my eyes, unabsorbable, pointless.

I do not need to read now.

XXXIII

Things were different on the top floor that day. The first edition of Micajah Culp's *At Gabriel's Command* was being photographed for some project or other, and so was not in its usual position under the display cabinet glass out on the library floor. Instead it was in a delicately lit side room, laid out on a table, while the photographer methodically worked his way through the book, his flash escaping from under the door every so often as he captured another image.

I was tidying the shelves, as I did every day, and had now done for... some years (I had been there for so long I was considered part of the furniture, to the extent that few other than the head librarian still bothered to speak to me, in the same way you wouldn't address a wardrobe. The top floor was quiet, as it was Reading Week and therefore no reading was taking place at all. I saw the photographer slipping out the side room door and exiting down the stairs and thought little of it. It was a big job and he had come and gone several times since I had been up there, either to fetch a forgotten piece of equipment from his car or just to make some coffee in the back office.

Once he had gone, I could tell from the particular type of deathly hush I was the only person now left on the floor. Just me and the books. I didn't mind it at all. You could drift in the dreamlike silence, carrying out actions as if still awake. It was in moments like this that my mind finally stopped, and I wasn't thinking about comics or databases, or PhDs or Lori or anything but the books and the correct order for them to go in. A pure calm, as fragile as a soap bubble. To even acknowledge it would break it.

Or if a very loud fire alarm went off, which is what happened. The noise went in one ear, through my skull, out the other, and back again as I struggled not to fall from the footstool I was standing on. As instructed in the mandatory fire safety training I had undergone soon after arrival, I stepped down and in the direction of the staircase the photographer had not long descended. I was about to walk purposefully towards it, but I did not.

Daddy held me back. There were only a few more books on the shelf to tidy. I could do that, and still get out in good time. It was obviously a false alarm, anyway. These things always are. Finish the row, boy. You've got to stick to the system.

I knew it was stupid. I knew I could get down and up again and carry on exactly where I left off because I never forgot where I had got to. But it was only twenty more books. Thirty at most. Two minutes' work. I'd be out of here in three minutes. Plenty of time.

I carried on tidying. The alarm continued to burrow its way between my ears. The sound of thundering feet on the staircase below came and went. But some of the books were wildly out of order and that needed sorting. Two minutes passed. Three. And there were only fifteen more books to go, but there was one that was misplaced from another row entirely, way at the back of the floor, and I just had to put that back in the right place. Four minutes gone. Five. A few more books, I told the incessant scold of the fire bell. And that one belonged on the shelf below. Off the footstool. Back up the footstool. And that one above. Six minutes. And done. See? It didn't take long.

I strode to the stairs, as quick as I could without breaking the library rules and running. And just as I was about to go through the two swinging fire doors and down to safety, out of the corner of my eye as I passed a window, I saw the smoke, rising from below. Thick and deathly black, its seeping taste noxious and chemical, coming out of what looked to be a ground floor window. Something below that was definitely not meant to be on fire was very much on fire. And I was on top of it.

It occurred to me that I might be in big trouble. That this might be as bad as it realistically got. Should I stay where I was, put my faith in fire doors and hope someone would get me? Or should I just dash for it? After all, the fire alarm was still ringing, and that did mean 'get out'.

I had made up my mind to go. And I was about to. But then I thought about that first edition of *At Gabriel's Command* by Micajah Culp, sitting there unprotected on that table in the side room. Although I felt no allegiance to my secret Vibratist benefactors, for the simple sake of history, could I leave such a rare document to perish, if not by fire then perhaps in the blast of a fireman's hose?

Running to the side room, I found it, just as I imagined it would be, laid out, vulnerable. Outside the glass case, it looked desperately fragile, its binding frayed, liable to turn to crumble if I touched it. Gingerly, I closed and picked the book up, feeling the little frisson of history as I did so, happy it did not fall apart in my hands.

Once again, I started for the swing doors. And once again, I stopped. Thinking about it, I was about to take a delicate and highly valuable book out through a building that looked to be on fire. I would need something to cover it. I could also benefit from something covering me.

There, slung over the back of a chair, was the photographer's leather jacket.

I knew what to do. Unlike my childhood jacket of old, this was not too tight, far from it (I was far too slight to ever consider myself a candidate for leather jacket-hood, even fake leather). And the zip was chunkier than any I had before handled. But still, within not too many seconds, the treasured book was hidden beneath the sealed jacket. I hugged it tight as I finally passed through the swing doors and down the stairs, my feet hammering on each one with urgency.

Somehow I made it down all four flights without falling. But there I was, coming towards the last set of double fire doors, where toxic air was escaping and the paintwork on the walls glowed ominously orange. There, through the thin strip of reinforced glass, I could see smoke, and through that, a photocopier, flaming magnificently, the walls and floor around it fiercely black. Not only that, the fire had spread to a trolley of books that had been awaiting my attention and would now never be reshelved. Around it, stray papers burned, plastic chairs melted and abandoned coats and bags shrivelled. Even through the doors, I could feel the heat.

So far, the fire was still contained within one area of the well-spaced floor. The problem was, that area was between me and the exit, tauntingly open to the world outside. I would have to run right past it to get out. Could I once more employ my fearsome inhalation skills so admired by Cam and make it across the floor on one big lungful of air now? I would have to run like that one time I was fast, as the bus came straight towards me all those years ago. But back then I was in the open air, not under a black fog of contaminants that even here were making it harder and harder to breathe normally.

And I think I was about to run, I was probably just seconds away from opening that door and legging it, when I saw something move in the smoke beyond the fire. At first, I thought it was something else burning and collapsing in on itself, but as I looked it took on the properties of an imprecise figure. They saw me through the glass door and waved.

'Hello?' I just about heard them crying through the glass door.

Not knowing what else to do, I waved back.

They said something. I couldn't hear them at all. There was no way around it. I would have to open the door a crack. The heat fried my eyebrows and the fumes seared my throat.

'Have you got my jacket?' was what they were saying under the T-shirt they had pulled up over their nose and mouth.

'Yes!' I shouted back at the figure who was the photographer.

'Don't have my camera too, do you?' he said, with the nonchalance of a man not in the immediate vicinity of an ignited photocopier.

'No!' I tried to say, and coughed instead.

'Hang on,' he said, and disappeared out of sight for a moment, and I once again closed the door. He reappeared soon enough, carrying a large fire extinguisher. He walked towards the fire, casually pulling out the pin.

There was something else I remembered from my mandatory

fire safety training. That there was in fact more than one type of fire extinguisher, and which one you used depended on the source of the fire. Now, I couldn't quite remember which was which, but I was reasonably sure that the biggest extinguisher contained water, and that could only be used on things like paper or wood and not on electrical fires because…

'Don't!' I shouted. I was about to open the door to make myself heard. But I never did. And because of that I was still alive when the fire fighters arrived minutes later (entering via the fire escape on the second floor I wish I'd remembered it being there from my mandatory fire safety training) and found me unconscious in the stairwell.

When they placed me on the stretcher in the car park outside and undid my jacket, revealing one of the three last surviving copies of the first edition of *At Gabriel's Command* by Micajah Culp, it was said that the head librarian cheered jubilantly.

The photographer, who had gone to the ground floor toilet for a long time when the fire broke out, and had a similarly lackadaisical attitude to alarms as myself, was seriously hurt. I, miraculously, was not. The fire doors protected me from the blast that occurred when the water from the extinguisher acted as a conduit, sending the poor man flying over a table and into the shelves of oversized books behind.

For the very first time in my life, I got to ride in an ambulance and go to hospital. It was odd, being the centre of attention, trained professionals fussing over me, making sure I was OK and not dying. For a second I felt like a proper citizen and not just an orbiter.

I was not long in A&E. Checked over and deemed fine enough not to take up a bed, I was discharged after a few hours. No ambulance ride home. I chose to walk in the cool night air, imagining it was cleaning my lungs, still wearing the photographer's leather jacket.

The next morning, I got up to go to work as always. I showered, dressed, and caught the bus. It was only when the library was in sight, and for the first time I saw the blackened bricks and the windows empty of glass and the red and white tape forbidding entry that I grasped that there was no work. For the time being, there was no library. I stood there, looking at the mauled building, not knowing what to do.

I headed into town.

XXXIV

The head librarian called me to a meeting at the main university site. In a borrowed office, she told me that, mainly due to the explosion caused by the unfortunate photographer (whose jacket I handed to her in the hope of it getting back to him), the old building was now structurally unsound, and would require renovations that could easily take years. The library's collection would be moved into portacabins in the library car park, a process that would itself take some weeks. In the meantime, I had a choice. I could either take another, undefined position in the university, or I could go on half-pay until the library reopened in its new location (I took the half-pay, naturally). And while she could not condone my staying behind in the library to ensure the safety of the first edition of *At Gabriel's Command*, and stipulated that I follow all fire regulations in future that, just between me and her, she was deeply appreciative of my doing so (I did not tell her that my saving the book was a by-product of my staying behind, and in no way the reason for it).

'Well, I think that covers everything I want to say,' she said, as I made moves to leave. 'But don't go. There's someone else who wants a word.'

She herself left the office. I sat there alone, wondering what was going on and if there was anything really stopping me from going if I felt like it.

There was shuffling in the corridor. Someone was coming in. Turning round, I saw, stepping through the door, frailer than he had been before, his hair still a magnificent mop of white, Christopher Hillesley. Inevitably, Dolf followed. He was jowlier, and now had a belly that bulged under his polo neck, making him look absurdly pregnant. It did not feel like much time had passed since I had last seen them, although it clearly had (I think now that I experience time differently to others, possibly because my life changes so little).

'No need to get up,' said Christopher, as if I had only seen him yesterday. He sat himself down behind the desk, Dolf standing behind, as he must have been doing for nearly twenty years now.

'You are still here?' said Dolf. 'It was only meant to be temporary.' Perhaps realising the harshness of this, he added, 'It is good to see you again,' albeit with as little emotion as he had said goodbye to me all those years before.

'Yes, it is,' I said, feeling like an animal in a trap and wishing I'd left when I had the chance.

'We have come because we think you're exceptional,' said Christopher, his fingers intermeshing under his chin.

'Um... thank you,' I said, surprised.

'We do not intend it to be a compliment,' said Dolf.

'Oh,' I said.

'What we mean,' continued Christopher, 'is that you are an exception to the norm. You think and act in ways that are not usual.'

'This is something we have observed,' added Dolf. 'A person does not, usually, leave a video playing that is causing another to have a seizure. Equally, a person does not, usually, delay leaving a burning building for ten minutes.'

I shrunk inwardly from the discomfort of being a subject of anyone's curiosity. That they were absolutely right about me only made it worse.

'I'm... sorry?' Is that what they wanted? If it would get me out of the room, I would happily give it to them.

'You do not have to be sorry,' said Dolf.

I gave up trying to work out what they wanted.

'Have you ever wondered why that might be?' asked Christopher.

It was only then that I saw that I actually had not and that in itself was quite odd. I had always simply accepted it as the way of things. Other people were one way, I was the other, and that was that.

'A little,' I said. They would never believe the truth.

'You see,' said Christopher, relaxing back in his chair, 'we are in search of answers too. I don't think I need to tell you who we... represent. We know, you see, that you have been making certain investigations on the internet, that you talked to Mo Lightman before he sadly passed away.'

'We have eyes and ears everywhere,' said Dolf. He must have realised it sounded more menacing than he intended as he quickly tried to soften it with an unnatural smile, which made things worse.

'You know,' continued Christopher, 'that we have some investment in Atom Comics. That they help us come into contact with individuals who might be of interest to us.'

'I myself used to be an Atom Comics reader,' said Dolf, surprisingly. 'I recall being partial to the Silent Scissor, or "Die Stille Schere" as she was known in my country.' Sensing he had achieved an unintended level of intimacy, he coughed and muttered, 'I long outgrew it all, obviously.'

'But there is something peculiar about our results in this area,' said Christopher, leaning forward now, as if stretching towards the point. 'Of all our ways of making contact with interesting people, Atom Comics readers tend to be the ones who are most resistant to… relaxing.'

'Some refuse outright,' Dolf interjected, 'such as your departed friend did, or like you, they withdraw from the process.'

'And now,' said Christopher, 'thanks to new developments in diagnostic criteria, we think we may understand why. The answer is, perhaps, neurological.'

'Your brain is different,' clarified Dolf.

'It is our belief,' said Christopher, 'that the very thing that attracts a significant subset of readers to the particularities of Atom Comics may also make them unsusceptible to the gifts we offer.'

'We just need to prove it,' said Dolf.

'Will you help us?' said Christopher. 'With this information, it will help us apply our resources more effectively.'

No, I thought. I had no interest in helping them. I just wanted to go home.

'I don't know…'

'If not for us, then why not for yourself? If there is something that would help even partially explain all that you have been through in life, provide even a small window of illumination, would you not like to know it?'

I thought about it.

XXXV

''Ere, expect you're broken up at the news. Can't say I blame 'em, calling time like that. Bet they thought the films would be good for sales, but anytime anyone in the forums checks out the comics, they say they're shit and don't make sense. They must have been losing so much cash. So, yeah, pulling the plug on all that bollocks was obviously the right decision but I can see why you'd be cut up about it…'

My orbit intersected with Olly's for the first time since the fire. At first we talked about the shock announcement in that week's editorial columns that all Atom Comics would cease in one month's time. Despite inadvertently contributing to their demise, I did not feel as bad about it as Olly thought I would. I had, after all, aimed for totality. Up until now, I had just always assumed it was impossible.

Olly took a sip of the coffee I had bought him, just long enough for me to begin talking.

I had not talked to anyone about any of it, but whatever the reason is I talk to Olly about anything, I talked to him. Not just about the blaze, the photographer, the explosion and the hospital but, albeit in a version of the story that left out Christopher, Dolf, or any hint of the Vibratist Assembly, the lengthy questionnaire, the comparably long appointment with the psychiatrist (how I could even afford to travel to London for the first terrifying time in order to visit a Harley Street doctor was thankfully a question he did not think to ask) and the conclusion that was reached. I gave just the bare facts. It was all I had at that moment (I don't know if I have much more than that now).

When I had finally finished speaking, Olly was oddly silent. The cogs were turning in his brain, I could see. Then he smiled, and sang

>'Heeees
>Fantasticus!
>Fantasticus!
>Fantasticus Autisticus!'

And with those words, Olly put me, the one who could never be contained by mere definitions, in a tidy little box, all wrapped up in a bow. Like Atom Comics, I had been finished. But unlike them, I would continue.

How to communicate what comes after the end, the weeks between that moment and now? The narrative method of the celebrity TV gardener is no good to me here. The linear thread has reached its end. And fairy tales... I think we can discard those now. But the case for the fragmentary technique of my much-missed *Radio Girl: Secret Signals* omnibus is compelling. Not because Daddy wants it. Not because of any established system. But because it's the best tool for the job. And while I have lost control of everything else, blood stains on the cuffs of my light new trousers the final nail, I can control this. One last fling with reason before I go down.

I sit in my flat, reading the informative leaflet from the psychiatrist. Books, websites, message boards, anything. And any moment in my life I care to dredge up, everything is reframed. And I feel that I have been running a race with a broken leg, but no one could see it, wondering instead why I would insist on falling down.

*

The psychiatrist advises me to seek out others like me to talk through our experiences. I do not like the idea, but as he is the doctor and I am not, and he understands what I am and I do not, I decide to try it once. I go to a meet-up in my fourth favourite coffee shop on the high street. The others are younger than me, but have known what they are for longer, having lived fewer years trying to survive in another creature's skin. They are earnest and enthused, wanting to change the world for the better for people like us. I have been going too long to be earnest or enthused. In their company I feel old and exhausted. They are a new breed, happy to flap and shake in public, ready to replace me with their talk of community and action, when my life is defined by the lack of both. They tell me about what things are like for them and I say I understand completely, but because I cannot pretend to feel something I do not I can see they don't believe me. Then I tell them about what things have been like for me, and they say they understand completely but because they cannot pretend to feel something they do not I do not believe them. One of them says my life sounds lonely and I should get a cat. She has a cat and is not lonely. I wish them well but I do not go back.

*

There is a television programme about a man who is like me (he is played by an actor who is not). Every week a problem arises in his life. He has many friends and mentors. He talks to all of them about his problem. They give him advice. He overcomes his problem with their help and everybody is happy. I stop watching this programme after a while.

*

While I can see him more clearly for what he is, Daddy does not go away. Although my life is invariably structureless without work, with mornings lost to flapping and shaking and showers that go on forever, he still tightly controls the remaining aspects – the orbiting, the comics, the haircuts. Sometimes I think I am holding on to him all the tighter, like a comfort blanket.

*

An email to the database. It is not about comics. It is polite, tentative, sprinkled with a youthful humour I don't quite get. It asks me if I remember Fred and Stuart. She says she is their daughter. At least, until recently, she thought she was. Stuart had died quite recently of a heart condition he did not know he had. This had panicked her, as she worried that she herself might have it or potentially one day pass it on to her own children. Fred had told her that she was not to worry about that. And it had all come out. Stuart was not her father, I was (I don't understand how I could be the only suspect but Fred is adamant about dates). And she would be interested in getting to know me a little bit, online at first, maybe meet up a bit later. I sit on the email for three days, not knowing what to do with it, or this new strange fact that changes everything about me, so soon after the last one. Eventually I answer. I say it is nice to hear from her. I don't know what else she could want me to say. I still don't.

I am stuck, but continuing now, in this reading room. I am

meeting my daughter in three quarters of an hour and I will destroy everything because of the state I am in, but I am here, mindlessly holding a magazine that is of no interest to me at all.

Except... As I scan the italicised bold text, there are certain words. Planes. Vibrations. Merging. This could be...

'Hello there, can I be of help to you?'

Behind me is a young woman, dressed as if she is trying to sell me a house. Her accent is American, or Canadian (I do not know the difference). I wonder how she has ended up here?

'I'm... just looking,' I say (as an inveterate browser, this is a phrase that I have found particularly useful over the years).

'No problem!' she says. 'You're welcome to just stop here anytime. And relax...'

That word again.

'We actually have some great relaxation techniques that we teach in our classes, if you want to take a free leaflet.'

She hands me a booklet. On the cover is a woman in yoga pants, her arms and legs stretched out straight, her fingers splayed, her eyes looking up to the ceiling. Repelled, the booklet is ejected from my hand, only my lack of coordination making its flight across the room less dramatic.

Of course, Atom Comics could not have been their only recruitment tool. But how many more are they? What other mysterious things in life are actually gateways to the Vibratist Assembly and their mission to influence world affairs? Not that any of it can be that successful. The world hurtles towards disaster despite all their efforts (although who knows if it would be still worse without them). In any case, I no longer want to be in this room.

'OK, you don't want the booklet, that's fine. Is there any

particular reason you came in today? Anything you would like help with?'

'No, I...'

Out the window, I see Teigan walking past, carrying a packed laundry bag. I leap out of the chair, nearly stepping on the Vibratist saleswoman's toes.

'I have to go now,' I say, and stumble out the door as she carries on trying to sign me up to special relaxation classes.

And I am outside in the blazing heat, crying out Teigan's name as she walks briskly down the high street, still fresh in her summer dress, until she hears me. She turns around, sees that it's me. Puzzled, she walks towards me slightly, but not that much as I must be in a frightening state with my face burning and my clothes rumpled with sweat. And I walk towards her and she does not back away, and then I am standing in front of her and...

I cannot speak. Again, the words will not come, as if there is some blockage between my brain and my mouth. Nothing meets the quality test. Everything is discarded.

'What is it?' she says, looking a bit more worried than she was already.

Still nothing comes. And I know nothing will. I made an act of faith (there, I said it) and was rewarded with an improbable result but here I am throwing it away right here in the high street and I see that I am squeezing my arm and who knows what my face is doing and

I feel a hand on mine.

'It's OK,' she says, 'take your time. Olly told me about... how you are. And it's fine.'

Olly told her? He didn't tell me he'd told her. All the things he says to me and he doesn't mention this? That would have been useful information.

'It's all OK...' Her soothing tone did not quite cover her nervousness, but I could tell she was really trying.

And then it all comes out, convulsively, as it sometimes does. I tell her about how I am meant to be meeting my daughter for the first time, but I can't because my face is on fire, and my clothes are drenched with sweat and there is blood on my trousers and I need to wash and I have hardly any money left because I had to give Ahmet his money and I have only three quarters of an hour to solve all these problems and I can't even solve one of them. And when I finish and look up I expect her not even to be there anymore because I'm something that shouldn't be there or even be at all. But she is there. She looks me up and down.

'I think we can fix this,' she says.

I am in a public toilet, washing myself at a sink. Beside me is a bag of charity shop clothes Teigan chose for me. I did not have time to try them on but Teigan said they would suit me and fit me because she had an eye for it. From the way she dresses I know she is right. She has already rubbed some unspecified cream on my face and neck. I will admit it was the most sensual experience I've had for some time. Invasive, but not unpleasantly so. I am still visibly cooking, but at least it stings a little less.

I dry myself with a paper towel and change in a cubicle. The clothes fit perfectly, and look a lot better on me than those I had bought for myself. These I bundle up and shove into the toilet bin. I never want to see them again. Stepping out gingerly over the urine-soaked floor and into the piercing sunshine, I feel something approaching hope.

Teigan waits for me outside. She can't help but smile at what she's achieved.

'Thanks,' I say. 'How much do I owe you?'

'Nothing,' she says, her shyness descending once again as our interaction moves beyond her area of expertise.

'Are you sure?'

'They cost practically nothing,' she says, 'and you need the money.'

'Yes. I do.'

I have checked my wallet. There is just enough in it to buy my daughter coffee and a cake, as long as she doesn't want one of the nice ones.

'You should take this,' says Teigan, reaching into her handbag and pulling out a ten pound note.

'I can't,' I say. 'I don't know when I can pay you back.'

She keeps on pushing the note towards me and I take it.

'It's good that you gave your money to Ahmet,' she says. 'Were you really in a fire?'

'Yes. No, not really. Sort of. I was above it. I didn't go in it. I nearly did.'

'That's very brave.'

I look at my watch. I have to go. In fact, I should have gone already. I'll be late. Daddy is saying run. Run or you'll be late and never mind that you'll turn up out of breath and sweating, you won't be late and that's all that matters. Run. Run now.

'Shut up!' I shout.

Teigan looks shocked, and edges away.

'No, not you!' I babble. 'It's difficult to explain but there's a voice in my head, not really a voice but like a voice and it's telling me I have to run or I'll be late but if I do that I'll ruin the clothes and…'

Teigan chews on her finger. If I don't run, she will, I can tell.

'I'm sorry,' I'm saying, and I'm squeezing myself again. 'I'll go now, stop bothering you…'

She chews, but she does not run.

'You could text her,' she says, quietly, 'and say you'll be a few minutes late.'

Daddy says no, says I have to be on time or the whole thing is ruined, the system is broken and I grab Daddy by the throat and smash him against the wall and then there is no Daddy, not then, only Teigan and Teigan is right. Her idea is better than Daddy's. I do as she says.

I look up and although she is looking away still she has not moved.

'Things get confusing in my head too sometimes,' she says at a volume I can barely hear. 'I understand.'

Somehow, I know that she does.

And then I am saying something I cannot believe I am saying, for several reasons.

'Do you like Atom Comics movies? There's a new one that's just come out. It'll be a while before I have enough money to go, and I wasn't going to see it because it's not canon, although that's not important, but what is important is… would you like to see it?'

I look at her face. She is not looking anywhere near me. She is going to say no.

'Sure,' she says, a slight smile breaking on her lips.

And I put her number in my phone.

I am in my least favourite coffee shop in town. My daughter (who says that she is sorry she did not leave home earlier, but sometimes she gets anxious and can't get going) is not here yet. Still a few minutes away. I would have run for nothing. I hope she gets here soon, or someone will ask what I want and I will have to find a way of assuring them I am a proper customer and not just some orbiter hiding from the sun.

I know I don't need to write her that book. I can just say what I am and move on. She will understand. The young people do, I think. I don't know if I ever properly thought I had to. It was just something I had to go through, before I could be here.

All this time I've been worrying about saying the wrong thing, but I missed the point. I am free to say anything. I am constant and unchanging, but within that I have been many things despite defying all labels and have changed constantly ('do I contradict myself?'). I can be something new again here. I can be a man who asks his newly-found daughter what he should call his fictional cat. Or I can be someone who tells her what a day he's had and laughingly explain why he's ended up lobster pink, maybe smoothing down some elements to make a nicer story. Or I can be somebody who asks her questions, letting her tell him about her life, who she is, what she wants to be.

I look at my watch. My phone has no messages. She needs to be here soon, or this fragile state of equilibrium I have arrived at will fade.

Out of the window, I see Ahmet in his puffer jacket with the hood right up. He has just come out of the expensive book shop. He must have been in there for the past hour, looking at the covers. He is talking and laughing with another man. A man with a rucksack on his back and a cap on his head. Ahmet reaches into one of his pockets that doesn't have a second-hand paperback shoved in it, and pulls out some money. My money. And hands it to the man with the rucksack and the baseball cap. The man turns, a familiar look of mischief in his eye.

Then, running from left to right, as if I am watching on a cinema screen, is a big, grey blur, heading straight towards the man's turned back. It rushes past Ahmet and knocks the man straight to the ground letting out a triumphant roar. It is Olly, in one of his less good suits. He wrenches the money from the man's fist and hands it back to Ahmet.

Olly leads Ahmet away by the shoulder, admonishing him for his gullibility, and as the baseball cap man pulls himself off the ground, Olly sees me staring at the tableau from my window seat. He gives me a thumbs up, then mimes a phone call. I nod in response, but he doesn't see. I hope he gets the job.

I check my phone again. Nothing. I think about answering those emails. But the door jingles as someone enters and there she is, the young woman whose face I have seen only in attached images and who does look slightly like me, but more like Lori and unnervingly like Fred, her inherited hawk nose softened by quieter eyes to something more inquisitive than raptorial. Tall but not broad, thinner, ganglier, almost awkward in her poise. Today she has the appearance of someone who has been stuck in a car under a blisteringly hot sun, hair sticking to her glistening forehead. At least she has dressed for it, in shorts and a light shirt.

She stands there, smiling, but not knowing what to do, suddenly even younger than she actually is. She has seen my photo, but am I what she was expecting? Is she going to turn and run now, before it's too late? She is still there by the door, waiting for something. Perhaps she is wanting me to be the parent and take charge of this peculiar situation. It is not my style. But I am Fantasticus Autisticus, my father's son, and I contain multitudes.

I stand and wave to her.

I open my mouth to speak.

Richard Blandford was born in Cardiff and grew up in Southampton. After a period spent studying and teaching Art History in Manchester and Winchester, his first novel, *Hound Dog*, was published in 2006 by Jonathan Cape. Detailing the adventures of a sociopathic Elvis impersonator, it was praised by author Dan Rhodes, who called it 'squalid, raucous and wildly entertaining' and was adapted into a script for an as-yet-unmade TV version by Simon Nye. It was followed by the coming-of-age story *Flying Saucer Rock and Roll* in 2008, also published by Cape.

Richard is also the author of two ebook short story collections, *The Shuffle* and *Erotic Nightmares*, that mix the banal with the extraordinary and humour with horror. Other projects include the art survey *London in the Company of Painters*, published by Laurence King in 2017, and 'The Fixer', a serialised story in David Lloyd's online comic anthology *Aces Weekly*. He has written articles for *The Guardian* and art periodicals *Frieze* and *Elephant*.

A third novel, *Whatever You Are is Beautiful*, in which a disease sweeps the world, compelling sufferers to turn into superheroes, was published as an ebook by Eye Books in 2021. He now lives in Worthing with his partner, Emily, and his daughter, Ella.